J.C.

THE FALL OF AN EAGLE

This novel of action and suspense, set in the wild, threatening uplands of Anatolia, centres round an attractive Australian woman archæologist whose search for the lost cities of the Hittite empire uncovers a great deal more than she bargained for. Few novelists possess Jon Cleary's enviable power of evoking distant and unfamiliar countries so that they become as real and substantial as the characters in his books. This is a hard land, parched and poor. In spite of the efforts of the Turkish Government, the inhabitants are resigned to a life that stretches back through centuries of hopelessness and poverty.

To this harsh, hot country comes Virginia, a young widow who, since the death of her husband, has made her career as a professional archæologist. She is kindly received by Meldrum, the American engineer who is building a dam, and the pretty Turkish woman doctor who, with the Chief of Police, comprise the English-speaking population of the little town. There is, however, another visitor, a Kurd educated at the American College in Istanbul, whose presence seems as disturbing to the authorities as it certainly is to Virginia'a affections. The passionate affair that develops between them, an affair which Meldrum watches with outward cynicism and inward concern, leads rapidly to a conclusion as unexpected as it is violent. 'Jon Cleary,' wrote Anthony Burgess in a recent review, 'is an expert story-teller.' No one who reads this book will disagree with him.

by the same author

YOU CAN'T SEE ROUND CORNERS
THE LONG SHADOW
JUST LET ME BE
THE SUNDOWNERS
THE CLIMATE OF COURAGE
JUSTIN BAYARD
THE GREEN HELMET
BACK OF SUNSET
NORTH FROM THURSDAY
THE COUNTRY OF MARRIAGE
FORESTS OF THE NIGHT
A FLIGHT OF CHARIOTS
THE PULSE OF DANGER
THE HIGH COMMISSIONER
THE LONG PURSUIT
SEASON OF DOUBT
REMEMBER JACK HOXIE
HELGA'S WEB
MASK OF THE ANDES
MAN'S ESTATE
RANSOM
PETER'S PENCE
THE SAFE HOUSE
A SOUND OF LIGHTNING
HIGH ROAD TO CHINA
VORTEX
THE BEAUFORT SISTERS
A VERY PRIVATE WAR
GOLDEN SABRE
THE FARAWAY DRUMS
SPEARFIELD'S DAUGHTER
THE PHOENIX TREE
THE CITY OF FADING LIGHT
DRAGONS AT THE PARTY
NOW AND THEN, AMEN

JON CLEARY

The Fall of an Eagle

COLLINS
8 Grafton Street, London W1

William Collins Sons & Co. Ltd
London · Glasgow · Sydney · Auckland
Toronto · Johannesburg

First published 1964
This reprint 1989

ISBN 0 00 221230 7

© Jon Cleary, 1964

Printed and bound in Great Britain
by Billings Book Plan, Worcester

To Evy and Gordon

So in the Libyan fable it is told
That once an eagle, stricken with a dart,
Said, when he saw the fashion of the shaft,
" With our own feathers, not by others' hands,
Are we now smitten".

AESCHYLUS

Chapter One

"Have you seen the skeleton? I am sitting on it."

Startled, Virginia Halstead dropped her torch, feeling it strike her foot and bounce off. She yelped a little with pain, then knelt down and felt for the torch on the dark floor of the cave. She could hear the man laughing in his throat, a mocking sound that made her angry; her hands swept the cave floor, panicky as blind wingless birds. Then suddenly she was swamped by light and she looked up into the bright beam of the torch. She was conscious of how ridiculous she must look crawling about on her hands and knees, like some pilgrim doing a penance in the tiny cave-church. She stood up, brushing the dirt from her knees, trying not to look too angry for fear that it would reduce further what little dignity she had left. She took the torch as it was held out to her and turned it on the man himself.

He was sitting on the sarcophagus hollowed out of the rock in the corner of the cave. He gestured beneath him, carelessly, like a man for whom the bones of the dead had no fear nor meaning. "Have you seen the skeleton?"

"Yes." She had been only two weeks here in the Anatolian plateau and she was still unsure of herself with Turkish men; they bludgeoned you with their indifference towards women. But this man did not seem indifferent to her: mocking, yes, but not incurious. He sat pressed against the wall by the yellow jet of her torch; the Virgin Mary looked over his shoulder with startled eyes. "Yes, of course I've seen it!"

He smiled, a flash of white in the dark-brown mask of his face. He belongs here, she thought irrelevantly: these cave-churches have been carved out of the solid rock and so has he. Then she was annoyed at herself for her flight of fantasy : it was giving the mocking man a dignity he did not deserve.

" You are angry with me ? "

" Of course not." She stood behind her torch, invisible to him ; in darkness, she thought, even fools have dignity. " Why should I be ? "

Then she turned away from him, shutting him out with her back as if it were a door. She made a step towards the entrance of the cave, then changed her mind. Why should she allow him to drive her out of this tiny primitive church ? In the narrow gorge below the mouth of the cave she could hear the murmur and occasional laugh of the German Boy Scouts ; and from across the gorge, where they were being photographed against the pock-marked cliff like so many brightly-plumaged birds, came the shouts and giggles of the party of French tourists. She had been resenting them up till this moment, but now all at once she found their presence comforting. She turned back, focusing her torch beam on the decorated wall in front of her.

" Do you find all that interesting ? " He had not moved from his seat on the sarcophagus ; he lolled, with one leg propped up, above the thousand-year-old bones of another man. " Why are people so interested in the past ? "

" It has something to teach us." Despite her irritation with him, she found herself answering him : Saint Barbara looked at her slyly, chiding her to be careful.

" What, for instance ? " Without turning to face him she knew that he was looking about the dim cave, at the carved pillars, the altar, the font, the work of monks who had lived here ten or twelve centuries ago. " Were these men of the old Cappadocia better than us ? "

She thought of a spiteful answer to that one, but kept it to herself. She turned towards him again, making a concession. " All this is part of the story of Man. Aren't you interested in the history of your ancestors ? "

He shook his big dark head, still smiling. " Not those who are strangers to me. My father, my grandfather—that is as far as I care to go back in history. This——" He dismissed the cave and its artists with a contemptuous hand. " This is what Turkey to-day is trying to escape."

Across the gorge one of the French girls shrieked and several men laughed : they, too, were not interested in the past, history was just a lot of holes in the cliffs to them. They moved on down the gorge, complaining about the heat, pining for a drink, asking why they had come all this way when Istanbul or Antalya had so much more to offer. The man nodded towards the door of the cave. " The French party think as I do."

" How many languages do you speak ? " He was the sort of man who provoked irrelevant thoughts ; the more one got to know him, the more questions he would ignite like sparks. But she would not allow herself to get to know him, and she wished she had not asked the question.

" English, French, German. And of course Turkish. Knowing languages helps me to know people. And people are more interesting than caves and ancient paintings on a wall. What languages do you speak ? Latin, Greek, Sanskrit, all the good old tongues ? " He laughed again and stood up, and she was surprised at his bigness : most Turkish men she had met were not really big. But he had the long arms of a Turk ; he stretched, and seemed to take in the whole width of the cave. " Allow me to buy you a drink. It is dry work being— are you an historian or just a tourist ? "

" I am an archæologist."

She had moved closer to the door of the cave and he looked at her in the bright reflection from the cliff across the gorge. " You are a very good-looking archæologist, much better than so many I have seen here in Turkey. Too many of them look like something they have just dug up themselves."

" If you have just paid me a compliment," she said tartly, defending her colleagues who were not here to defend themselves, even though she knew so many of them would not have cared in the least what he thought of them, " then thank you."

He laughed, the sound reverberating in the cave ; a trick of light made some of the saints on the walls turn their heads and look at him reproachfully. " You have some fire in you. The dust of the past has not choked you up. Come, I shall buy you a drink."

Though he mocked her, there were flashes of formality about him that suggested an old-fashioned politeness. He took her elbow, before she could decline his invitation, and gently pushed her ahead of him out the narrow doorway. The German Boy Scouts, in leather shorts and with their shirts tied like cummerbunds round their middles, brimming with that Teutonic healthiness that she always had to admire and yet found disturbing, a defeated people of nearly twenty years ago who looked as if they had no memory of defeat, came up the rough steps to the ledge just outside the cave. They stood aside for her and the Turk to pass, looking at him with frank curiosity and at her with equally frank admiration. Once again her mind went off at a tangent : the look they gave her would not have commended itself to Baden Powell. She could not speak for the rest of the Boy Scout movement, but these German boys were interested in more than just tying knots in ropes.

The Turk helped her down the rough-hewn steps worn smooth by a thousand years of treading. " I think I rescued you from the cave just in time. You are safer with one forty-year-old man than with eight teenage boys."

" Boy Scouts don't attack women."

" Why not ? Scoutmasters attack boys. I am always reading of it in the English newspapers. Perhaps it is why a Scout's motto is *Be Prepared*." This man mocked everything ; she wondered if he had any respect for anything. " Sex affects everyone, even Boy Scouts. Those German boys looked perfectly healthy and normal." He stopped at the bottom of the steps and looked back up at the eight half-naked boys standing looking down at them; brown as the cliff behind them, they looked like young savages ready to attack. Then they all smiled, waved to her and the Turk, and turned and went into the cave. " I like the Germans. There is no subtlety about them. They stared at you quite without disguise. Could you imagine an English Boy Scout staring at you like that ? "

" I have had no experience of English Boy Scouts," she said, sounding prim in her effort to stifle a giggle. " I am an Australian."

" Ah, an Australian ! " He looked at her with new interest; the clutch of his huge hand almost crushed her elbow. " My father fought against the Australians at Gallipoli. He killed four of them with the bayonet. He had great admiration for them."

" Sounds like it," she said, and took her elbow out of his hand before it was reduced to pulp.

They walked up the gorge towards the steps that led up to the parking level. The sun poured into the gorge, drowning them in heat; she gasped for air, beating her hands against the currents of dust that floated up around them. Thistles, so dark blue that they were almost purple, looking like patches of shade cast by some invisible creatures, perhaps the ghosts of the long-dead monks, grew among the rocks. The cliffs leaned in, offering no shade, only menace; she saw where the rock had cracked, stood waiting through the years for the signal to fall. Pigeons fluttered in and out of small caves high in the cliffs, haunting the still air with their sad sound; high above the gorge a hawk punctuated the raw blue page of the sky, waiting with the patience of death to strike at one of the unwary birds below. A car came down the twist of road above the parking level, its brakes echoing the squeal of one of the French girls.

Virginia made a face. " Why do people like that bother to visit places like this ? "

"Conscience perhaps. You people from the new countries always have a conscience about what you call culture."

"France a new country?" She asked the question as an Australian; then answered herself as an archæologist. "Of course compared to this part of the world it is new. But the French would not like to hear you say it."

"Especially General de Gaulle," he said, and laughed again, filling the gorge with his mirth; the pigeons exploded from the cliffs in grey and brown clouds that for a moment blocked out the sun.

She looked at him and, infected by his good humour, suddenly laughed with him. They climbed the steps and crossed the cobbled road to the small outdoor café on a ledge outside another cave. They found a table in the shade of the tattered awning, ordered beer from the one-eyed boy who came grinning at them out of the cave, and sat down. She took out her comb and ran it through her blonde hair, made dry and wiry by the dust and heat.

"I like to see women combing their hair," he said in a suddenly soft voice. "Some women, that is. They make a very beautiful movement of it. You are one of those."

It was a long time since she had been paid compliments; and one did not expect them at all here in Turkey. She had seen how the women here in Anatolia were treated, part of a man's possessions, two-legged beasts of burden. She scrutinised this man with the sudden change of moods, wondering where he had learned to appreciate the small charms of a woman.

"Do you come from around here? Malayan?"

The dark face closed up, turned to rock again. A truck went down the road below them, carrying half a dozen soldiers to the valley beyond. He looked down at them, his eyes cold as quartz; funny, she thought, how everything about him suggests this hard unyielding landscape. He looked back at her and said in a voice that crackled with pride, "I am a Kurd."

That explained his bigness; she had read of the tall men from the eastern mountains. "You are a long way from home," she said, not curiously, but feeling she had to say something. Silence, with this man, was a barbed-wire fence that had to be crossed. She felt uncomfortable and wished she had not come up here with him; but he held her without effort on his part, the secrets of him a magnet that would not allow her to get up and walk away. She had read of men who had had this effect on women, and she had scoffed; now she put her own weakness down to lethargy brought on by the heat. The one-eyed boy, all his friendliness concentrated in one bright blue orb, brought their beer and she retreated behind her glass.

"Much farther than you think," he said, and raised his glass to her, another unexpected gesture. He smiled again, and the dark quartz eyes turned soft with appreciation of her. "Maybe even farther than you are."

He had expected her to be puzzled by that remark, but she had her own secrets. "We might have a bet on that. I'm a terribly long way from home——" The pain all at once came back, something she had not experienced in months, filling her body like the killing heat. She sat back in her rickety chair, feeling faint and sick. One could never really escape the pain of grief: one could retreat a thousand years, or three thousand, as she had in Greece and Crete last year, but the pain of loss was always there.

He leaned forward, concerned for her. "Are you ill? Did I say something to upset you?"

She shook her head, took a sip of the thin light beer. "No, it's the heat."

He stared at her, then he turned away and looked down the gorge towards the valley, white as a vast boneyard under the glare of the noon sun. In the distance the rock chimneys that were the village of Kasrik stood like thigh-bones among the scarce trees. Beyond the valley and its eroded hills, folded upon each other like thick strips of flesh, the snow-streaked peak of the extinct volcano Erjiyes Dagh glimmered behind the dusty plate-glass haze of heat. Anatolia lay unconscious under the weight of the sun.

" Yes, it is much hotter than usual. Earthquake weather."

" Is there such a thing ? " she asked, feeling a little afraid, glad to have something, even fear, to replace the pain.

He smiled, picked up a nut from the bowl on the table and cracked it between his strong white teeth. There was a suggestion of strength about him that she had not found in many men, perhaps in none at all : the men in her life had never really been in need of rock-hard strength. He was not handsome in a way that she had become accustomed to appreciate ; in repose his face had a fierce cruelty to it, the look of a man who would demand rather than ask. His skin was burnt almost black, leather stretched over bones that were aggressive ; in death his skull would still be a challenge to life. He had thick black hair, slightly curly and in need of a cut ; dark eyes that sometimes appeared blue, sometimes black, that looked as if they could change their mood with the quickness of a spinning coin : heads, I love you, tails, I hate you ; a nose not as long as the usual Turkish nose but just as dogmatic and more aquiline ; and a big wide mouth made for argument. He was over six feet in height, wide in the shoulders and chest and narrow in the waist and hips, a man built to fight. He was a man, she guessed, who would have as many enemies as friends.

" It's a superstition. When the air is as still as this, the peasants always expect something to happen. Even sophisticated people talk of the calm before the storm, don't they ? But how often does the storm come ? " He rubbed the stubble of dark beard on his chin ; she had noticed that most Turkish men seemed to consider it effeminate to shave more than once or twice a week ; the message of Gillette had not yet got through to this part of the world. " But I cannot understand why you should come to Cappadocia in August. Spring is the time to come up here."

"I have to wait on my helpers. I have six students who are coming out from England to help me dig. They have been delayed—permission from Ankara has been a bit slow in coming through."

"That is how it is with all governments, eh? A good argument for anarchy."

"I doubt if I want to go that far," she said dryly, and took another sip of her beer.

"Did you drive all the way out here from England? I have seen your Land-Rover in Malavan, with its English number-plates."

"You are observant," she said, and he nodded his head, as if to say that it was natural for him to be so observant. "No, I didn't drive out. The Land-Rover was shipped out to Istanbul. I have been down there for two months. Before that I was in Greece and Crete for a few weeks. I spent some time there last year."

"At Knossos?" He smiled at her look of surprise. "I have been to Crete. Oh, not digging up the past. I was a smuggler," he said, smiling still, and she was not sure if he was joking or not. He stood up, the top of his head touching the sagging awning. He threw some money on the table, patted the shoulder of the one-eyed boy, and walked round and stood at the back of her chair, ready to pull it back as she stood up. "Come, I shall drive you back to Malavan. It is not good for you to be walking around in this midday heat."

Surprised at her own meekness, she stood up and followed him down to his car in the parking level. She had left the Land-Rover in the town this morning to be serviced and had come out here by taxi, trusting to get a lift back in one of the taxis or buses that brought out the tourists. The Kurd's car was a Volkswagen, almost brand new, and he fitted into it as into a mobile suit of armour. She was not a small woman, and the two of them seemed to fill the interior of the car.

"How did you know I was staying in Malavan?"

" I have been observing you."

" Did you follow me out here ? "

He laughed, taking the car up the winding road with fine disregard for anything that might be coming in the opposite direction, riding on the wrong side of the road in what she had come to recognise as the Turkish habit. The system worked so long as no one took it into his head to be a conformist. " Why else should I come out here to these caves ? "

She did not believe him, but she went along with his flattery. " You are different from most Turkish men I have met. They wouldn't cross the road to have a second look at a woman."

" I told you, I am a Kurd. That makes me different from a Turk."

She knew there were still some Turks who looked upon the Kurds as a race apart, who still remembered them with hatred for the revolt of 1926 ; but till now she had never met a Kurd, had never known if the Kurds thought of themselves as someone apart. This man evidently did, not with resentment but with pride. He had a certain veneer of culture, but it was no more than a cloak thrown casually over a man who still retained, without embarrassment, some of the primitive attitudes of his wild forebears.

He slowed the car as a wave of goats flowed down the road ; horns tossed on either side of the car like flotsam. A small boy, made of dust, adorned with rags, ran behind the goats, yelling at them in a hoarse piping voice. The Kurd shouted at him and laughed, and the boy stopped, laughing back at them as the car picked up speed again and sped on up the white, eye-cracking road.

" That boy is so innocent. He has no future, yet he can still laugh." He looked at the wedding ring on her finger. " Do you have children ? "

She shook her head, feeling the pain again. " My husband is dead. He died before we could have children. Before——"

But then she stopped : why tell this stranger about her miscarriage after Tom's death? Yet her tongue wanted to go on talking: somehow this man sparked questions or confessions in her.

"Children are fortunate in your country. Here——" He looked about him as they drove up along the top of a ridge. In a field that looked as if it could have grown nothing but rocks, a man, two women and several small children were threshing a small harvest of corn. The man was winnowing the crop, throwing it into the still air in wide yellow fans that caught the sun; the women, dark scarecrows, were bagging it; and the children, perched on the threshing board, shouted at the thin brown ox as it pulled them round and round in circles among the golden hummocks of straw. Beyond the hummocks stood home: a mud and rock pile that had less dignity than the troglodytes' caves from which Virginia had just come.

"It takes time," she said, feeling fatuous as she always did when asked to comment on another's country.

"It is taking too long," he said angrily. "There are still too many people here in these hills who want to live in the past——"

She smiled, taking the anger out of him, a little frightened by it. "Like me?"

He grinned. "Not like you, no. Your interest in the past is a luxury. These people cling to it out of fear of the present."

If only he knew, she thought: an attempt to forget grief and a sense of guilt was not her idea of luxury. But then they had come over the brow of a hill and were coming down into the wide valley where the town of Malavan lay. It was an old town wrapped round a broken conical hill that made a tentative challenge to the sky, like an old man's crumpled arthritic fist. A few new buildings had been erected in the last ten years, smug and stolid as middle-class burghers, but the rest of the town was a history of housing back through the centuries. They passed the remains of the small Seljuk fort that was now the outer wall of the town goal; through the open gateway Virginia glimpsed the inner stockade where the prisoners lolled like men on holiday. The road wound down the hill, past the wine factory, the mosque, the bank, through the town square with its ring of walnut trees, and down to the newer end of town by the river. They pulled up before Virginia's hotel, the newest building in Malavan.

Virginia got out, feeling the sun fall on her with almost physical force. " Thank you, Mr. —— ? I'm sorry, I don't know your name. Mine is Mrs. Halstead."

" Mine is Dursun. Yashar Dursun."

She smiled, could think of nothing further to say, then crossed in front of the car and walked up the steps to the terrace. Dursun stared up at her for a moment, his face darkening again, then he let in the gears, turned the car round and drove back up into the town.

Nick Meldrum was sitting at a table beneath one of the big sun umbrellas on the terrace. " You shouldn't have done that."

" Done what ? " The heat and Dursun's strange effect on her had worn her patience thin ; she was in no mood for Meldrum's small cynicisms.

He smiled his patient tolerant smile that could be so infuriating ; the sun winked slyly on his dark glasses. " Don't bark at me, honey. I'm only offering advice. A woman should never cross the path of a man here in Anatolia. You should have walked around in *back* of his car. He won't forgive you if you've broken his luck."

" I don't think he is the sort of man who worries about superstition," she said, her voice tart with irritation at both men, the Kurd and the American. " But I'll make sure I don't walk in front of *you*."

Meldrum grinned and raised his glass of beer. " Honey, your temper is showing. Have a shower, come back and I'll buy you a drink."

2

She got out from under the shower and dried herself before the long mirror on the bathroom door. The mirror was of poor glass, but despite its distortion there was little to criticise in what she saw. She looked at herself frankly; vanity had never been one of her faults. She was tall, but her tallness did not make her appear thin. She was full-breasted, perhaps a little too much so: Robert Faber had delighted in her bosom, rhapsodising that she reminded him of Minoan women who had made a feature of their breasts by not covering them.

"You will never be an archæologist," he had said, brutal as ever in his professionalism, even while in bed, "but you pass with honours in everything else."

She had passed with honours as an Amazon, flattening him with her shoe in their fierce final row. She smiled now, the first time she had smiled about Faber since their break-up. He had turned up the next day at the London Museum with a large patch of plaster on his head; he had said he had suffered the wound surfacing in the Thames, where he had been diving to look at a sunken Roman galley. He had never been lost for a good lie.

Whether her face was beautiful, she did not know nor did it worry her; at least she knew she was not ugly and she was more than just plain. Every man had his own idea of beauty; the blind man was not denied it because he could not see it. She had been beautiful to Tom, and that had been all that mattered. Faber had called her beautiful, but everything he had said had turned out to be lies and that could have been another of them. She wondered what Yashar Dursun thought of her, then chided herself for her conceit.

She put on the white linen dress that showed up her tan. She was always glad to get out of her working clothes, the jeans and khaki bush jacket that she invariably wore; she hoped she would never lose her femininity, as so many of the woman archæologists she had met had done. She combed her hair, which she had had cut short once she had landed in Istanbul and realised how hot Turkey was going to be; put on lipstick and darkened her thick eyebrows; then went downstairs to have her drink with Nick Meldrum, a man from whom she could never expect a compliment.

He, too, was a big man, as big as Dursun. His bigness was one of the few comforting facts about him. She always felt uneasy with his slow mocking smile, his complete cynicism, his cool detachment. She wondered if his misanthropic attitude ever hindered him in his job.

" Once upon a time I was an idealist," he said now, halfway through their drinks, eating from a handful of olives. " That benighted period lasted about six months. My first job abroad, in Peru. I went back to the States, saw truckloads of food being carted away to feed pigs, remembered the Indians I'd seen who had to survive on a handful of meal, and began to wonder about the mercy of God. I could have become a Communist, but I became a cynic instead. I was never a Democrat nor a Republican, and I couldn't become a Commie. Cynics have no party. That's one of the attractions of our beliefs. Or disbeliefs, if you like."

He smiled at her, one caterpillar eyebrow coming up from behind the large dark glasses. He ran a slow hand over his crew-cut dark hair, then raised a finger at one of the waiters, asking for more drinks. All his movements were unhurried; he had the slow grace of a large sleepy animal. Virginia envied him his grace; she herself, she knew, was only graceful in the water. Faber had told her that when they had been diving in the Thames.

But there was no opportunity for swimming here in these dry hills. She looked down towards the river, at the couple of inches of water running over the shining rocks. A man was digging a trench, trying to create a small dam in which his wife, squatting patiently on the low bank, could wash their clothes. Virginia thought suddenly of Antalya, of the long beach beneath the towering mountains, of the sea that stretched like rippled silk to the horizon of time, the oldest sea in the world. Stone Age men had bathed there, the Mycenæans, the Persians, the Romans. She herself had bathed there for a week in July, diving with an American expedition who were investigating a Phœnician ship they had found. Perhaps she would have done better to remain down there, seeking the comfort of the past in comfort. Why had she chosen the penance of coming here to the Anatolian hills in the heat of summer? That was it, of course: she was always looking for penance of some sort.

"Any news of your crew?" Meldrum asked.

"There was a letter from them to-day. I understand they are virtually camped on London Airport, just waiting to hop aboard a plane as soon as they are okayed by the Turkish government."

"Who's paying for this expedition?"

"I am."

He raised the eyebrow again. "That must be costing you plenty."

"I can afford it." Her voice was tart again: in countries where poverty was part of the atmosphere she always found herself on the defensive about her wealth. She was not really wealthy, not even perhaps by Meldrum's standards, but she would be considered rich beyond dreams by—well, by that woman squatting down there beside the river washing her ragged clothes in four or five inches of mountain water.

"Why are you doing it?"

"I want my Ph.D. I am writing a thesis. The Study of the Historical Geography of Cappadocia Based on Archæological Evidence."

"A nice title for a piece of light fiction. But that wasn't the answer to the question, and you know it. I'll put it another way. What is a good-looking woman like you——"

"Thank you. You've just spoiled your reputation by complimenting me."

" I never claimed to be a misogynist, honey. Why is a good-looking woman like you wasting her time among a lot of ruins ? "

" I don't think a cynic is in a position to criticise what anyone else does."

" I am a split personality. Part of me is a water conservation engineer. I do something constructive." He looked around the valley spread below them, at the meagre vineyards covering the shoulders of the hills like threadbare green sweaters. " Though sometimes I wonder when, if ever, I'll see some results."

He was here on loan from the United States Government, advising the local authorities on how they could use the water that would some day be available to them from the big dam being constructed at Bebek, thirty miles from Malavan. He had been staying at the hotel when Virginia had arrived here, and after the first few days, despite her discomfort with him, she had been glad of his company. At least he could speak English, and she had grown tired of stumbling in Turkish with the manager of the hotel. The engineers on the dam construction staff were German and they rarely came into Malavan, preferring to stay on the dam site during the week, then at the weekend belt hell-for-leather in their big Mercedes up the main road to Ankara two hundred miles away. All the other visitors to the hotel were French or German, and her command of their languages was not enough for easy conversation. Most of her conversation with Meldrum was an argument, but at least it was in a language that gave her no difficulty.

There was suddenly the sound of music, and from the small barracks across the street an eight-man band, ragged in looks as well as sound, came marching out, followed by a platoon of soldiers. The soldiers, their uniforms neatly pressed, their belts and gaiters white as the sashes and socks of first communicants, made the band look even shabbier ; it was the town band, dressed in uniforms that had clothed several generations, and it made this weekly march not out of pride or duty but only because in a town under martial law it had no option but to do what it was told. At the rear of the squad marched Captain Arif, as immaculate as a military museum dummy, his white-gloved fists trying to swing in time to the broken rhythm of the band. A herd of small boys, ragged and disrespectful as goats, marched behind in a parody of the captain and his platoon.

" There he goes, Captain Arif," said Meldrum. " He's like one or two American generals I've met in various parts of the world. They forget they're soldiers and make a career of being symbols."

" I shouldn't let the generals hear you say that. Nor Captain Arif, either. Have you seen the gaol here ? "

Meldrum watched the small procession march up the street towards the square, trailed by its growing wake of impudent boys. " Arif would never arrest me. He's too ambitious, too career-minded. He's scared of what Ankara might do to him. He wouldn't want to spoil his record by arresting someone who's here as the guest of the government."

" Even a guest who doesn't mind his manners ? "

Meldrum looked back at her and grinned. " Oh, I mind my manners all right, honey. When I'm with the Turks I'm the epitome of old Southern hospitality. I left the South a long time ago, but I still remember my grandpappy, who bowed every time he met a lady." He stood up and bowed. " Shall we eat ? "

" You *are* a split personality," she said, suddenly warming to him. " I've never seen the Southern gentleman before."

" He died a long time ago. You just caught a glimpse of the ghost of him."

" Ghosts are my constant companions," she said before she could stop herself.

The smile and the banter left him. He took off his dark glasses and looked at her with compassion, an expression that fitted oddly on the face that had for so long worn the mask of cynicism. " I suspected as much. Exorcise them, honey. They are never really good company."

3

" I'd never think of coming here on my own," said Latife, looking around the crowded *lokanta*. It was not a large restaurant, but it was the most popular of the town's three and each evening it was crowded, even though most of its patrons came in only for coffee and talk and a game of backgammon.

Virginia smiled at the woman doctor. " It must be lonely here for you in the winter. I mean, when all the visitors like us are gone."

Latife Altinbash shrugged. " I still have to find that out. I've not yet spent a winter here. Maybe halfway through the winter I'll give up and go back to Izmir. Turkey has no tradition of heroines."

She smiled at herself and at them, enjoying the small joke against herself. After five months in Malavan she still had her sense of humour, something she found she needed more and more each day. She was a small slim woman in her late twenties, with a long nose, dark pretty eyes and black curly hair cut short. Even her looks went against her with these peasant men of the hills; they liked their women plump, strong and with their hair long. So far, in all the months she had been here, no man had allowed her to attend him. No matter how ill they were, what pain they were in, the men always waited till Dr. Niyazi, the male doctor, could look at them. She had volunteered for this post out of a sense of duty that women should play their part in the new Turkey; but sometimes in the dark doubt of the night she wondered if Ankara had not made a mistake in accepting her. The government was doing all it could to hasten the emancipation of women, but it was battling prejudices that were centuries old. What the law in Ankara said about women and what a man in the hills thought were generations apart.

" You should make a pass at Captain Arif," said Meldrum.
" You could spend your nights down at the barracks with him,
comparing your ostracism."

Arif had been standing in the doorway when Meldrum
spoke, but by the time the women had turned round he had
gone. They were staring at the doorway when Dursun came
in. He saw Virginia looking at him, hesitated, smiled, then
came towards them, pushing his way between the crowded
tables like a man striding through a swamp of reeds. Some of
the men he pushed aside looked at him angrily, but his back
was already towards them, he was oblivious of them.

" Mrs. Halstead ! They told me at the hotel I should find
you here. I was going to ask you to dinner." He looked down
at the empty plates on the table. " But you have already
eaten ! "

" It's a bad habit Australians and Americans have," Virginia said, already beginning to feel the abrasive side of this
man again. " We always eat much too early. And we are
getting Dr. Altinbash into the habit, too."

She introduced him to Latife and Meldrum, and without
invitation he sat down at their table.

" Won't you join us ? " said Meldrum.

Dursun looked at him and laughed. " Your sarcasm is not
lost on me, Mr. Meldrum. But I was afraid you might *not* ask
me. And I was looking forward to the pleasure of Mrs.
Halstead's company this evening."

Meldrum looked at Latife. " I think we better go, doc.
Four's a crowd."

" You stay right where you are," said Virginia, and looked
at Dursun. " Mr. Dursun, have you met with many rebuffs in
your life ? "

" Rebuffs ? " He pondered the word, then understood it.
He laughed again, leaning back in his chair till he seemed in
danger of toppling over backwards. There were four soldiers
at the next table and they turned round as he almost leaned
back into their circle. But he was as oblivious of them as he

had been of the men he had brushed aside on his way in from the doorway. " My life has been a chain of rebuffs, Mrs. Halstead. Dr. Altinbash should look at my bruises. She would see that they are recurring ones, like hives or shingles."

" I'll be glad to look at them," said Latife. " Anything for a male patient."

Dursun looked at her and winked. " Doctor, I'll report in the morning for a full examination."

Virginia was surprised to see Latife blush. Then she realised that Latife herself, despite her emancipation, was still constrained by old customs : a man did not make risqué jokes with a woman. She looked back at Dursun, angry at him for having embarrassed Latife. Then she saw the look of contrition on his face, and she knew his joke had been an act of bravado to impress the foreigners that he now regretted. It was no wonder he was so bruised by rebuffs, his tongue invited them.

" I'm sorry, doctor. I am always telling my friends they should respect women, then I make mistakes like this." He looked at Virginia. " I don't know what Mrs. Halstead will think of me."

She forgave him, fascinated once again by these sudden changes of mood he showed. " Still you might go to Dr. Altinbash with some sort of ailment. Just to set an example to the other men around here."

He looked about the *lokanta*. The room was lit by faintly blue globes ; everyone had the pallor of death. Mouths were opening and shutting, suggesting a convention of fish, but all the talk was lost in the blare of the radio : a girl in Ankara dominated the room with a nasal whine, singing to these men who did not care of a man who had left her to die in battle. Streamers of fly-paper hung like black crêpe from the ceiling ; the fog of smoke was thickening about the blue globes. The heat was stifling : the glisten of sweat was the only sign that many of the silent faces, those who sat against the wall watching the backgammon games, were alive. From the wall above the bar Kemal Ataturk, fly-stained, faded, dressed in dated evening clothes, gazed out over the room with the cold tired eyes of a dictator weary of the battle of trying to haul his people out of the past.

Virginia and Latife were the only women in the room, but their chairs could have been empty for all the attention they drew ; the men ignored them, turned a collective back on them that was even more of an insult than any stares would have been. All but two men, dressed in nondescript blue suits, shirts without ties, and the floppy-crowned cloth caps that were still worn in Turkey but had gone out of date in other countries in the Twenties. They sat at a table just beyond the four soldiers and stared at Dursun, Meldrum and the two women with the patient blank gaze that reminded Virginia, when she noticed them, of the stare of carrion birds. Unaccountably she shivered when she saw them, but Dursun had evidently not noticed them. He turned back to the table.

" This town will change. When the dam is finished, when the farms begin to blossom and money starts to flow into this district, the town will change. Some day, Dr. Altinbash, you will have men patients. We'll drink to the day."

He turned, raising a hand high in the air and shouting for a waiter to bring a bottle of wine. As he did so one of the soldiers behind him snarled something and stood up, leaning over his table in the direction of the two men beyond him. Dursun dropped his arm and looked quickly over his shoulder.

" What's up ? " Meldrum asked, but Dursun did not answer him. He was turned round, looking directly at the two men who were now on their feet facing the belligerent soldier.

" The soldier wants to know what the two strangers are staring at," Latife said.

One of the men said something, and Meldrum asked, "And what sort of answer did the soldier get ? That sounded like a dirty crack to me."

Latife had picked up her handbag and motioned to Virginia

to do the same. " I think we should be leaving. There is going to be a fight in a moment."

" Maybe you'll get a patient or two," Virginia said.

" Maybe we'll be patients," said Latife. " When Turks fight, they don't take time out to check the sex of whom they are knocking down. You evidently don't know that Turks love to fight."

Dursun was still turned round and now a second soldier looked at him. He said something in Turkish : there was no mistaking the challenge in his voice, but Dursun only smiled, said something conciliatory, and turned back to Meldrum and the women. " I think we had better go." Then he looked down at his feet and said something in Turkish. Virginia, already on her feet, leaned over the table and looked down. A dwarf with crippled legs, with pads on his hands and roller skates fitted to his knees, crouched between Dursun's legs, a roll of lottery tickets held in his mouth like a dog delivering letters to its master. The wizened face looked up at Dursun, terror turning the big eyes to streaked marbles. Dursun put a hand on the hunched shoulders, then looked quickly up at Virginia. " Get out of here quickly ! "

But Meldrum and the women had not moved quickly enough. There was a bellow of rage from one of the soldiers, and next moment they were caught up in a boiling whirlpool of fighting men. The whole room came to its feet, pressing in towards the centre of the fight. Virginia was flung forward ; a fist brushed by her ear on its way to someone's jaw. She tripped and would have fallen had not Meldrum grabbed her. Everything was a confusion of distorted faces and flailing arms ; Latife abruptly disappeared into an onrushing surf of men. Meldrum held Virginia tightly against him, yelling at the top of his voice, swearing furiously ; suddenly he leaned over her and threw a fist into the face of one of the soldiers as the latter came at him. Then, half-carrying her, half-dragging her, he began to beat his way through the struggling crowd towards the doorway. And all the time the girl on the radio sang of her love for the man who had gone away, and Kemal Ataturk, the greatest fighter of them all, suddenly seemed to smile through the fly-stained glass of his picture.

Meldrum and Virginia reached the doorway to be halted by a blast of whistles in their faces. Captain Arif and a sergeant stood there, blowing whistles with almost comic desperation. Suddenly the fighting stopped, just as half a dozen soldiers with rifles came running up and pushed their way into the *lokanta* past the group in the doorway. Meldrum halted, still with his arm about Virginia, and turned round to put another arm about Latife as she stumbled through the crowd towards them. Arif blew his whistle again, pointed to the radio on the shelf behind the bar and the girl singer was cut off in mid-note. There was silence in the room now but for the shifting of feet.

All the men were turned towards the doorway, waiting sullenly on Arif's next move. Virginia, no longer frightened, looked at the blank, tightly-closed faces turned towards her: Captain Arif was going to get nothing out of them. He seemed to realise this, for he looked at once at Meldrum.

" What caused this fight, Mr. Meldrum ? " He spoke with plodding care, the foreign words falling from his tongue as if he were spitting out olive pits.

Meldrum looked about the room, then back at Arif. " I haven't the faintest idea, Captain."

Arif's long nose twitched above his small toothbrush moustache. He was not a tall man, he was considerably shorter than any of the soldiers he commanded here in the town, and his lack of height embarrassed him every time he had to exercise his authority. He looked up at Meldrum, a good six inches taller than himself, and decided not to call the American a liar. In a yard across the town square behind him a donkey bellowed : it sounded like a hoarse mocking laugh, an echo of the laugh that had haunted him all his days at the Ankara war college. He wanted to weep : his life was plagued by jeers, by men who mocked his authority, by spies. . . .

He smiled, almost tearing the muscles in his face. " A fight relieves the monotony. One cannot blame them." He looked about the room, trying to look sympathetic towards the townsmen, rupturing himself with the effort. Then he saw the four soldiers, hair dishevelled, uniforms torn open, standing among the crush of men in the centre of the room. He snapped something to the sergeant beside him, spun abruptly on his heel and went out of the *lokanta*. Then he instantly reappeared, saluted Meldrum and the women, and disappeared again. He could not even manage a dignified exit.

Meldrum took another look around the room, then ushered the women ahead of him out into the cooler, but still warm, air of the square. " I'll come back to-morrow and pay the check. Time we went home, I think."

He walked between the women as they crossed the cobbled stones of the square ; the cobbles were polished smooth and the light from the surrounding shops was reflected from them as from a rippling lagoon. On top of the hill above the town the giant head of Ataturk, profiled in electric lights, stood out against the night sky ; some of the globes had gone out, electric leprosy, and the late dictator had no nose. Radios were blaring in shops and houses, all carrying the same song : the night was filled with the plaint of the lovelorn girl, pining for yet another lost lover : women knew no happiness in this country. A blind lottery seller came towards them, led by a small boy : destitute of fortune himself, he offered them a chance of riches. Meldrum bought half a dozen tickets, and the lottery seller went on across the square, led by the eye of a child already suffering from glaucoma. A donkey hawed, a sad cry of pain now, not a mocking laugh.

" I hope that crippled seller wasn't hurt in the fight," Virginia said. " And I wonder what happened to Mr. Dursun ? "

The soldiers had now formed up in front of the *lokanta*, the four soldiers who had been in the fight in their midst. The sergeant barked an order and the squad went off down the street, their boots echoing like a tattoo of bones against the cobbles.

" A good question, honey. What happened to the other two guys, too ? All of them lit out before Arif even got to blowing his whistle."

" Together ? " Latife had a dark bruise on her upper arm, but she did not appear to have been upset by what had gone on in the *lokanta*. Violence was always just below the surface in these men of the hills, and she had not been surprised by what had happened. " You think Mr. Dursun knew those two men ? "

Meldrum shrugged. " I wouldn't know. Maybe he didn't. But he sure didn't want to be mixed up in any riots." He looked at Virginia. " He fooled me. The last thing I'd have taken him for was a peaceable man."

" Me, too," Virginia admitted, and unaccountably felt disappointed in Dursun. She was not a woman who admired aggressive men, but somehow it was as if, with Dursun's sudden abandonment of them, she had discovered a flaw in his character. He could have at least made sure I was safe, she thought ; then wondered at herself for her demand on him. She once again felt angry at herself for her interest in him ; his personality clutched at her like the thistles that grew on the hills around Malavan. She shut him out of her mind, turning to Meldrum and Latife with an abrupt comment on the heat that took them both by surprise.

Latife glanced at her, a woman's look of mixed curiosity and understanding, then she said, " The heat must break soon. It has never gone on as long as this before. So the peasants tell me."

" Does it worry them ? " Virginia asked.

" Some of them have begun to buy charms from the *hojas*. That is a bad sign. When one has to rely on religious teachers to break the weather, it means one is getting desperate."

" Even with these people ? " Virginia asked. " I thought they were filled with superstition ? "

" They are. But they don't spend money as they once did on charms. They have become a little more educated, a little more sceptical of what the *hojas* can do for them. That is why I say it is a bad sign that they are going back to buying charms. It is almost as if they are becoming frightened by the heat. There was a terrible drought and famine up here over fifty years ago, and some of the old folk are remembering that and spreading the tales of it."

" Maybe I'll buy a charm myself," said Meldrum. " I'm not frightened by the heat, but I'm fed up with it. I don't mind it during the day, but I'd buy a dozen charms for a cool night."

" A cynic buying charms ? " Virginia said. " That *would* be a victory for the *hojas*."

They left Latife at the hospital, the yellow peeling building that stood in its scrub of garden like a derelict barracks ; Virginia had never been inside the hospital, but she wondered if its interior was as depressing as its exterior. It was significant, she thought, that Latife had never invited them inside. She and Meldrum waited at the gate till Latife had gone up the broken concrete path and disappeared in the front doorway, then they walked on down towards the hotel.

Ahead of them a dark shape suddenly scooted across the road ; it looked like a large dog frightened by something. Then they heard the whirr of the skates on the cobbles. " Well, the dwarf got out of the fight okay," Meldrum said. " I thought he might have been a patient for Latife in the morning."

" I feel sorry for Latife."

" It's a battle for her, sure. But at least she's *doing* something."

" Touché," said Virginia without resentment. " But I could have stayed home, you know, and been no more than a social butterfly." But that wasn't true : she could not have stayed at home, no matter what she had been.

" It might have been better. Even social butterflies have their uses. A good one provides entertainment."

She looked at him sideways. " Were you ever in love with a social butterfly ? "

His face was a mask, but still relaxed. " What makes you ask that ? "

" Your tolerance towards such a creature."

" Honey, a good cynic is tolerant towards everything."

He hadn't answered her question, but there was no time to pursue it. Dursun was waiting for them, sitting at a table on the hotel terrace among the chattering sparrows of the French tourists. He rose as they came up the steps, hailing them with a shout that was like the bark of a gun amidst the jabber around him ; the talk suddenly stopped and everyone looked at him, then, reassured, went back to their conversations. Virginia hesitated, but Meldrum pushed her towards Dursun. They sat down, neither of them responding to the broad smile of Dursun. He ordered a bottle of wine from a passing waiter, then turned back to them.

" We'll have that drink we were going to have in the *lokanta*. Where is Dr. Altinbash ? "

" She was ground to a pulp in the fight," said Meldrum. " We left her there."

Dursun's face contracted with concern ; then it relaxed. He laughed, but not loudly this time. " Jokes like that don't amuse me, Mr. Meldrum."

" I wasn't amused, either, when you left me to look after Mrs. Halstead and Dr. Altinbash on my own." Meldrum stood up, unhurried as ever. He appeared relaxed and at ease, but there was a hardness to his voice that Virginia had never heard before. " Women are not third-class citizens in my book, Dursun. They're entitled to some protection."

Dursun leapt to his feet, but Meldrum, with a nod at Virginia, had already turned and made his way across the terrace and through the front door of the hotel. Dursun went to follow him, but Virginia grabbed his sleeve.

" Sit down, Mr. Dursun. Please ! "

He looked down at her, his dark face almost black with anger. " I have killed men for talking to me like that ! "

Later she would wonder that she had not been surprised at what he had said. But now she looked quickly around at the French tourists, still tangled in the skeins of their voluble conversation, then pulled his sleeve again. " Please sit down. You have to understand that Mr. Meldrum sees things differently."

He slowly lowered himself into his chair. She let go his sleeve, but not before she could feel the rage still quivering in him. In the side light from the dining-room behind the terrace his face looked more than ever as if it were carved from rock : it looked a face incapable of love, charity, sympathy. Then suddenly the rock crumpled as he leaned forward. " Mrs. Halstead, you think I should have stayed with you ? "

Virginia hesitated. She had never before had to reproach a man for cowardice ; the white feather would have moulted in her fingers before she could have given it to any man. But something told her that this man had not acted as he had done out of cowardice. " I think you should have stayed. Even these local men, even though they treat their women the way they do, I think they would have stayed."

He still leant forward, searching her face with eyes that now had an unexpected doubt about them. But it was not doubt of her : all at once she realised it was doubt of himself. " I was concerned for the lottery seller, the little dwarf," he said, but she could see that his mind was only half on what he was saying : it was an excuse that he only half-believed in himself. Then he sat back as the waiter brought the wine. He waited till the man poured their drinks and had gone. He then raised his glass. " I have never begged a woman's forgiveness before, Mrs. Halstead. I beg yours."

She raised her own glass because she could find no words to acknowledge the gesture that she knew must have cost him so much. They sat in silence for a while, then at last she said, " Were they friends of yours? Those two strangers? "

The conversation of the French tourists swirled about them like eddies of breeze : an occasional word emerged, like a familiar object thrown up on the currents of air. Down by the river a donkey hawed, sawing at the night ; in the tourist coach parked in the hotel parking lot the driver turned on the radio full blast. The night air was torn with noise, and for a moment Virginia thought he had not heard her. Then he shook his head. " They were strangers to me, also." But his voice was too direct : he's lying, she thought, experienced in the lies of men, or anyway of one man. She felt a sense of betrayal, then wondered why : she hadn't yet reached the stage of placing her trust in this strange man. Yet, she discovered now, all her reactions to him ever since meeting him had been anticipatory.

" I myself am a stranger in Malavan," he said, speaking as if from a prepared script. " Some day I hope to be doing business here. It would not be good for me to be involved in any trouble with the law. When I saw Captain Arif in the doorway, I picked up the dwarf and went out through the kitchen. I am sorry. I thought discretion the better part of chivalry."

" Prettily put, but not very flattering." She saw the concern in his face, and she put a quick hand on his arm. " No, I'm not still angry. I was only joking."

He looked down at the hand on his arm, then closed his own huge hand over it. She could feel the strength in his fingers, the roughness of his palm, but he was doing his best to be gentle.

" I am not accustomed to kindness," he said simply.

Chapter Two

Virginia drove well, with almost prim precision, handling the heavy Land-Rover almost as if it were a light car. She avoided the bumps in the rough valley road with uncanny anticipation, her foot holding the vehicle to the same steady speed. " Put your arm out the window. It will act as a scoop, give you some air."

Latife did as she was told, felt the air scooped in against her cheek. It was still warm air, but it gave some relief from the oven of the Land-Rover's cabin. " You are learning all the tricks."

" I'll have to, if I'm going to go on living this sort of life. It's one of the drawbacks to archæology, that all the best sources are in filthy climates, either baking hot like this or freezing cold like it was when I was up in the Hebrides. A nice dig right in the heart of Paris, just off the Champs-Élysées, would be just the thing."

" How long is it since you left Australia, Virginia ? "

" Almost four years." She was surprised when she said it : the time had gone so quickly, it seemed only a few months since she had boarded the aircraft at Sydney : perhaps it was because the grief and pain were still there. Love still inhabited her under its other cloak of suffering ; and in such a condition under either name, time lost its meaning. " I've been in London most of that time, studying at London University, working part-time at the London Museum. I've had one or two trips. To Luxor in Egypt, to Greece and Crete. I spent a month on the island of Islay in the Hebrides." Which was where the affair with Faber had begun, on a camp bed in a tent with a fifty-mile-an-hour gale threatening to expose them to the elements at any moment. She smiled inwardly at the thought, and felt pleased that she could smile : the ability to laugh at a man was the best way to purge him from one's system. " After this dig, if I get my Ph.D., I'd like to branch out. Perhaps try South America."

Latife looked at her questioningly, but said nothing. She liked this Australian woman with her direct friendly approach, her sympathy for Latife's own loneliness ; and she knew that Virginia carried some pain within her, that behind the smile of the day there were tears in the night. But she would not ask : all her life she had never been able to cross the border into the intimacy of real friendship. She was determined to succeed as a doctor : ambition had replaced friendship. And sometimes she regretted the substitution, especially when it seemed that ambition was getting her nowhere. Emancipation had its problems : it threw one open to the conflicts of decision.

Up ahead the village began to appear out of the haze, like something seen through a silken veil. " I'm never happy in Kasrik," Virginia said. " I've been down here twice, but each time they let me know I'm not wanted."

" Have they chased you out ? "

" Not exactly. But the *Muhtar*, an old man with a white beard——"

" I know him. Kel Hasan. He doesn't make me welcome, also. He thinks I should be wearing a *yashmak* still, should have on *shalvar* trousers instead of this skirt. What did he say to you ? "

" I didn't understand a word he said, but I got his meaning. Out ! " She jerked her thumb. " These old men don't waste time on politeness to women."

Behind them, among the jumble of picks and shovels, Ismet Javid, the male nurse, smiled blankly at them, having no English but trying to belong to their conversation. Small and thin, no bigger than Latife, he was as dedicated to the health care of these hill people as Latife herself. He could not understand why the Australian woman should be coming out here to Kasrik with them in this heat, but he welcomed her. Anyone who showed interest in what he and the doctor were trying to do was welcome.

The Land-Rover entered the village, moved up the winding dirt street between the tall rock chimneys. They stood forty to fifty feet high, tall eroded monoliths that men had turned to use : windows and doors marked them as homes. A few houses stood among the pyramids and cones, but even these looked as ancient as the natural rock. Nobody knew how long Kasrik had been inhabited. Hittites might have lived here two thousand years before Christ was born in another cave in another land. A spring supplied the only water for the village : in succeeding centuries before Christ, Phrygians, Persians, Macedonians and Romans might have drunk from it as they stopped on their way to conquest. Virginia dreamed of the discoveries she might make, of emulating Schliemann and Evans and opening up the past for modern man. But in her heart she knew she was not really looking for discoveries. She was here to dig for a suspected Hittite settlement, to put the final touches on her thesis ; but she was really only seeking escape. Kasrik, timeless itself, was only another way of filling in time. Till what ?

She parked the Land-Rover beneath the purple shade of the walnut tree that stood in the middle of the village square. Some old men, squatting on stones at the base of the tree, their *shalvar* trousers bagging beneath them like collapsed balloons, looked at the Land-Rover resentfully as it spread dust on them, but they did not move. One could read their attitude in the walnut of their faces : they had been here before cars had come to the village, they would be here when all the cars had gone. They hitched up their trousers, chewed on their toothless gums and went back to their silent communion with each other.

" We have some calls to make," said Latife. " Do you want to come with us ? "

The Fall of an Eagle

" I'll look around for a while." Virginia stepped out of the blessed shade of the tree, putting on her dark glasses against the bruising glare. She slung a peasant's woven bag over her shoulder ; it contained her camera, her note-book and the Martin-Clark resistivity meter. She took two resistivity rods from the back of the Land-Rover, put on the gay wide-brimmed straw hat she had bought in Crete, and securely fastened the ropes that held the canvas flaps at the back of the vehicle. She knew the ropes would not stop any thief intent on pilfering, and she was aware of the old men watching her out of the corners of their eyes. But she knew she could employ no one in this village to stand guard over the Land-Rover, and so she had to take the risk of losing things. " The children will lead me to you when I want to find you."

" Watch out for the *Muhtar*." Latife said something to Ismet, they both laughed and moved off, followed by the disapproving stares of the old men. Virginia looked at the ancients, nonplussed by their passive antagonism towards her, then she turned and began to make up her way up the winding street towards the far end of the village. Children attached themselves to her, trailing her like curious goats : kids was the right word for them, she thought. She smiled at them, tried to talk to them, but they were the proper descendants of their grandfathers : she was an outsider, someone to be distrusted.

She walked to the edge of the village and came to where the chimneys thickened, were broken in size and more closely grouped together. Here the valley floor began to slope upwards, turning abruptly into ridges that, smooth and naked, stretched like a profusion of voluptuous limbs into the giant body of the flat-topped hill that dominated the village.

The road here ran up through a narrow gulch. A rough path, a donkey's tracing among the scramble of rocks and thistles, led up to the top of a ridge. Up there was where she hoped, when her party really began to dig, they would find some evidence of Hittite occupation. Down in Istanbul she had plotted all the finds in Turkey; the density of dots on her map had pointed to a possible route leading through here from Hattusas, the ancient capital of the Hittites, in the north down to Carchemish, a great fortress conquered by the Hittites, in the south. She knew that the main trading route had been farther east, but the salt of Tuz Gölü might have drawn the traders this way. While still on her own, waiting on her student helpers to arrive, she could look for little more than clues of pottery types. The famous Amber Route, from the Baltic to Greece and Italy, had been plotted by pieces of amber found in the regions through which the traders, carrying amber to exchange for bronze and vice versa, had plodded their way. She hoped for no more than a small trading post or fort to be hidden here under the bald hills, but whatever it was it would give extra point to her reason for being here. She had reached the stage of having to convince herself as much as anyone else.

She had just turned off the road, putting a tentative foot on the rocky path, already feeling the effect of the fierce heat in this rock cauldron, when there was the sound of a shot. She looked around her, startled by the sharp sound; but at once another sound assailed her ears. It was the beating of what seemed like a million wings. The sky suddenly darkened, and she looked up to see the pigeons, thousands of them, coming out of the cliffs and rock chimneys in great grey and brown clouds, rising to block out the sun in a swift-moving thunder-head that threatened to engulf the whole sky. On the trip through Central Australia she and Tom had once seen a vast flock of birds rising at dawn from a billabong, lifting against the rising sun and turning the early morning into night again; but she had been only half awake and had seen the sight from a distance, and it had caused no fear in her. And Tom had been there, too.

But she was frightened now by the unexpectedness of what had happened, heightened by the strangeness of her surroundings and the hostile atmosphere through which she had passed

as she had made her way up through the village. The storm of
pigeons had turned bright day into violet dusk; the rock
chimneys were a battalion of strange shapes closing in on
her. The sound of the countless wings filled the tiny gorge;
it was almost as if the sound were a physical thing beating
her into hysteria. She spun round and round, frantic, felt
herself getting giddy with heat and panic. The naked ridges,
grey now like dead flesh, seemed to be sliding down on her;
she lurched to the side of the road, stumbling through a
dark purple clutch of thistles but not feeling them. Her
dark glasses fell off, but the day seemed no lighter: the storm
of birds had swallowed the sun, in a moment they would
descend on her, smother her with their myriad wings. Panic
and heat had now brought her to the verge of hysteria. She
opened her mouth to scream, knowing she was going to faint,
then felt the arms close about her. In the moment before
blackness fell in on her she saw the man's face, strange yet
familiar, close to her own. She tried to force the scream
from her throat, to shout for help, but it was too late. She
was unconscious.

When she came to, she was lying on the slope of the shallow
ditch beside the road and Dursun was leaning over her. She
started up in fear, but he gently pressed her back. " Keep
still, Mrs Halstead. Here, drink this." He put a small leather
drinking bottle to her lips and she swallowed the cool water
that trickled into her mouth. She lay for a moment, gasping,
feeling the sweat running on her, then she slowly sat up.
" Do you feel better ? "

She nodded, still dazed, still feeling that she was on the
edge of some nightmare, on the trembling border between
sleep and waking. She shut her eyes against the blast of the
sun, then felt him put her dark glasses on her, his rough hands
gently fitting the side-pieces over her ears. She opened her
eyes again, found his face close to hers and his eyes clouded
with concern. He peered at her for a moment, then leaned back
on his haunches.

" Who was the man ? " she asked. " Was it you ? "

" What man ? "

" I thought a man grabbed me—— " Or had it been an illusion, something that had come back out of memory, an impression that had come loose from the broken mosaic of her mind in the panic-filled moment before she had fainted ? She was not even sure what the face had looked like. She struggled to her feet, resting on his arm as the giddiness overcame her again. He gave her another sip of water from the leather bottle, and she smiled her thanks. She looked up at the sky, now blazing again. The pigeons were drifting back to the hundreds of small coops that, she saw now, had been chipped out of the cliffs and rock chimneys for them. They fluttered down, small ragged clouds that were all that remained of the storm that had terrified her, and disappeared into the rock faces, leaving behind them only the faint sound of their cooing. She looked at Dursun, suddenly embarrassed for having fainted : she wondered if Kurdish women ever succumbed to such a womanly weakness. " I heard a shot— then millions of birds came from nowhere—it was silly of me, but what with the heat—— "

He picked up her straw hat and put it on her head. He smiled, not mockingly but understandingly. " It would shock anyone who was not expecting them." He looked up and around at the pock-marked cliffs and chimneys. " The villagers keep the pigeons for their guano. It's the only fertiliser they have for their vines. You might say the pigeons keep the soil alive here in the valley."

She bent down and picked up her shoulder-bag. As she did so, she saw the other bootprints in the soft white dust beside the road, too many to have been made by one man. She saw also the gleam of the empty cartridge shell, one that had been ejected from a rifle only in the last few minutes ; it rested on a clump of thistles, its brassy surface completely free of the dust that usually covered everything here within an hour or two. She straightened up, convinced now that another man had

been here only moments before she had regained consciousness. She looked at her watch, but she could only guess at
how long she had been blacked out : it could have been half
a minute or ten minutes. She looked up and about her, but
the chimneys and cliffs looked back at her with eyes in which
the pigeons moved like dark irises. There was no sign of any
man.

They began to walk back down the road to the village. She
felt in no mood now for exploration ; the Hittites, who had
waited centuries for her to discover them, could wait another
day. Children came running up the road, ragged wraiths in
the shimmering glare flung up from the white road. Dursun
spoke to them and laughed ; the children shrieked with
merriment and spun round the man and woman. Dursun
made as if to slap the behind of the nearest boy ; there was
another shriek of laughter and the children sped off down the
road. Dursun looked after them, the rock of his face splin-
tered by laughter. And something more, Virginia thought.
Compassion.

" You love children, don't you ? " She could not contain
the surprise in her voice, but he did not seem to notice it.

" I should like a dozen children ! "

" All boys ? Is it true that some men here in Anatolia don't
count girls as children ? "

He grinned at her. " No, I should count the girls. Just so
long as there were not more of them than boys." Then he
looked down the road again, at the children fading into the
cracked mirror of the glare. The laughter left his face and
he put his hand abstractedly into his pocket. He brought the
hand out again and she was surprised to see the yellow prayer
beads crawling like a small snake round his fingers. Somehow
she had not expected him to be a man who believed in prayer.

" I should not want my children to live as these children do.
I lived like this once, a long time ago. For a whole winter
I lived on bulgur wheat and boiled weeds. It is not as bad
as that for these children, but sometimes it is not much better,

either. Not in a famine year." The beads tightened on his fingers; his eyes were brilliant with his depth of feeling. He stared down the road at the children, skeletons no more substantial than the dust they stirred up as they ran. "It would save a man's soul to be able to rescue even one child from this misery."

"Are you concerned for your soul?"

He looked cautiously at her before he replied, then he nodded. "I haven't always been a good man and I may still go against the ways of God. But I have never given up the hope of Heaven. Have you?"

"No. I am a Roman Catholic. Perhaps not a good one, but I try."

"One should never measure goodness. There are too many yardsticks."

They were walking down the village street, and all at once the question occurred to her: "Why are you here in Kasrik? How did you come to find me up there?"

"I was visiting a friend. The children told me a foreign woman with pale hair had gone for a walk up the road. Then I saw your Land-Rover down in the square. I followed you. Again," he said with a grin.

But again she knew he was lying. She was completely composed again now; she was hardly even aware of the heat. She knew, too, that the man's face had not been an illusion: the man who had grabbed her in the moment before she had fainted had been one of the strangers from the *lokanta* last night. "I didn't know you had friends in Kasrik."

"Why should you?" He was mocking her again: his mood had changed completely with her questioning.

She shook her head, trying to get out of the awkward situation into which she had talked herself. "I don't know. I thought you were as much a stranger here as I am."

"I'll never be that," he said with something like reproach. "But perhaps I make friends quicker than you do. Would you like to meet my friend?"

44

She hesitated, afraid : did she really want to meet the two men she had seen last night ? But he had taken her arm, was leading her up a side lane through the almost solid shadows of the rock chimneys. They came to a house cut out of one of the larger chimneys ; it had a neat wooden door, windows, even a window box with a straggle of red geranium hanging from it ; it looked unreal to Virginia, like something from a Walt Disney cartoon film. A small girl crouched on her haunches outside the door, cleaning a copper pot with sand, Cinderella sketched in broken wavering lines.

But the young man who opened the door was real enough ; and so was the poverty behind him. Dursun escorted Virginia into the cave, for that was all it was, despite its façade. A dirt floor, shelves and seats carved from the soft rock walls, a table of rock on which was opened Latife's medical bag. Latife herself turned from the woman who lay in one of the three beds hacked out of the wall.

" This is Ahmet," said Dursun, and the young man smiled shyly at Virginia. He was short and slimly built, the bones showing through his flesh like a reminder of the proximity of death. His dark quick eyes had an intelligence about them that Virginia had not found too often with these peasants of the hills, a curiosity that acknowledged the existence of another way of life. " And his mother Behije. Friends of mine." Dursun put his arm about the shoulders of Ahmet, and the young man smiled up at him with what seemed to Virginia to be a mixture of awe, admiration and love. The polite formality went from Dursun's voice as he looked about the sad dark cave. " Friends who deserve better than this ! "

" No speeches," said Latife, and turned back to the woman. At first Virginia had thought the woman was old, but now she saw that she could be no more than middle-aged. But every year of her life had marked her face : she wore the cicatrice of misery. " How long have you known Ahmet and his mother ? "

Dursun said something in Turkish to Ahmet and they both

laughed. Then he looked at Latife. " Two days. Friendship is a swift flower in the right soil."

Latife turned from the woman and began to scrub her hands in the bowl of water on the rock table. " Anatolia is full of aphorisms. Words grow more easily in this country than anything else."

" Isn't it true ? " Dursun asked.

" I'm tired of words ! Promises, arguments, aphorisms——" She dried her hands and began to pack her medical case. She looked at Virginia. " This woman has a dropped womb, has had for years, since the birth of that little girl outside. She could have been helped, if there had been a doctor in this region when the government first promised there would be one. No doubt the boy's father, he's dead now, would have argued against her being touched by a doctor. Words, words, words ! And now that I'm here, it's too late. She's not going to die, not yet anyway, but her whole belly now is just a mess of pain. The worst of it is, I can't offer her much more than words, too."

" The boy can be offered more," said Dursun quietly. " He wants to teach."

The woman moaned, and Ahmet moved to her. Latife picked up her case and moved to the door. She looked back at the woman and young man, shook her head, then opened the door and stepped out into the narrow lane. Virginia followed her. The small girl still scrubbed at her copper pot, head downcast, trapped already in the net of her mother's life. Several other children appeared from nowhere, materialising out of the glare, and stood in a line against the wall that formed one side of the lane. Latife smiled at them absent-mindedly and put on her dark glasses. " Ahmet is a bright boy, the brightest by far in this village. He could be a good teacher. But it would mean going to Ankara or Adana to study. He has no money and it would mean leaving his mother and sister behind. So he doesn't go. He stays here and tends the few vines they have out in the hills, grows a little corn, looks after her and

46

eats his heart out. He can't escape till she dies, and by then it may be too late. He may be married, have children of his own——" She looked at the small girl, at the children lined up against the wall as if facing a firing squad. She bit her lip and raised a hand to her glasses, as if her sight had just become fogged. "It's one long cycle of despair." Then she looked at Virginia and smiled wryly. "More words."

Dursun came out of the house, closing the door behind him. He looked at the children, who stared back at him with half-frightened smiles on their dusty brown faces ; then he clashed his hands together and laughed aloud as they scampered away down the lane. Their laughter came back, light as tinkling glass on the still air : they were not frightened, it was a game that they and the big man enjoyed. Ignorance still protected their innocence.

"What can Behije eat, Dr. Altinbash ?" Dursun asked.

"Anything, I suppose." Latife shrugged. "But I doubt if she has any taste left. Why ?"

"I'll bring her something from Malavan. The last good meal she ever had was probably her wedding feast."

They had reached the end of the lane, turned into the street. Captain Arif was coming towards them, picking his way carefully over the ruts in the road like a prize cockerel. Dursun dropped his voice, but it only seemed to heighten the sudden mockery in his tone. "The army on manœuvres !"

Captain Arif came up to them, saluting the women as if they were generals. He came from Istanbul and had long ago accepted women as necessary equals ; Kemal Ataturk was his god and what Ataturk had preached was his bible. Only privately did he sometimes wonder if Ataturk had meant that *all* women should be treated as equals. The beautiful and the intelligent, yes ; but *all* women ? "It is a pleasure to meet beauty and intelligence in such surroundings," he said, the compliment as awkward as an apology would have been in his mouth. "One forgets the heat and dust."

Virginia wondered who was Beauty and who Intelligence of

herself and Latife; but she could see that the compliment had cost Captain Arif an effort and she did not want to be mean. She smiled in acknowledgment, then introduced Dursun.

Arif tried to stand taller as he looked up at the smiling Kurd. " I heard you had arrived in our district. Welcome."

He had spoken in English, as if in a further compliment to Virginia, and Dursun replied in the same language. " Nothing escapes you, Captain Arif? You have the eagle eye, I'm told."

Arif stiffened, his nose twitching as if it might at any moment fly off his face. He snapped something in Turkish, saluted the two women and stalked stick-legged and board-backed, pompous as a wooden doll, off up the street. His shadow scurried beneath him, more human, less ridiculous than the man himself.

" You insulted him," Virginia said. " Why did you have to do that? "

" I hate soldiers," said Dursun, no longer smiling, staring after the retreating figure of the captain. " They killed my parents."

Virginia had no immediate answer to that brutal information. One could not say, " I'm sorry to hear that "; one did not acknowledge a tragedy with a polite platitude. She herself had been on the receiving end of such stupidities and knew how angry they had made her. But the human tongue had not the capacity for sympathy that the human heart had; the vocabulary of comfort and pity was a small one. So now she said, " What did Captain Arif say to you in Turkish? I hope he didn't threaten you? "

But Dursun ignored her question. " I am driving out to the dam at Bebek. Would you care to come with me? "

" I'm sorry. I am driving Dr. Altinbash back to Mala-van——"

" I shall be another hour or so," Latife said. " I have four more women to look at. Why don't you go with Mr. Dursun? "

Virginia hesitated. She had not even begun her search here

in Kasrik. But another day would not crumble the Hittite ruins, if they were here, into dust. And this man attracted her in a way that no other man ever had, not even Tom. She was curious about him, and the curiosity was too strong to be denied. She took out the keys of the Land-Rover. "If we aren't back by the time you're finished, drive yourself back to Malavan. You can drive?"

"Very slowly and very cautiously," Latife said with a smile and took the keys. "I shall look after your truck." She looked at Dursun. "Where is your car?"

"Down in the square."

"Bring it up here," Latife said, and put a hand on Virginia's arm. "Mrs. Halstead doesn't want to walk too far in this heat. We'll wait here."

Dursun stared at her for a moment, obviously unused to taking orders from women, then he nodded and went off down the street. Virginia looked at Latife, aware of the slight tension in the other woman's grip on her arm. "What's the matter, Latife? I thought you wanted me to go with him?"

"I had second thoughts. Perhaps it is none of my business, Virginia. But are you being sensible about him?"

Virginia felt a moment of temper at Latife's interference, but she managed to keep the irritation from her voice. It was a long time since anyone had concerned themselves with any foolishness of hers; she tried to tell herself that Latife was acting only in her own interests. But it did not improve her temper to know that Latife was possibly right. "I'm not a young girl, Latife. I came here to Turkey looking for ruins, not romance."

Latife smiled. "I'm sorry, Virginia. But it wasn't just that he might sweep you off your feet—I am not as much against that as you might think. Turkish women dream of romance, even the emancipated ones."

Virginia put out an impulsive hand. She had had no girl friends since she had left school; all at once she felt a rush of affection for this lonely woman doctor; they were like two lost strangers meeting in an endless waste of desert. "I'm sorry, Latife! I didn't mean to sound spiteful——"

Latife nodded and looked down the street. Dursun's cream Volkswagen had pulled out of the square and was coming up the narrow rutted road. "Captain Arif said something to Mr. Dursun that you did not catch. It was in Turkish. He said that his eagle eye would miss nothing of what Mr. Dursun and his friends, whoever they were, might do."

"His friends? Who are they?"

Latife shrugged. "Captain Arif didn't say. And neither did Mr. Dursun. But I noticed he didn't answer your question when you asked him what Arif had said to him."

"You have a suspicious mind, Latife."

"It's a Turkish habit." The car had almost reached them; it pulled up and the dust rolled forward like pale outriders. "Just be careful, Virginia. He could be a government man sent down here to check on Arif. Or he could be——"

"What?"

Latife shrugged again, the Mediterranean gesture that Virginia found so frustrating: it answered everything yet answered nothing. "Go and enjoy yourself, Virginia. Don't concern yourself with ruins to-day."

2

"I am what you call a developer. I have a small hotel on a beach near Antalya—some day I hope it will be a big hotel. Tourists are coming to Turkey now in big numbers. Americans, Germans, French, a few English. Turkey is taking the place of Greece and Yugoslavia for those people who have been everywhere else. With Western tourists it is—what do Americans call it? A status symbol? To go to places where other tourists have not been. For the next few years Turkey will be *the* place to visit. Not just Istanbul and Izmir, but up here in Anatolia, to look at the caves at Goreme and those near Malavan. I came up here to look at the dam they are building at Bebek. Perhaps it could be turned into a resort. A hotel, a beach, perhaps a casino, if the government would allow it."

" Somehow I had never thought of you as a hotel pro-prietor. I just can't see you being polite to complaining guests. What would happen if some general, or even a captain, came to stay at your hotel ? "

The car swerved on the road as he leaned back to let the laugh burst out of him. " You have no respect for me, have you, Mrs. Halstead ? "

Virginia raised her eyebrows in surprise. " Respect ? So you really do think I should be wearing the *yashmak* ? "

He looked sideways at her, the laugh still rumbling in his deep chest. " Did you not respect your husband ? "

" I loved him. That included everything else. Respect, admiration, whatever you like."

" He was a fortunate man."

She looked away, out the car window at the blue lake of the dam just coming into view among the shimmering naked hills. She had not discussed Tom with anyone since his death ; somehow it had seemed like trying to revive a corpse. And Tom's corpse had been an ugly one, smashed terribly, nothing like the living Tom. " Not so fortunate," she said. " I was his unlucky charm."

He made no comment, but took the car down the winding road to the edge of the lake. They got out and walked down to where the water, still and dark, utterly without bird life, cut into the yellow earth like a huge sheet of glass. Half a mile, perhaps a mile, to the south of them (Virginia had no idea of distances in this trembling landscape where hills advanced and retreated like dancing elephants) they could see the rim of the dam wall, still friezed with scaffolding. Trucks crawled along the top of the dam wall, and from the gorge beyond the dam there came the sound of invisible bulldozers. On one hill flanking the dam wall stood a half-completed power station, its gaunt frame making it look already a ruin ; on the opposite hill a small mosque stood beneath the ancient challenge of its minaret, the relic of an age when God's power alone had been important. A siren blew and a moment later the sound of the bulldozers ceased. Silence settled like a giant dark bird on the oil-smooth lake.

" They will be finished in another two or three months," Dursun said. " There are two thousand men working on this dam."

" You'd never know," Virginia said, looking at the bald hills around the lake, glad to forget Tom again.

" They are all down in the.gorge. For most of them it is the only steady work they have ever had in all their lives. When the work is finished, they have to go back to their fields." He looked around the lake, incredibly blue amidst the yellow hills. There was no sign of vegetation ; trees were still only a mirage here. " It is to be hoped that their fields will be greener because of what they have done here."

He spoke sometimes like a man quoting from a pamphlet or making a political speech ; she wondered for a moment if he belonged to some political party. That, perhaps, would explain some of the mystery of him : she knew that politics in Turkey was not the cut-and-dried variety that she had been accustomed to in Australia. Even British politics, with its recent scandals, did not have the intrigue that distinguished politics in this country. But she had no time to pursue the thought. She saw Dursun gazing over her shoulder into the distance and she turned.

The jeep was coming towards them along the edge of the lake, seeming, caught between the glare of water and sand, to be skimming along a foot or so above the ground. It pulled up, was engulfed in its following cloud of dust ; then Meldrum emerged from the dust, his unhurried gait contrasting strangely with the speed with which he had brought the jeep along the lake edge. He nodded at Dursun, then looked at Virginia.

" I had the glasses on you from back there." He nodded

towards the dam site. " You were lucky it was me saw you and not one of the soldiers."

" Why ? "

" You might have had a bullet or two whistling past you." He looked at Dursun. " Didn't you know this is a restricted area ? How did you get this far ? "

Dursun nodded over his shoulder. " We came in by a back road."

" Deliberately ? "

Dursun smiled. " Perhaps I took the wrong fork in the road. It is so easy in these hills."

" I'm sure Mr. Dursun didn't know it was a restricted area. Why should it be ? Are you expecting someone to blow it up ? "

Meldrum pushed back his hat. It was a broad-brimmed bush hat, old and battered, with a puggaree that had once been crimson and was now pale pink. Virginia had noticed before that it was a hat he used as another man might use a gesture of the hand or an expression of the eyes : he pushed it forward again, as if frowning with it. " Maybe the government is. There are a lot of people in this country who want to cause trouble. What's your business out here, Dursun?"

Surprisingly, Dursun seemed well in control of his temper. Meldrum's tone had enough bite to invite a fight, but all at once Dursun seemed the more composed, almost a little amused by the other's only half-hidden aggression. " I think the lake could be put to more use than you have so far planned."

" Mr. Dursun would like to build a hotel here, develop a holiday resort," Virginia said, anxious to keep the peace between the two men.

" A good idea, don't you think ? " Dursun said.

" I wouldn't know." The hat was pushed forward farther still ; its shadow and the dark glasses he wore obliterated any expression from Meldrum's face. " I came here to help the farmers get a little more out of their land than rocks and a few poor crops. I'm not interested in the pleasures of those that can afford vacations."

" Are you a Communist, Mr. Meldrum ? "

" Watch it," said Virginia hurriedly. " He's an American."

Suddenly Meldrum grinned and shook his head at Virginia. Her naïve remark seemed to take the tension from him ; he pushed his hat back again. " Honey, there are still one or two American Commies left. I'm not one of them, but they aren't an extinct species." He looked at Dursun, still grinning. " I'm just not interested in middle class folks, that's all, Dursun. I have only a small capacity for sympathy and I prefer not to waste it on them."

" You and I have something in common, Mr. Meldrum."

" I'd never have guessed it," said Meldrum, and turned to go back to his jeep. " I'll be coming back around five, honey. Have a drink with me ? "

" Glad to," said Virginia, and watched him walk away across the hard-baked earth, get into the jeep and drive back towards the dam site. Beside her she was aware of Dursun also staring after the disappearing American ; aware, too, that the Kurd's mood had begun to change. Meldrum had left just in time.

" Do you like him ? " Dursun said abruptly.

Virginia looked up in surprise. " Like him ? I suppose so. I hadn't really thought about it. Why ? "

" He likes you."

" He just wants someone to have a drink with. Anyone who can speak English." She stared at the dark set of his face and all at once took an unaccountable risk : " Does it upset you that he might like me ? "

" Yes."

She did not look at him till they were in the car and driving away from the lake. Then, still confused by her own involuntary question, she said, " Don't take anything for granted, Mr. Dursun."

" I never do." There was a stiff formality to him now, as if he felt he had gone too far and was trying to withdraw. But he halted for a moment on the path of retreat : " But I'm beginning to wonder now if one shouldn't. It would save time."

Then abruptly the car began to slow. Dursun looked mystified, then all at once his stiff mood fell from him. The car rolled to a halt, and he looked sideways at her with a half-smile on his lips. " This is a very old joke. We've run out of petrol ! "

Virginia's exasperation got the better of her. " Well, you'd better damn' well do something ! We're going to be baked alive if we sit here all day in this tin oven ! Do something, dammit ! "

He spread his hands, unworried. " What can I do ? We are twenty or more kilometres from Malavan. Relax, Mrs. Halstead. I am not going to take you—" he paused a moment, the half-smile still on his lips "—for granted."

He got out of the car and looked about him. The road here ran through a shallow gorge between steep cliffs that cupped the heat like a crucible. They were in a silent burning world of their own ; the horizon was only a stone's throw away in any direction. High above them an eagle roamed the sky like a dark brigand ; it glided recklessly into the sun and was devoured. Virginia got out of the car and looked across at Dursun.

" Whom do we wait for ? "

" Mr. Meldrum. He will be coming back this way this afternoon."

She looked at her watch. She could feel the heat striking at her even through her straw hat ; reflected from the bright earth it engulfed her like a suffocating tide. Anger and the heat made her dizzy again, and she put a hand on the car to steady herself. And cried out with pain as the metal burnt her. Dursun came round the car on the run.

" You and your joke ! God Almighty, why did you have to

be so bloody careless! Don't touch me—keep your hands to yourself!" He had gone to take her hand, but she pulled away from him. She stumbled away from the car towards the side of the road, looking for somewhere to sit down, but thistles blocked her, taunting her like a barricade of further baleful jokes. She stood helplessly, watching Dursun as he suddenly turned from her, reached into the car, took out the leather water bottle, her own bag and another small leather bag, then came towards her. He nodded up towards the cliffs.

"There is a cave up there. We'll wait there."

"Four or five hours!"

"It will pass quickly enough. I should have thought that an archæologist would have more patience than most people. Don't you measure time in centuries?"

When she had burnt herself on the car and he had rushed towards her, his face had been anguished with concern for her. But her angry rebuff had flushed that away; he was now as distant and mocking as he had been on their first meeting. He stepped on the thistles, crushing them with his boots, making a path for her but offering no other help. He made his way ahead of her up through the rock and she, after a moment's angry hesitation, stumbled after him. Dizzy though she was with heat and temper, she was still detached enough to view their progress with a sourly amused eye. This was the Middle East, the ancient, way : man in front, woman bringing up the rear. He had put her in her place by just stepping into his traditional character. For one wild moment she wanted to hurl a stone at his broad superior back.

The last few yards up to the cave were a steep climb and here at last he turned and waited for her. He put out a hand to help her, his face expressionless; but she scrambled up past him, rubbing one knee painfully against a sharp rock, and almost fell into the cool womb of the cave. She heard him chuckle, then he came up into the cave, blocking out the light for a moment as he stepped through the narrow entrance. He put down the bags, then held out the water bottle to her.

" Have a drink. You will feel better."

Her first reaction was to refuse, but she knew that would only be stupid. She drank from the bottle, feeling the water run down over her chin on to her shirt. She handed the bottle back to him without a word ; and while he drank she looked about the cave. It was low and narrow, so that Dursun seemed to fill it with his bulk, and it appeared to run back into the cliff for a considerable distance. Ten feet from the mouth of the cave one escaped completely from the searing heat of the narrow gorge. She sat down, drawing her knees up in front of her, and looked up at him. If they were to be stuck here for several hours, some sort of truce had to be made.

" Didn't you think to check the petrol before you left Malavan ? "

He was still standing against the glare beyond the cave's entrance, but she saw him turn his head and look down at her. " Little details I forget. It is a bad habit—it has got me into trouble before." He put down the water bottle, searched in his leather bag for something, then came towards her. " Some dates. And bread and goat's cheese."

She suddenly discovered she was hungry. He sat down beside her as they began to chew on the stale coarse bread and the white crumbling cheese. " I lived on this for a whole winter once down in Izmir. Yet I still haven't lost my taste for it."

" When was that ? " Her curiosity about him was still there : it was like an itching sore that she took delight in rubbing.

" When I was young. Seventeen, eighteen. I was waiting to get a job on a ship. I was going to escape from Turkey."

" Escape ? Why ? " She was interested in why other people had their reasons for escape.

" Turkey had offered me nothing up till then. Kurds were not trusted. I would sit in a *lokanta* all day, it was the only place where I could go to be warm, and dream of Brazil."

" Why Brazil ? "

" Why not ? The war, your war, was on—where else was

there to go but to South America ? Kurds are fighters," he said with almost boyish pride, "but we are not mercenaries, we like to fight our own wars. If I had gone to America, England or even Australia, what would have happened ? I'd have been interned or conscripted. Excuse my selfishness, but I was not interested in your war."

" Didn't you hate the Nazis ? "

" Why should I ? They had done nothing to us Turks."

" But their cruelty, what they did to the Jews, didn't you feel something about that ? " She had never had to argue the case against neutrality before : everything she learned about this man only made him even more of a stranger to her.

" Why should I be concerned for the Jews ? Were the Jews concerned for us Kurds when we tried to rebel back in 1926 ? In this part of the world, Mrs. Halstead, a man doesn't fight for other people's rights, he fights for his own. It may be selfish, but it is honest."

" All right," she said resignedly : it was like talking to someone in another century. " But what were you going to do in Brazil ? "

" I was going to make my fortune, build a mansion, have a dozen passionate wives, have banquets every night, eat bread and cheese only as a rare delicacy, bathe every day, wear nothing but silk. I was going to be the Sultan of Brazil." He looked at her and his smile was almost shy. " Do I sound stupid, Mrs. Halstead ? "

" Dreams are never stupid." Her anger towards him had now completely gone. Once more she found herself being drawn towards him, magnetised by her inexplicable curiosity about him. Everyone, she knew, had his own mystery ; even the idiot infant held some secret. But no man, not even Tom, had had the effect on her that this man had. She was frightened by her curiosity of him, but there was no question of drawing back. " You said your parents were killed by soldiers. Was that because you were a Kurd ? "

He nodded. " In the Kurd revolt. My father fought in it.

Perhaps he deserved to be shot, I don't know. But not the way the soldiers did it. They came to our house early one morning, took my mother and father from their bed and shot them on our doorstep. I was three years old then. I sat there in their blood and waited till my father's people came for me. I was too young to know how long it was, but they told me it was late afternoon before they came. To sit all day in the pool of your parents' blood is not a happy childhood memory. And no matter how young you might be, you do remember it."

She was not prepared to argue with that. The memories of her own childhood were not tragic ones; so bland and sweet were they that she found it difficult to remember anything that had happened to her before she had gone to school at the age of six. Her parents had not been rebels: a wool broker, as her father had been, fought only against the possibility of bankruptcy. And it had never been much of a battle for her father, at least not in her lifetime. Her mother and father, though she had loved them dearly, she knew now had been smug and selfish in their attitude towards the rest of the world. Snug in their comfortable wealth, they had had occasional sympathy but little else for the poor of the world. No soldiers had ever come to their door; only the parish priest, the Salvation Army officer, the charities fund collector. Each had been given a donation and had gone away satisfied: no blood shed, only a pound or two from the bank account that never missed it. Perhaps because her parents had never known suffering, they had never known their own depths. She knew from her own experience that happiness, accepted without question, was a delusion: to be appreciated it needed the salt of the occasional pessimism and doubt.

" Where are your parents ? "

" They are dead, too." They had not even known the pain of grief: they had died suddenly within hours of each other.

" And your husband, too ? That explains, then, why you always have that lonely look about you."

She was surprised to learn she looked like that. "Do I really?"

"Don't you *feel* lonely?"

"Of course," she said, as if she expected him to understand.

"What happened? To your husband, I mean."

She looked at the glare beyond the entrance to the cave. It was so fierce, so concentrated by the eye of the cave, that she could see nothing of the other side of the gorge. She stared into a furnace of light that almost hypnotised her: the cave, the man beside her, the present, all shrank beyond the edge of her consciousness, like images of wax melted by the heat and sliding out of a tilted frame. "It was all so stupid and meaningless. We had been married eighteen months, I was four months pregnant, we had money, a home, he had a good job—he was a lawyer. Everything was perfect. Too perfect, maybe. I don't think I could really enjoy perfect happiness again—I'd always be expecting something to happen."

"We Kurds have a saying—death is the only true happiness. But I don't believe it."

"I don't think I could be *that* pessimistic. Anyway. We lived in Darling Point—that wouldn't mean anything to you, but it is a very good part of Sydney, on the harbour. Like the part of Istanbul along the Bosphorus, out where all the Americans live. Tom went out one morning on his way to the office, got the car out and pulled up on the other side of the road to wave good-bye to me. I called to him—I remember I wanted him to bring me home some hair spray from town. He couldn't hear me, so he got out of the car to come back across the road to me. A car came along——" She stopped, seeing in the blaze of light ten feet from her all that had happened five years before. She looked down a telescope of time, saw Tom's blood burst from him as he hit the roadway like red sauce spilling from a shattered bottle, and opened her mouth to echo the scream of long ago. Then she felt Dursun's arm about her, as she had felt someone's arm about her that other time, and she leaned weakly against him, shuddering with remembered shock.

"I am sorry," Dursun's voice was a deep gentle whisper. "I should not have asked you about him."

She was silent for a while, then she sat back and he let his arm fall from about her shoulders. "No, it's all right. It's just that it's so long since I let myself think about it so clearly——" She leaned back against the wall of the cave, aware of the cool rock through her shirt. "I lost the baby, too. Everything was taken from me at once. These things happen, I know, but you never think they will happen to you." She looked at him from the corners of her eyes, conscious of his reserve. "Isn't that right?"

He shook his head slowly. "You and I grew up in different worlds, Mrs. Halstead. I am not a pessimist, not like the people who believe that proverb about happiness. But in my world I have expected everything to happen to me—I have *had* to. Even death, my own death. And there's still time for that."

"Don't talk like that!" She put out an impulsive hand, felt the thick hairs on the massive forearm beneath her fingers, felt the muscles of the arm suddenly stiffen like snakes beneath the skin.

He looked directly at her. "Everything I say disturbs you. I am not used to a woman like you——" He took his arm from beneath her hand, stood up and walked to the cave entrance. He stood there, seemingly unaware of the heat that struck at him, instead almost savouring it. Virginia saw again the contrast between themselves : she relished the cool shadows of the cave, but he seemed ready to flee them, as if they were some sort of trap. "You disturb me, too. Just being near you——"

"It's only because I am a foreigner," she said defensively, the words sounding foolish in her own ears ; she drew back into herself, into the shell she had carried with her for so long.

"Perhaps. I have not been used to dealing with women much at all. Not on your terms. I mean the terms of a Western woman."

None of the men she had known outside her marriage, and she had not known many, had ever professed less than a great deal of experience with women. Even Tom, the most innocent of men, had never admitted to innocence. She was a little nonplussed to find this man, so sure of himself in other ways, fumbling in his approach to her like a schoolboy. She was trying to find a way of answering him, of discouraging him without making him angry or hurting him, when he came back and sat down beside her again. He didn't look at her, but spoke to the opposite wall of the cave.

"Have you ever wanted to go to Brazil?"

The question so startled her that she laughed. She saw him flush, and at once she was contrite. Her hand, as if it had an instinctive will of its own, moved once more to touch him; with an effort she kept it by her side. She was frightened of the physical appeal this man had for her. She and Tom, in their marriage, had both allowed full rein to the devil in the flesh; the affair with Faber in London had had the same wild passion. But she had been in love with Tom, and had been seeking love with the other man; and what had happened in the bed had been an end and not a beginning. Then she laughed again, this time to herself: at what, she did not know. Nervousness, perhaps; or at her conceit in being frightened of seduction before it had even been suggested. Because he had not made any move towards her in that way. The man himself could not be blamed for the physical effect he had on her; his behaviour had all the polite circumspection of a Jane Austen hero. She sat back against the wall, stiffening herself against its hard cool surface.

"I am sorry I laughed. No, I've never wanted to go to Brazil. Peru, maybe, but not Brazil."

" Peru ? The Incas ? You try to drug yourself with the past, don't you ? "

" Where did you get your education ? " She had steered him away from herself ; she was safe for a while longer. Her only danger now lay in herself.

He had turned to face her, but now he looked away again, at the wall opposite. He had recognised that she had turned the conversation away from herself ; whatever else he had been going to ask her, he now kept to himself. " I worked for two years at the American College in Istanbul."

" Studying or teaching ? "

It was his turn to laugh ; the cave reverberated with the thunder of his mirth. It was some time before he could gasp, " I was the janitor's assistant." Then she, too, laughed ; and the merriment broke up the tension between them. He went on, " The students lent me books, but never enough. I was hungry for reading. I would steal books from the library. That was why I lost my job there. They came to my room one day, down in the basement, and found all the books I had there. Two hundred and seventy-eight of them, a library of my own. I was always going to return them, but I hated to be without them."

" What did you read ? "

" Everything. Politics, history, novels. I even read a book by Emily Post. Very funny, to a Kurd." He gurgled with laughter again.

" Did they call the police ? "

" Not at first. I think the principal was pleased to learn I was so keen to be educated. Unfortunately my temper had got the better of me. I had hit the librarian before I found out they were not going to call the police. I broke his jaw. *Then* they called the police."

" What happened then ? Did you go to gaol ? "

" Oh, no. I got away," he said carelessly, as if escaping from the police was a daily habit.

The afternoon wore on. The sun dropped lower, its rays

striking deeper into the cave, pushing the heat in towards them where they lay on the hard floor. She had lain down, with her hat beneath her head for a pillow, and dozed off. Dursun sat unmoving against the wall of the cave, looking down at her with the uncertain attention of a man seeking an answer to a question he still had to ask. She looked up at him once, aware of his stare, but she was now too languid, too worn out by the heat and the boredom of waiting, to be afraid of him. She dozed off into a dream in which he walked through the white nude hills that had become her own flesh.

She came out of the sleep slowly, as if rising to the surface of a warm sea. She opened her eyes and looked up past the hard curve of his cheek, black against the golden reflection on the cave roof, the stubble on his cheek and jaw catching the light like a mineral sheen. She could feel the weight of his body pressing on her; she murmured and stirred, only half in protest at what she knew she would welcome. The sunlight had now penetrated the interior of the cave, so that they lay in a blaze of concentrated light; she could feel the heat wrapping itself round her, a golden coil that held her bound to the cave's floor. Her mind had stopped, and she responded out of instinct. She raised one arm, an instinctive defensive gesture that turned into an embrace.

Then Dursun sat up, turning away from her to stare out of the cave's mouth. She whimpered, the dream suddenly ending; then she came fully awake, sitting up beside him. They heard the jeep coming down the road through the gorge, the changing down of the gears, then silence. Dursun, without looking at her, doing up his belt, got to his feet and walked to the mouth of the cave.

" Mr. Meldrum ! " Then he looked back at Virginia. " I'll go down first, give you time to do your hair and compose yourself." Even disconcerted as she was, she remarked the stilted phrase that occasionally intruded itself into his speech. " I'll tell him you were not feeling well."

" You have lipstick on your mouth."

They spoke to each other without embarrassment, but almost formally : they might have been exchanging job instructions. He wet his handkerchief from the water bottle, wiped his mouth, looked at her for approval, then turned quickly and went out of the cave. She heard him talking to Meldrum as he approached the American, then his voice died away as he reached the road. She stood up, pulled up her jeans and did up the buttons of her shirt ; during the daytime heat she had given up wearing brassières, glad to be rid of their constriction. She put on her desert boots, tying the laces carefully and unhurriedly. She ran a comb through her hair, wiped her mouth as Dursun had wiped his, put on fresh lipstick and picked up her hat and bag.

Then she started to tremble, feeling giddy and faint again. She leaned against the cave wall, assaulted by the savage sunlight, ravished by the thought and not the deed of what had almost happened. She was shaking all over, still feeling the touch of Dursun's hand on her. Sensuality still gripped her like a fever, but now she was sick with the disgust of it. Or rather not with *it*, but with her own surrender to it. She was not prudish enough to see any sin in sensuality itself : she knew the demands of the blood. She had never thought of herself as promiscuous, not even with Faber, but she had almost given herself to Dursun as any whore might give herself to some bull of a man who attracted her. She had bankrupted herself of self-respect.

Meldrum was leaning against the jeep, his broad-brimmed hat pushed back on his head. " Dursun tells me you're not feeling well. A touch of the sun ? "

She nodded, glad of the dark glasses that hid her embarrassment. " We've been waiting hours―― "

" I'd have come sooner if I'd known." The sarcasm in his voice was almost non-existent ; she only detected it because she was straining to hear it. He was smiling as he got into the jeep. Dursun clambered into the back seat and Virginia sat beside Meldrum. He looked at her before he switched on the motor. " You want to be careful, honey. This country's tough on women. That's right, eh, Dursun ? "

3

The knock on the door was peremptory, that of someone used to knocking on doors and having them opened at once. Virginia put down her pen and closed her note-book, almost glad of the interruption. For the past hour, trying to get her mind off Dursun, she had been classifying the potsherds and soil specimens she had collected since her arrival here in Malavan. Nothing she had discovered was exciting, but she had learned long ago that archæology was a profession that required patience, a patience she was beginning to suspect she did not have.

She got up and opened the door. Captain Arif, cap tucked under one arm in an old-fashioned pose that suggested he was about to have his photograph taken, stood outside in the hall.

" I should like to converse with you, Mrs. Halstead. In private, please."

She stood aside and gestured for him to enter her room. Only when she had closed the door behind him did she re-member she was in her dressing-gown. She had been so sur-prised to see the captain that she had invited him in without thinking. She drew the gown tighter about her, wondering how strictly the proprieties were observed here in Malavan. Arif noticed her movement and drew himself up to his full height.

" You are perfectly safe, Mrs. Halstead. Turkish officers are gentlemans. *Men*."

" I am sure you are." Virginia sat down on the edge of a chair. Through the open door that led out on to the small balcony there came the hollow clop-clop of a home-going donkey, the sound so light and nervous that one expected the legs of the donkey to buckle at any moment. In the barracks across the road a radio blared : a Western number this time,

Elvis Presley conquering where a dozen other invaders had failed. " Why did you want to—to talk with me ? " She almost said *converse*, but checked herself just in time.

Arif looked around, then sat down on the edge of a chair facing her ; they sat perched like two birds ready to fly off as soon as the other made a move. He sat with his knees close together, just as Virginia had been taught to sit by the convent nuns, his cap held neatly with both hands on his thighs, posed again for the invisible camera. Ambition cloaked him like a plastic bag, kept him brushed, blancoed and laundered for immediate departure for Ankara as soon as the promotion came. Only the eyes gave him away : the doubt of himself, the distrust of others.

" Mrs. Halstead, how much do you know Mr. Dursun ? "

Virginia could not stop the blush that flooded through her ; she hoped that in the weak light of the electric bulb it would only look like a reflection from her pink dressing-gown. She had been thinking of Dursun when the knock had come at the door, re-living with a mixture of shame and pleasure, the half-dream, half-reality, in which he had almost forced himself upon her this afternoon. She knew that if Meldrum had not come along when he had, she would have allowed Dursun to make love to her. The sense of physical disgust that had gripped her this afternoon immediately after the interruption had passed ; she knew now that it had been disgust at the shame of possibly being caught by Meldrum in the actual act that had made her so sick. But a feeling of shame still troubled her, that she had been on the point of committing herself to a relationship that had no foreseeable future. She had shivered at the thought, too, that she could have been made pregnant. That cold realisation had had hold of her when Arif had knocked on the door.

" Not much—not well at all." She was involuntarily following his speech patterns ; she must get a better grip on herself. Across the road Presley told her to-night was so right for love. That boy was a menace, a pied pop-singer

leading women like herself to destruction with his advice.
" I met Mr. Dursun only yesterday. Out at the ruins. We are
only acquaintances."

" Acquaintances ? " He thought about the word, did not
recognise it, but accepted it. He held his cap even more
precisely on his thighs, a down-turned begging bowl : he
would not beg for information on Dursun. " Has he told you
much about himself ? "

She began to gain a little in confidence : Captain Arif was
not as sure of himself as she had thought. He had not come
here to make trouble for her—then she wondered why she
should have thought *that* ? What had she done that would
merit any censure from Arif ? I'm developing a guilt complex
about this afternoon, she thought. But to allow a man to make
love to you was not a crime. Or was it here in Turkey ? Here
in these hills a woman had so few rights, no matter what the
law said, that perhaps she did not even have the right to give
herself to a man if she chose.

" He has told me very little. I told you, we are only acquaintances."

" You spent all day with him, Mrs. Halstead."

How on earth did he know that ? But she wasn't going to
ask him : that would only arouse his suspicions, although he
probably had them already. But she was becoming more
expert in defence in cross-examination : Tom would have been
proud of her. Or would he have, defending her part in an
affair with a strange man ? " By accident, Captain Arif, not
design."

He pondered on that one, fitting the words into the proper
slots of meaning in his mind. She suddenly realised that she
was at an advantage as long as the conversation was kept in
English. Abruptly he said, " Do you know if he comes from
Ankara ? "

She shook her head. " I don't think so." But she did not
say that Dursun had told her he came from near Antalya.
Without really thinking about it, she committed herself to

Dursun's side ; she became an accomplice, if only by omission.

"He does not talk about the government?" He shifted the cap on his lap again, perched a little more precariously on the edge of his chair. Why, he's scared stiff, she thought ; and suddenly felt sorry for the little man with his brittle vanity. He was only another who wanted to escape : from this hill town, from the limbo of being forgotten by Headquarters. But now he was afraid that he was only too clearly *not* forgotten, that Dursun had been sent here to spy on him.

But, whatever else he might be, she could not see Dursun as a government spy. The rebel was inherent in him, was as much part of him as his sudden changes of mood ; and the spy could never be anything more than a slave, not even when he turned. "No, Captain, he never mentions the government." She took a chance and offered him sympathy : "I don't think you have anything to worry about."

He looked at her at an angle, past his long nervous nose. "I am not worried," he said defensively, but he might just as well tried to deny his name was Arif. He stood up and at once threw away his defence : "You will not tell Mr. Dursun I was here?"

But she found herself unable to make promises to him ; without thinking why, she knew her loyalty was to Dursun. "Why should I, Captain?"

He turned to go, posed once again for the camera : she wondered how many actual photographs he had of himself. "If he says anything about the government, will you come and tell me, please?"

"No, Captain. I'm only a visitor here. I don't want to become involved in anything." But she was already involved, though not in any way that should disturb Arif.

He hesitated, then said, "There are two other strangers in this district. Do you know *them*?" She shook her head, surprised at the question. "Do not get to know them, Mrs. Halstead. They are dangerous men, political outlaws. They will be gaoled when I catch them."

"Do you think Mr. Dursun has something to do with them? How can he, if you think he works secretly for the government?"

"I cover all possibilities, Mrs. Halstead. One has to."

He bowed, marched to the door and opened it. He looked out, careful of the proprieties, then stepped quickly out into the hall and closed the door softly behind him. She giggled at his rapid exit, then she sat down on the bed and stared at the two suitcases on the other side of the room, wondering if now was the time to pack them.

Across the road Elvis Presley had been replaced by a Turkish singer, a man whose voice was full of sadness.

Chapter Three

The bank manager, Mahmut Yusun, came towards Virginia, his smile managing to look friendly and warm despite his terrible false teeth. He was a small squat man with a freckled bald head, steel-rimmed spectacles and a continual look of concern ; he had not developed a defence against the debts and plights of his clients. If he had not been so conscientious, he would have been a poor bank manager. Money in itself did not interest him : had he been a Catholic, Virginia thought, you could have compared him to a father confessor who sat behind the grille of a bank counter instead of that of a confessional. His smile of welcome for her was not because she brought money into the bank, but because he was pleased that she had no worries. Or none that he could see.

"Good morning, Mrs. Halstead, how is you ? " His English was poor, but he was learning ; he had been told by Ankara that, with the gradual increase of foreign tourists to Malavan, someone at the bank would need to speak English or some other foreign tongue. He had taken on the task himself, learning a certain number of words each night in the same way as he had, as a child, learned numbers. He had reached an age where, without losing any of his sympathy for his local clients, he would welcome meeting someone with money to spare. He did not envy anyone their wealth, but was glad that God had smiled on them in such a way. God had smiled broadly on this Australian woman : she had money, beauty and health ; and there was no one in Malavan who had all three. " You want money ? "

Virginia followed him round the counter to his desk, taking her travellers' cheques from her bag. She never changed many cheques at once, preferring to come in every three or four days when she needed cash. It was not that she was afraid of having a large sum stolen from her; it was just that she would have felt embarrassed walking out of the bank with a lot of money in her bag. Each time she came into the bank the two clerks and the girl typist looked up and smiled at her, but she could never tell what they thought of her. Accustomed to money all her life, growing up in a time of affluence in Australia, she knew she would feel ill at ease if she showed evidence of her wealth in front of people who had to live on a wage that was less than the price of a bottle of perfume or a pair of gloves, purchases she made often and extravagantly.

She wrote out a cheque for five pounds and pushed it across the table to Yusun. The manager called to one of the clerks to get the money, then looked back at Virginia, his teeth clicking like soft castanets in his mouth. " How long you are staying, Mrs. Halstead ? "

" I don't know. Perhaps not long now."

" You have found what you find for ? " She had told him that she was here to seek out some evidence of Hittite ruins, and had been pleased to see he had been interested. There were other people in the town who were interested in the local history, but their enthusiasm had struck her as mainly commercial.

But right now she was thinking of something else but Hittite ruins. " I don't think so, Mr. Yusun."

Then she looked up as Captain Arif came through from the rear of the bank. It was not a large building, having only two rooms on each of its two floors, and she wondered what Arif had been doing in the back room. On her second visit to the bank she had wandered in there by accident looking for Yusun and had been bustled out without ceremony by the more officious of the two clerks. But Arif looked as if he owned the bank. But then, of course, he did : he owned everything in town, in the name of the government.

He saluted Virginia, said something in Turkish to Yusun and went on out of the bank, his boot-heels clicking like steel-thimbled impatient fingers on the tiled floor. Yusun looked after him. " We are fortunate to have a man like Captain Arif. He is very serious with his duty."

Virginia was not really interested in Arif, but she wanted to be polite to Yusun while she waited for her money. " He is connected with the bank ? "

" Oh, no." Yusun smiled, almost losing his teeth ; he sucked them back in, and Virginia tried not to look at his mouth. " Only one time in a month. Money comes from Ankara to pay the men out at the dam at Bebek. It stays here one night, then Captain Arif and the soldiers take it out to the dam. He comes to make sure the bank is safe." He smiled again, keeping hold of his teeth this time. " He counts the bars in the windows."

The clerk returned with Virginia's money. She stood up, to turn and face Dursun as he leaned on the counter behind her. He smiled at her, not apologetically, not possessively, as if yesterday had not occurred. But yesterday *had* occurred : the memory of it went through her like a rush of blood. She looked at him coldly, falling back on the hypocritical mask because she had no other answer to him here in front of the curious bank clerks. They were all looking at him and her, and she wondered if they knew something. Had he been boasting in the *lokanta*? Her look turned colder at the thought.

Dursun dropped a note on the counter. " I've come for change. My car is over at the garage." He spoke in Turkish to Yusun, and the latter signalled to one of the clerks. He continued to speak to Yusun, then the bank manager turned to Virginia. " Mr. Dursun tell me he show you our district. Very good. You should let him show you more."

Dursun looked at her, still smiling ; but the old hint of mockery was there again. " I know where there is an old wall that might interest you. Out towards Arashehir."

" Mr. Yusun told me about it when I first came here. I don't think it is what I am looking for."

" You should see it, Mrs. Halstead," Yusun said, eager to help this Australian woman, eager to sell his district. " It is very old."

" I'll take you out there," said Dursun, taking, without counting, the small notes the clerk handed him in exchange for the large note. He was still smiling, challenging her now. " I have plenty of petrol to-day. Nothing will go wrong, I promise you."

" Go with Mr. Dursun," urged Yusun, a small enthusiastic fate with false teeth. " Our district has history. You should find it everywhere. Go with Mr. Dursun."

He accompanied them to the door, pushing Virginia out into the heat, into history. " Miss nothing of our district, Mrs. Halstead. Very much history. Go with Mr. Dursun." He smiled at her, holding his teeth in with the corners of his mouth as if performing some party trick. " You will not regret it, Mrs. Halstead, I promise you."

Not wanting to create a scene nor offend this friendly little man, Virginia allowed herself to be almost thrust down the steps of the bank towards the Volkswagen parked outside the garage on the opposite side of the road.

" You must take back some of Turkey with you, Mrs. Halstead." Behind her Yusun opened and shut his mouth in a fanfare of clicks. " Good luck ! "

" I want to get my camera and note-books," she said to Dursun when they had crossed the road and stood beside his car. " To tell you the truth, I don't really want to go with you."

" I know." He spoke gently ; the mockery had gone. " But I do want to talk to you. And out in the country it is more private than here in town. Please, Mrs. Halstead." She wondered if he had ever said *Please* to a woman before, and doubted it. She remarked, too, that though he had tried to make love to her yesterday, he still called her Mrs. Halstead.

That gave her still some advantage, though she was not quite sure how.

" Righto, drive me down to the hotel."

When she came down from her room with her camera and note-books, Meldrum stood at the door to the dining-room. Behind him on a table were some papers and a glass of beer. " You're a glutton for punishment, aren't you, honey ? "

" What do you mean ? "

He grinned. " The heat, honey. What else would I mean ? It's even hotter to-day than yesterday. And that was hot enough, wasn't it ? "

" I'm going out to look at a new ruin."

" A *new* ruin ? I thought all ruins were old. Are they manufacturing them now ? "

" I meant——"

" I know what you meant, honey." The mocking grin left his face, but the expression that replaced it was unreadable ; for the first time she realised he could be as impassive as Dursun.

She went down the hotel steps, got into the car and slammed the door. Dursun glanced at her, then looked up at the front door of the hotel ; but there was no sign of Meldrum, and she was glad of that. She was furious at him, but she did not want Dursun taking her side against him.

They drove up the deserted street. " Are you really so interested in what went on thousands of years ago ? "

" Yes," she said emphatically, and despised herself for striving so much to sound convincing. She went on, doubting a little what she said, " For one thing, it gives me a sense of perspective."

He laughed at that, but more incredulously than mockingly. " What happened here in Turkey thousands of years ago helps you see things better in Australia ? That's a long perspective, Mrs. Halstead."

She had noticed in Crete and down on the Ionian coast the same carelessness, almost contempt of the past. Peasant people who lived among the debris of history, who used the ruins of a Seljuk fort to house their livestock, who grew their vines along the wind-break of a fallen Hellenic wall, people such as they she could understand : the cord of inheritance had been cut for them and they were faced with the battle of each day as it dawned. They found no comfort or sustenance in past glories ; a Minoan relic meant nothing if it could not be sold to some archæologist or tourist. But Dursun had professed to some education, no matter how informal, and she was disappointed in him. It widened the gap between them, made them even more foreign to each other.

" You should be proud of what you have here. That's what we miss in Australia—any identification with the past. We have to borrow from the English—which is wrong. What pride can we Australians feel in what the Elizabethans did ? "

" What pride can you Australians feel in what the Hittites did ? "

But before she could argue that, the present took hold of them again. Up ahead two figures suddenly appeared on the road, vague shadows in the white glare. They were waving their arms, signalling the car to slow down ; but abruptly Dursun put his foot down and the car gained speed. He drove straight at the two men, who had now come out into the middle of the road. They leapt aside as the car bore down on them, and as she swept by them Virginia could see the startled look on the familiar faces. Then dust obliterated them, and when she looked back, peering through the settling blizzard of dust, the men had disappeared from the road. She turned back to Dursun.

" They were the two men who were in the *lokanta* the other night ! The ones who started the fight with the soldiers."

" Were they ? I didn't recognise them." He had slowed the car again, but his face was as set and intent as if he were driving to save their lives. Then she realised he was angry and was trying to contain himself.

" Who are those men ? "

He shrugged, the old answer that annoyed her so much. " How should I know ? "

She had no right to accuse him of her suspicions, although she was sure that the men had come out into the road to flag him down, thinking he was travelling alone in the car. She resorted to a shrug, appreciating its value now as an answer.

They stopped in Kasrik, at the one tiny store the village possessed. They had a beer to wash the dust from their throats, bought some food and wine, then got back into the car. They drove on, disturbing the thousands of pigeons as they whined up the narrow road out of the gorge above the village, moving for a few moments beneath a dark cloud that gave the illusion that the heat had suddenly lessened. Then they were out in the glare again, but after a while Virginia noticed that the country had begun to improve, that the hills and fields were a little less bare.

" We're following the river that runs down to Bebek," Dursun told her. " When the dam is finished, when your Mr. Meldrum has taught the farmers all about irrigation, this will be a good place to live."

" He's not *my* Mr. Meldrum."

He looked sideways at her, suddenly smiling. The anger had gone from him, and he seemed now only to be concerned with the pleasure of being with her. " I am glad to hear that. I do not like too many complications."

She did not ask him what complications he expected. She was too preoccupied with her own.

2

The wall, as she had expected, was much too recent to be connected with the Hittites. Its stones ran up from a grove of poplar trees to peter away in a field of burnt stubble ; one could only guess at the dust of how many harvests had blown over them. But the wall had not been built by the Hittites ;

more probably by later Phrygians who had ventured as far east as this; but half an hour's searching convinced her there was nothing but the wall left here. And in itself it was not important: stones of the past lay dotted all over Turkey like pebbles left by time's tide. She walked down to the poplar grove where Dursun sat with his back against a tree.

"You got me out here under false pretences."

He shook his head, smiling up at her. "I am no expert. I just knew this wall was old, that was all. A few centuries do not mean as much to me as they do to you."

She took off her hat and sunglasses and sat down opposite him, her back against another tree. She shook out her hair, feeling it wet with perspiration against the nape of her neck. The day lay becalmed around them; the trees stood like tall green-sailed masts waiting for a breath of breeze. Through the pale shafts of the trunks, fifty yards away, she could see the silver glitter of the river, the only movement in the whole dead landscape. She took the cheese roll and the bottle of wine he handed her. Turk-like he had not waited for her, but had already begun to eat and had drunk from the bottle. She wiped the mouth of the bottle and raised it to her lips.

"Your hair loose like that, a wine bottle at your mouth—you look reckless."

She took the bottle quickly from her mouth and a trickle of wine ran down her chin. "Don't get any ideas, Mr. Dursun. I assure you I am anything but reckless."

"Mr. Dursun. Are Australians always so formal? From what little I've read about them, I thought they slapped even strangers on the back and called them by their first name. Can't you call me Yashar? And I like your name. Virginia. That comes from virgin, doesn't it?"

"I think so. But names don't mean much." She began to chew on the bread and cheese.

"I'm glad of that. I've never been very interested in virgins."

She didn't look at him at that, giving him no encouragement. She finished the bread and cheese, had another mouthful of wine, put down the bottle and leaned back on one elbow to look up through the trees. The leaves were a black blur against the bright faded blue of the sky ; she wondered when they had last moved to the slap of a strong wind. Then she saw something move in the sky, a small dark shape that floated across an open patch between the tops of the trees. At first she thought it was a leaf, letting go of the tree with the reluctance of a living thing that knew it was going to die ; then it was joined by other shapes, and now she saw they were birds high in the sky. They hung there, dozens of them, waiting like dark angels for the end of this part of the world.

She pointed upwards. " Those birds—what are they ? "

He rolled on his back beside her ; they lay on the brittle grass as on a bed and looked up at the ceiling of the sky. " Eagles. They are waiting for the storks."

" The *what* ? "

" The storks. They come south every year towards the end of summer, from Russia, Poland, Rumania. I have seen them in other parts of Turkey—this must be one of their migration lanes. And the eagles wait for them, just like the brigands used to wait for the travellers on the old roads through Turkey years ago."

" And kill them ? "

" What else ? " Again the shrug. " It's nature. You wait and see. The eagles do not have an easy fight of it."

Repelled but fascinated, she got up and walked through the trees to the eastern side of the grove. The sun had swung over so that she still stood in shade but the sky above was open to her. There was now no mistaking the eagles for dead leaves ; they cruised lazily but menacingly on the limitless plains of the burning sky. Even more now than ever, Virginia was aware of the deathly stillness ; fifty yards away she heard the river rippling over its stones, tearing itself into silver scarves against projecting rocks. She looked around at the surrounding fields and hills, waiting like the eagles, then she looked up again at the sky. The huge birds had begun to draw together in a tight circle.

Dursun came up behind her, put one hand on her hip and pointed to the north with his other hand. " There they come! "

She looked beyond the hills, saw through the shimmering haze the distant snow-streaked landmark that was Erjiyes Dagh. It rose out of the hills around it like a frozen explosion, the haze seeming to make it still be trembling from its ages-old eruption ; the snow on it looked incredible in this heat, one thought of it as the bones of the mountain laid bare to the bleaching sun. A wisp of cloud hung round the mountain's peak ; from it another cloud was drifting towards her. She put on her dark glasses and stood watching as the cloud, getting whiter as it got closer, constantly changing shape but never changing direction, came down the trail of sky across the shining plain where the eagles waited. There was an inevitability, a frightening resignation, about the line of flight of the storks. They had been coming this way for centuries ; this ambush always lay in wait for them ; some of them would never reach the south. In myths, Virginia thought, storks are the carriers of life. But the birds themselves knew that death was a part of life.

Dursun took his hand from her hip and lay down. He had taken off his jacket, making a pillow of it on a small hummock of dry grass. He rested his head on it, nodding for her to do the same. " The fight will go on for hours. This is the most comfortable way to watch it."

She hesitated, then sat down but did not lie down beside him. He had brought the bottle of wine with him ; he offered it to her, but she shook her head. He took a mouthful of wine, then lay back again, almost bored by what was about to happen above him. She looked at him, feeling a little disgusted at his indifference ; then she sat back against a tree, straining her neck to stare upwards. She knew she would hate what she was about to see, but she could not shut her eyes against it.

The eagles had begun to quicken their flight, rising and falling on the waves of heat-disturbed air. The white cloud was now quite distinctly a flight of storks: she guessed at their number, perhaps two hundred of them. They outnumbered the eagles three to one, but she had never thought of storks as fighting birds. To her the scene presented an Australian analogy: a flock of sheep running into an ambush of dingoes.

Suddenly she rebelled at the thought of the massacre to come. " Stop them ! "

He rolled his head to look up and back at her. " How ? Even if I had a gun, they are too high to shoot. Nothing can stop it, Virginia. This has nothing to do with us down here. It has been going on for centuries. I doubt even if a man in an aeroplane could stop it. It is in their blood, the storks' as well as the eagles'. Don't things like this happen in Australia ? "

" I don't know. I'm a city girl. Maybe it does, I don't know."

" City people are too protected. Every one of them is full of blood, but they all faint at the sight of it."

" Doesn't *anything* upset you ? " she said tartly.

" Yes," he said quietly. " Poverty."

She looked back up at the sky, left without an answer: she was no more accustomed to the sight of poverty than she was to the sight of blood. The storks came on, now bunched more tightly together, a white phalanx flying with slow grace to what Virginia thought was certain death. The eagles had begun to climb higher, still circling, their movements a little more jerky, as if nervous and impatient for the coming slaughter. The strain of looking up began to tell on Virginia's neck, and she lay back. Dursun moved his head aside on his improvised pillow, and after a moment's hesitation she laid her head beside his. She could feel the closeness of him, the sound of his breathing and the heat of his body, but she was not disturbed by it : what was about to happen in the sky took all her attention.

The dark circle of eagles had lifted, standing still in the air now, poised for the plunging kill. The storks were flying so close together that it was impossible to see between them ; they were airborne on the one huge shining wing. Virginia, staring up at them through her dark glasses, lost all consciousness of the earth on which she lay. It was as if she, too, were floating in the air, above the sun-glazed hills, a spectator and yet also a part of the death that was about to happen. She prayed for the storks as she might have prayed for children about to be massacred.

Then the storks were immediately beneath the eagles. There was an instant when both flights of birds seemed to stand frozen in the still air ; then the eagles plunged like dark arrowheads at the white body of the storks. And suddenly, as if on command, the storks split up ; not in confusion, but as if instinct, inherited over centuries, had trained them for this particular combat. They flapped heavily through the air, twisting and turning in slow ungainly flight, but somehow managing to avoid the first savage attack of the eagles.

No storks had fallen in the first assault, and now the eagles were climbing, coming in again. But the storks turned to meet them ; and Virginia, seeing what they were doing, gasped at what looked like suicide. She had read of this suicide impulse in wild creatures : the lemmings of Norway were the classic example. Self-destruction, to her, was the worst of deaths ; even in her blackest moments after the death of Tom she had not once thought of taking her own life. She shivered, and Dursun reached for her hand and pressed it.

" Just watch."

But it was impossible to watch the whole battle. The sky above her seemed full of birds, dark and white, whirling in a storm of wings and screams; despite her horror and disgust, she felt a strange mounting excitement take hold of her. Spittle thickened in her mouth, and she reached for the bottle and took a mouthful of wine. She could see feathers beginning to float in the air, like tiny puffs of smoke; birds locked together and rode the sky as the one piebald beast. Then she saw that the storks were not accepting their fate; they were fighting with the same savagery as their attackers. She gasped aloud with delight and surprise: she had always thought of storks as passive, peaceful birds. But now she saw that they were not resigned to 'death, that the urge to survive was as strong in them as in any living creature. Her hand tightened on Dursun's as she saw the battle was not going to be as one-sided as she had expected.

The air immediately above them was a turmoil of birds, plunging, weaving, twisting, falling, screaming: an intensely local storm in the vast glittering sky. A stork stumbled away from the mêlée, an eagle clinging tŏ its long neck; another stork dived, its huge beak aimed like a javelin, and the eagle fell away. It came slowly down, its great wings flapping despairingly, then it died while still in the air and dropped like a boulder to the earth some three or four hundred yards from the poplar grove.

A stork followed it, ridden down by an eagle. The white wings beat the air all the way, but it was a hopeless struggle: the eagle had made its kill. Virginia turned away as she saw the two birds hit the ground in a field on the other side of the river: she could not bear the final cruelty. Dursun sat up, then stood up, looking down at her with concern.

"Let's go back into the trees. You don't want to watch this."

Wordlessly she stood up, feeling a little dizzy with the effects of the wine she had drunk and the battle she had seen. She followed him back to where she had left her camera and bag, her hand in his, led by him as if she were a child being led away from some terrible accident. She did not look up, but she could hear the battle going on above her, the birds screaming in exultation and fear, killing and dying. She sat down against a tree and Dursun sat beside her.

"You must not let it upset you." He held her hand in both of his, and she did not draw it away. "This is nature. It has been happening forever, even long before that wall was built——" He nodded out into the glare at the long ridge of stones lying like the exposed backbone of some long-buried monster. "Just don't look up. The fight may go on for another hour. But they'll drift away. It is a running fight that could go on for miles, all up and down the valley."

There was one terrifying scream that rent the air: like that of a soul plunging into hell, Virginia thought; and she clutched Dursun's hand, digging her nails into him. "Why can't something be done, Yashar?" It was the first time she had called him by his first name, but no reaction showed on his face. "If it happens every year, why can't something be done to protect the storks?"

"What? Kill all the eagles in Turkey? Wouldn't that be wrong, too? The eagle is the most magnificent bird there is, the king of birds. Would you kill all the lions and tigers of the world? Destroy so much beauty?"

She was surprised to hear him talk of beauty; but then perhaps he thought only of beauty in terms of strength: she wondered if he would see beauty in a rose. "Why does there have to be so much killing, so much cruelty?"

"You are being stupid, Virginia," he said matter-of-factly. She waited for resentment to rise in her, but there was none; after a moment she nodded in agreement. "Men are just as cruel as those eagles. What about your heroes of the past? Look at the Greeks. They killed their prisoners to save themselves the trouble of feeding them or having to take them with them. And the Ottomans, they made those eagles up there look like pet lovebirds. They had one small, very entertaining custom—all the younger brothers of a Sultan were put to death

84

so that he had no heirs but those he produced himself. Brotherly love, eh ? And the Nazis——"

" Don't go on." The sound of the battle had drifted away ; she glanced up through the trees and saw that the sky was clear.

" Cruelty is a part of life, Virginia," he said, still holding her hand. " You accept it when you live the sort of life some of us have to live."

She looked at him, hoping for some revelation ; for all the strong physical presence of him, he was surrounded by a fog that baffled and frustrated her. " Who *are* you, Yashar ? "

He smiled at her, taking his hand from hers and putting his arm round her shoulders. A part of her rebelled against the intimacy, but the rebellion was not strong enough ; she stirred a little, but allowed his arm to remain where it was. " Does it matter ? I don't know who *you* are."

" I haven't hidden anything."

" You must have some secrets." She admitted that to herself, but said nothing. " But I haven't asked about them, have I ? I don't want to know."

She stiffened in his arm, but he didn't let her go ; she could feel his grip on her strengthen, even though gently. " You mean you are just looking for a quick affair ? I'm not like that, that's one secret you had better get to know about me now ! "

His hand came up to turn her face towards his ; she felt the calloused palm, not the palm of a hotel owner, against her cheek. " Virginia, I have tried to stay away from you. No, believe me, please——" as she tried to strain her cheek out of the rough bowl of his hand. " I watched you for two days before I spoke to you in the cave of the churches. I told myself that nothing could come of it—even if you allowed it. But I couldn't help myself—I *had* to speak to you, to get to know you——"

" You didn't go about it in the friendliest way." She remembered his mockery of her at their first meeting.

He nodded, the dark eyes that could be so fierce in their anger now tender, almost humble. " I am not used to approaching women cap in hand." She wondered where he got his English colloquial phrases, but she said nothing ; all at once, for this moment and this day, she did not want the fog surrounding him to be cleared. Perversely, the mystery of him suddenly had its own appeal. " The point is, I wanted to meet you."

" I didn't want to meet *you*."

" Did you want to meet any man ? " he said with a quick flash of insight. " Even Mr. Meldrum ? "

" Why do you keep harping on him ? He is there at the hotel, that's all."

" Perhaps I am jealous. Yes, I *am* jealous ! " He spoke with sudden fierceness, pulling her face round towards his so that their noses brushed.

She stared at him, afraid, yet too far gone to draw back. A movement far out in the fields caught her eye, but it was not enough : it was as if a lasso of thread was being thrown to her to prevent her stepping over a precipice. She saw the stork hit the ground like a white meteor, then the eagle was on it, tearing into it.

It seemed a long time later that they lay beside each other, he on his back and she with her head resting on the pillow of his arm. Far away they could hear the birds still screaming as they fought ; idly she wondered how they could stay in the air so long. She rolled on her back and looked up at the trees above them. " These poplar groves are always so neatly planted. Why is that ? "

" Do you notice the different heights of the trees ? A tree is planted every time a baby is born. The grove grows as the family grows."

" What a lovely idea ! " She turned her head, amused, not frightened by the prospect of her question : " Would you plant a tree if I had a baby, Yashar ? "

She noticed the hesitation before he replied. " Not in Turkey."

" Where, then ? "

" Brazil, perhaps." He smiled, but she recognised it as an attempt to throw her off any further questions.

But she was not going to be put off : he owed her some of himself now, she wanted the fog dispersed. " What about Australia ? "

He didn't mind that question : he continued to smile. " Perhaps. What would people say if I planted a tree in Sydney every time you had a baby ? "

" They'd probably enjoy it. We're a young country, we don't have many customs. But why would you not plant a tree in Turkey ? "

The smile went. He took his arm from beneath her, stood up and began to dress. " My future isn't here."

" You sound sad when you say that."

He shrugged, as if sadness was another of the things he was accustomed to. " I wish I could take you to my home."

" Why don't you, then ? "

" You had better get dressed," he said, and turned away.

When she was dressed, she looked at him and said, " Why haven't you any future here in Turkey, Yashar ? Don't you work for the government ? "

His face opened with surprise. " What makes you think that ? "

" Captain Arif thinks you might."

He shook his head, grinning to himself. " Yes, it's a thought. I could be working for the government."

" But you're not, are you ? " He didn't answer, and then she said, " You're not working with the two strangers who were in the fight in the *lokanta*, the men we passed this morning ? "

" I told you, I have nothing to do with them ! " He wiped a dribble of spittle from his mouth with the back of his hand, a peasant's gesture. Once more she felt the abrasive effect of his sudden changes of mood. Then he smiled, took her arm and led her out of the poplar grove. " No regrets ? "

" I'm not a schoolgirl, Yashar," she said, but she knew she was only evading his question.

3

The battle of the birds had ended. She looked up as they came out into the open glare and saw the white cloud of storks, now greatly diminished, heading south. They flew close together, a little sluggishly, wearied by the long flight ; the leaders, she guessed, were already looking for a place to settle and spend the night. She looked around for the eagles, but they had split up, were now individual specks in the blue glass of the sky. They planed aimlessly in the upper stories of the air, as if bewildered and lost now that the fight was over ; then they began to move away towards the hills, the remnants of an ambush that had been defeated. And suddenly she felt a surge of admiration, almost of awe, for the storks. Birds of peace, they had fought the birds of prey, had had their casualties but had not lost the battle. The survivors, and there were many more of them than those that had died, had won through to the south and another year of living.

Dursun drove the car up the narrow track beside the old wall and turned on to the road. In the cool screen of the poplar grove they had been protected from the worst of the afternoon's heat ; now it struck at them again with all the fierceness of the ambushing eagles. " Do people ever die from this heat ? "

" Sometimes. And from the cold. And hunger and sickness and childbirth. And sometimes just from despair. People die, Virginia. One cause is as good or bad as another."

" You're too fatalistic for me. You'll have to change."

" It may be difficult. But for you, I'll try."

Ahead of them two eagles tore at a white mound of feathers in the middle of the road. Dursun blew the horn loudly, but the eagles were too intent on devouring their kill; the car went by only a foot from them, and Virginia looked out and saw the horrifying mess of blood, feathers, claws and savagely ripping beaks. She shut her eyes, feeling the sickness rise in her throat, and kept them closed till they had driven another mile or so. Then she opened them and leaned back in the seat, breathing heavily.

" You should not have looked," Dursun said. " You did the right thing to keep your eyes closed after we passed those first birds. We have passed eight or nine others, in the fields and on the roads. I can see now you will never be used to things like this."

" Would you want me to be ? " She thought she detected a note of criticism in his voice.

But she had been wrong. He took a hand from the wheel and pressed her arm. " Virginia, I should not want you to be any different from what you are. A man should never try to change what he loves."

She could not help her look of suspicion. The echo of the lies of Faber was still in her ears ; life was made up of echoes, an experience of recurring whispers. " You don't love me, Yashar."

They were coming into a small town through which they had passed on their way out. It lay crumpled on either side of the road like debris ; once again she experienced the incredulity that people could pass their whole life in hovels like these. But just outside the town there had been evidence of the government's endeavour to pull these people into the twentieth century : a new school where children played in the yard, already halfway lost to their illiterate parents. That was the tragedy, of course : the children grew up with a new sense of discovery that led them away from their towns and villages to the cities, so that the towns and villages never really progressed at all. Was that why Yashar did not want to plant a tree for his child in Turkey ?

Dursun had to concentrate on his driving as a line of women

came towards them, driving their donkeys ahead of them. Virginia looked out at the women as she went past them, wondered how many of them had had love confessed to them. They stared back at her above the black veils drawn up about their faces : did they envy her the man who sat beside her ?

"How do you know I do not love you ? " Dursun asked without rancour ; she had expected him to be angry. " Is love something you can read like a book ? What if it is a language you don't know ? Do you know how a Kurd feels his love ? "

"No," she said hesitantly, and wondered why she had doubted him. Then knew : " But what's the good of love if it has no future ? What happens to us, Yashar, if we go on seeing each other ? "

"How long are you staying in Turkey ? "

"Maybe two months, maybe more. It depends on how successful our dig is."

"You cannot leave right away ? "

She looked at him in surprise. "Not a chance. I can't let down the youngsters I'm bringing out here. They're looking forward to it so much—I couldn't call the whole thing off at a moment's notice."

"Why not ? What is more important, our happiness or some old ruins ? "

"It's not that, Yashar. It's—well, I've *promised* these young people. God knows, they get let down enough these days. I don't want to be one to add to their disappointment and disillusion. Some of them would never be able to make it out here on their own—they could never afford it. I deliberately picked kids who had no money——"

"They would get over it. Young people are used to disappointment."

"My God, you sound just like some of the old stuffed shirts in England ! Of course they get over it, but does that mean that they have to be subjected to it ? "

He was silent as they drove slowly through the town, careful of the boys who kicked the patched and almost deflated rubber ball up and down the street. She looked out at them and said sourly, " I thought you were a man who was interested in young people who had no opportunity. Or was all that talk about Ahmet just to impress me ? "

He slapped his hand angrily on the horn as a boy ran in front of the car. " Do not talk to me like that ! "

" I beg your pardon ? " She sat up. " I'll talk to you how I damned well like ! What do you think you're running—a harem ? You're not the Sultan of Brazil yet ! "

He stared ahead, breathing heavily. At last, and the effort strained every muscle in his face, he said, " I am sorry, Virginia."

" Well, watch yourself." She was only slightly mollified.

" I shall not be staying long in Malavan. That is why I am impatient."

" Where are you going ? "

He shrugged, then smiled, trying to break down the barrier again between them. " Brazil, perhaps."

" Not back to your hotel near Antalya ? "

He looked sharply at her, as if suspecting her of being too shrewd. " Perhaps," he said after a moment. " I might even go home."

" Is home still there ? "

" Oh, yes." He nodded towards the east. " Almost five hundred miles from here. Beyond Lake Van, near the Persian border. Oh, it is there all right."

" That's the second time to-day you have mentioned home."

" To-day is the first time I have thought of it—oh, for many years. Nobody there would remember me now, but I still think of it as home. I should like to show it to you, but I don't think you would like it. It is wild country, beautiful but wild. Eagle country."

" What do people do there ? "

" Raise sheep mostly." Then he grinned boyishly, young with the memory of his youth. She had noticed this with several men of her acquaintance, the more active ones : a reminiscence of their youth suddenly seemed to shed years from them, as if for a moment all the virility and passion and enjoyment of those years had flared up in them again. " The best brigands and smugglers in all Turkey are also raised there."

Well, *that* was a youthful memory none of her other men friends had had. Then she remembered the remark he had made a day or two ago. " Was that where you did your smuggling ? "

He nodded. " I started at fourteen. We used to steal sheep, smuggle them over the border and sell them to the Persians. Then we would go back a month or so later, steal the sheep from the Persians, smuggle them over the border again and sell them back to the men we had stolen them from in the first place. It was very funny and very profitable. Sometimes the owners recognised their sheep, but not often. There would be a fight and we would have to run." There was no boasting and no remorse : it had been a way of life he had enjoyed. " Then the police finally caught up with us. I got away, but my friends didn't. They hung my best friend, because they said he was the leader. But he wasn't. I was."

" You didn't go back to try and save him ? "

" There was not time. Justice out there is quick. They caught him one day and hung him the next. I was up in the mountains—I didn't learn about it till a week later."

She wondered how she could sit here beside him and listen to this recital of crime without being shocked ; she knew how she would have felt if some juvenile delinquent back home in Australia had tried to tell her of his exploits. She was becoming acclimatised. She remembered the advice that an uncle, an old traveller of far countries, had given her before she had left Australia : Never take your home standards with you, not if you want to enjoy and understand the country you are visiting. She wondered how many thieves and smugglers her uncle had met and enjoyed and understood.

" That was when you went to Istanbul ? " He nodded. She looked at him, at the hard, almost savage profile that, it seemed to her, had been carved as much by experience as by inheritance. She searched for a word to describe him : arrogant, dominant, superior : she discarded them all. Then she settled on *intact*. It was not exact, but it described him better than anything else she could think of at the moment. He was intact, armoured by the years he had lived.

She was still staring at his profile when, beyond him, she saw the other car come out of the lane at the end of the town, setting off a flurry of chickens like an explosion of small land-mines, and turn into the main road behind them. She twisted in her seat to look back. " We're being followed. By Captain Arif."

" I know." He did not appear concerned.

" Yashar, why is he so interested in you ? "

He shook his head and smiled, looking in the rear-vision mirror. " You had better ask Arif.'"

They had left the town now. Suddenly he put his foot down hard and the car leapt forward. The next twenty minutes were the most frightening Virginia had ever experienced. She wanted to cry out in protest, to plead with him to slow down, but one look at his face told her she would not even get an answer from him. An expression of wild exultation had possessed him ; she had the feeling she had been forgotten. This, she guessed, was how he must have looked on wild rides through the mountains when chased by the police in his smuggling days ; he was re-living the past, experiencing again what must have been one of the great joys of his life. He was not a good driver, but somehow he held the skidding, speeding car on the road ; he rode it as he might have ridden a horse, almost letting it find its own way round the treacherous bends of the gravelled road. Virginia looked back once to see if Arif and his driver were still following them, but the Volks-wagen was throwing up so much dust that the road behind it was lost in a boiling yellow cloud.

Then Kasrik appeared ahead of them, a battalion of giant white sentries guarding the road. The car went roaring down into the narrow gulch; the pigeons burst from the cliffs in a violent detonation of wings. They went down into the village under a storm of birds, like a ketch running before a gale. Children appeared in the road ahead of them and Dursun suddenly thumped his foot on the brake pedal; the car swerved, its back end breaking away, and for a moment Virginia thought they were going to roll over. But somehow, God, Allah or someone smiling on them, the car remained on the road and upright. Dursun drove almost decorously through the village, waving and smiling to the children as they ran shouting alongside the car.

Beyond the village Dursun picked up speed again, but did not drive so fast and recklessly this time. He had had his burst of high spirits; he had thumbed his nose at Arif, if that was what he had intended. He's like a kid, Virginia thought, not displeased: every woman likes to see something of a son in her lover. He was like the "ton-up" boys who sped up the Kingston By-pass for the thrill and to show their contempt for authority. Except, and she was sure of this, underneath Dursun's contempt for Arif there was more than the aimless rebellion of the "ton-up" boys. She looked back and saw that Arif's car was now about a hundred yards behind them, just far enough back to miss the worst of their dust. The two cars drove in convoy towards Malavan.

As Dursun pulled the Volkswagen in before Virginia's hotel, she glanced across the road and saw the other car turn into the barracks. Arif sat stiffly in the front seat, returning the salute of the guard on the front gate; he stared straight ahead, seemingly oblivious of the car he had been following for the last twenty miles. An image sprang into Virginia's mind: he was like a man walking down a dark lane, turning his face against whatever he feared. She looked at Dursun and wondered what there was about him that frightened Arif. Would a man who had been a thief and a smuggler in his youth now be working for the government? But she was applying home standards; this wasn't Australia or England. Here, just beyond the Levant, where Europe merged into Asia, respectability was a thing of the moment: one was not expected to declare it as an inheritance.

" Will you have dinner with me to-night? "

She declined his invitation and saw the instant hurt look on his face; but she had surrendered more than her body this afternoon and she wanted time to think. She invented another date and hoped she could make it a fact: " I promised Dr Altinbash and Mr. Meldrum I'd have dinner with them."

" You spend a lot of time with Meldrum."

She put a hand on his arm. " Don't be like that, Yashar." She was conscious of Mustafa, the portly little hotel porter, standing on the terrace watching them with deep interest: life had become much fuller for him since the foreigners had started coming to Malavan. " You will just have to get used to the idea that I am not a Turkish wóman. Australian women are used to having men friends."

" Is adultery a habit with Australian women? "

She couldn't be angry with him: the question was so ridiculous. She laughed, thinking how naïve he could sometimes be. " Not a habit, Yashar. It happens occasionally, but it isn't a national custom. There is a very strong streak of the Puritan in Australian women, and very little sophistication. Some people call Australia the world's largest suburb. " She felt a spasm of treachery; but she knew it was true. " But that may not be entirely a bad thing."

" Is there a streak of the Puritan in you, too? "

She laughed again, wondering what the hotel porter would make of their conversation if he could hear it. " You ask me that, after this afternoon? " Then she pressed his arm again, reassuringly. " Yes, I think there is, Yashar. I have never been public spirited when it comes to love."

He still had the look of a hurt and suspicious youth; then he smiled. " I trust you, Virginia."

" Oh, thank you very much," she said, mocking him now, feeling more certain of herself with him ; but she got out of the car before he could say something else that would make her angry. " I think your education in women is just about to begin."

She turned and went up the steps to the terrace, past Mustafa, who smiled at her enigmatically : politely, mockingly, admiringly, she wasn't sure which. Her own education, in the men of Turkey, was also just beginning.

4

" Honey," said Meldrum, spearing another meat ball, " a long time ago a guy named Lasus said that, quote, the cleverest thing in the world is taking pains, unquote. That applies to the heart as well as to the mind and hands. Take pains before you feel pain."

" When I start collecting aphorisms, I'll know where to come."

He had been much more talkative than usual, but she welcomed his conversation : it occupied her attention while she prepared herself for the thinking she would have to do when she retired to her room. In the silent courtroom of the night she would have a long argument with herself, but she was not ready for it just yet. " Where did you get all this potted advice ? "

" I once spent a summer in Boston, the Athens of America. I was known as the Oracle of Boston Common. I used to sit there on a bench every day and distribute advice to the bums."

" What happened to them ? "

" They all left town and moved to the Bowery in New York. Bums have their own wisdom, the wisdom of wishing to remain ignorant."

" Why were you in Boston ? "

" I was making up my mind whether to go to M.I.T. That's the Massachusetts Institute of Technology. I was in love with a girl and I didn't know whether to go to college or get married."

" What happened ? "

" Do you like these ? " He pointed at the meat balls. " Kadin Budu. Also known as Lady's Thigh."

" How nice." He was talkative to-night, but he was not going to be informative, not about himself.

" For dessert I've ordered Kadin Göbeği. Lady's Navel."

" Quite an anatomical meal. Is this how the Turks dispose of their women ?" She looked up, regretting the question as soon as she had put it. She did not have his talent for keeping oneself to oneself.

He gazed steadily at her across the table. " I wouldn't know how they dispose of them. If you happen to learn, I hope the lesson isn't too tough."

" I wish you'd mind your own business. I'm sorry I asked you to have dinner with me."

" I'm not. You obviously asked me for some purpose. It helps take the ennui out of my boring evenings here."

" And what do you think my purpose was ? "

" I could shoot a dozen guesses. I think the ones most on target would be those dealing with friend Dursun. Right ? "

She had first called up Latife to have dinner with her, but the doctor was on duty to-night at the hospital. She had hesitated for some time before going down to Meldrum's room and knocking on his door. The hotel did not run to telephones in the bedrooms, and she had felt even more embarrassed having to knock on his door and ask him to have dinner with her. But he had not increased her embarrassment by any mocking query. " Honey," he had said, and she had not been sure whether he was lying or telling the truth, " I was just about to come up to your room and ask *you*."

" I got here first," she had said, keeping the mood between them light.

" Okay. They say the woman always pays, but this will be the first time I'll have seen evidence of it." He was grinning at her and his tone hadn't changed; but she was certain his words had a second meaning. " Do you mind if I do the ordering? I know these dishes here. They've got Turkish food on to-night for the benefit of the new load of French tourists who got in to-day. They're Catholic pilgrims, trying to taste what St. Paul tasted."

Now at dinner, dodging his remark about Dursun, she said, " Did St. Paul eat Lady's Thigh, do you think? "

" I must look up his Letters to the Ephesians. If it's mentioned, I've never heard any priest read it in the pulpit."

" You didn't tell me you were a Catholic."

" Did I say I was? "

" No-o. Come to think of it, you've never really said much at all about yourself. Just what are you, Nick? "

He shook his head and gave her that annoying smile. " No guy should ever attempt to describe himself. He leaves himself open to the risk of self-slander or self-delusion."

A rude word bubbled on her lips, but she held it back.

" I *am* sorry I asked you for dinner. Aphorisms with Lady's Thighs and Navels—I can't imagine a more indigestible diet."

He said nothing, but took another sip of his wine. They were sitting out on the terrace; the only other diners out here were a young German couple. The French pilgrims, fifty or sixty of them, had finished their dinner in the big dining room and had turned their chairs to face the priest who was leader of their party. A small fat man in khaki, he suggested nothing spiritual; one could see him any Sunday in the pulpit, using himself as an example of the sin of gluttony. He stood at the end of the dining room, bald head bowed to catch the light, and began to mutter into his chins. A moment later the people at the dining tables began to answer him in the same garbled mutter. Then Virginia recognised that the whole party was reciting the Rosary.

" Good God," she said, " they've got a hide! Taking over the dining room to say their prayers! "

" Why not? Who else is using it? You're a typical Anglo-

Saxon. Religion is only for the church and chapel. It's not like that out here. A man puts down his prayer mat wherever he is and prays when he has to. Those pilgrims have got the idea. You think St. Paul waited till he found a church?" The waiter came and took away their plates, holding the dishes carefully together as if he didn't want to disturb the people at prayer. "You really don't care what they're doing. You're just so edgy to-night you'd snarl at the Virgin Mary. What happened to-day?"

"Nothing."

"I've seen Dursun a couple of times out along the road to the dam. What's he up to?"

"I don't know. We didn't go out to the dam to-day."

"So what *did* you do?"

"Nothing. I *told* you. Oh, yes, we saw a pretty horrible sight——" She went on to tell him about the battle between the storks and the eagles.

But he was still not convinced. "More than that happened. If you don't want to talk about it, why did you ask me to have dinner with you?"

"I'm not going to talk about it," she said emphatically. "But—well, I didn't want to see *him* to-night. Does that mean I'm making use of you?"

"I'm used to it."

"What?"

"Being made use of. But don't let it worry you," he said as he saw the question forming on her face. "I've gotten very used to it. I respond automatically, and there's no harm done to my ego."

"You're not very helpful."

"Do you want me to be helpful? You don't, honey. I tried a moment ago to be helpful and you told me to mind my own business. I like you, Virginia——" It was the first time he had used her first name, and she recognised it as a concession on his part: he was offering her friendship, and she knew, without really knowing how or why, that he had not offered friendship to many people. " When you arrived here a few weeks ago the place suddenly began to look up. A good-looking woman always improves a place——"

She looked up, surprised. " Aphorisms, compliments—Are you drunk to-night, Nick ? "

" Honey——" He had retreated, and she realised she had rebuffed him ; he was more sensitive than she had imagined, and for the first time she began to wonder who had hurt him so long ago. Her curiosity of him began to sprout, like a seed watered by a chance rain, and for the first time in the evening she began to concentrate on him. At last he was providing her with the distraction she had sought. " You'll know when I'm drunk. I say nothing, absolutely nothing at all. *In vino veritas* just ain't true with me. The truth in me sinks to the bottom when I'm awash with liquor."

" Nick, were you in Peru when your wife or your girl friend, whatever she was, called it off ? " It was a wild shot in the dark, but it was on target.

His face darkened and set ; he reacted in exactly the same way as Dursun to the question that hit home. " Why Peru ? "

" Because you said it was there that you first became a cynic. Or rather, after you went home from there, back to America. It really had nothing to do with starving Indians, did it ? "

" You're wrong there. I felt very bad about the Indians."

" Who was the girl ? "

He looked up as the waiter came back. " Here's the Lady's Navel. Be a cannibal."

" You don't even admit the truth when you're sober, do you ? " she persisted. " How could you have helped me if I'd wanted you to ? "

He drained his glass, looked at the bottle as if debating whether to refill the glass, then decided against it. " I was married to the one girl for ten long, very happy years. *Very* happy. Or so I thought."

" Was she the girl you thought about on Boston Common?"

He nodded. " I decided to marry her, but I also went to M.I.T. She came to Boston and worked while I got through college. Then we went to Texas while I did post-graduate work down there. You see, I was almost through at M.I.T. before I decided to concentrate on water conservation. Maybe she resented that, I don't know. I mean, her having to go on working while I was still being a college boy. She never mentioned it, but maybe it was there all the time. Anyhow ——" He poured himself some more wine, suddenly reaching for the bottle. " This is the truth, honey. Nobody's ever heard it before, but maybe I do need a little wine to bring it out."

" Don't get drunk for my sake, Nick."

He smiled at her. " I like you, Virginia. You're short-tempered at times, but you have a talent for sympathy. I think you also have a talent for loving too much, am I right ? " He didn't wait for her answer. " That was how it was with me and Libby. That was her name. Libby Fisher, from Georgia. Macon High, Class of '41. Or maybe '40, I don't know. You never remember those kind of facts about the girl you once were in love with. I remember her bust measurement but not her age."

" You're getting crude."

" No, honey, I'm not. I'm just remembering the physical facts of her—or, no, the physical *fact* of her. Singular, not plural. Well, anyway. I was so much in love with her—and her with me, or so I thought—that I never saw another dame. Pardon me, woman. I even gave up my men friends. I finished college and we moved around from job to job, and there was always just the two of us and that was enough. Oh, we made friends, went out with other people, but they never really mattered to us. Then we went off to Peru, my first big job. But she couldn't take the climate. She went home after six months, but I didn't mind. I figured I had only another six months to go, that the money was too good to throw away, and that we could live without each other for that time. She agreed with me. I put her on the plane in Lima and that was the last time I ever saw her."

Virginia felt an echo of her own horror of long ago. " You mean she was *killed*? The plane crashed ? "

He shook his head, staring down at his wine glass. " No, she met someone else and went away with him. She wrote me, blaming herself, but she made one comment that stuck in my mind. She said I had monopolised her so much that her love had become numb. Maybe she was right."

She was silent for a while, then she said, " It was like that with Tom and me. When he died, I found I couldn't turn to any of my friends. I'd neglected them so much while Tom had been alive. Being in love is no preparation for loneliness."

" Have you tried anyone since your husband died ? "

" My teacher in London, a professor of archæology. He told me I was a dishonest archæologist, that I didn't have my heart in it, and I found out he was a dishonest lover, he didn't have his heart in it, either."

" I think he was right about you as an archæologist. I think you're kidding yourself, honey." He noticed the resentment in her eyes as she looked up. " Okay, I apologise. If I criticise, it's only because I worry about you. Why did you fall for the professor ? "

" I told you, I was lonely."

" And you still are ? "

" I was."

" And you're not any more ? " She did not answer, and after a moment he said, " You might be again, Virginia. That's the thing to watch out for."

Chapter Four

Dursun called for her the next morning and she went out with him. This went on for several days : he always eager, she reluctant but agreeable. She would not go back to the poplar grove ; she told herself, without conviction, that the remembered sight of the dead birds kept her away. She was impatient for the arrival of the students who were to help her with the dig ; they would provide her with a distraction, would anchor her while she tried to regain some perspective. She wrote off again to Ankara ; but she knew the answer might take a week or even a month. No one in Ankara knew nor cared that she might be throwing her life away.

Irked by Meldrum's comment on her as an archæologist, she threw herself into an exploration of everything the district offered her. Dursun, grinning, uninterested but uncomplaining, followed the pattern she set for filling in their days. They drove miles through the hot exposed hills in the yellow Volkswagen. The heat had not abated ; the countryside seemed to pulsate in the bruising glare ; the horizon was a gallery of mirages. They visited Goreme, Nevsehir, Haci Bektas : she drenched herself with the past, but Dursun remained untouched. She filled her books with notes, but she wrote like a woman preparing a long defence brief. And always the day ended with him making love to her. They were lovers by circumstance, a liaison that she had always thought only occurred with bored promiscuous people. She was neither bored nor promiscuous ; then she sought her excuse in loneliness. But she knew it was more than that that had thrown her at Dursun, even though it might have made her vulnerable to him. The man himself was the magnet.

But she could not go on drifting like this, and one morning she decided she would go back to Kasrik and take up her preliminary work again. If the students should suddenly arrive, she did not want them to think she had been wasting her time while waiting for them.

She had seen Meldrum only fleetingly since the night of their dinner together, but this morning she had breakfast with him.

" Any distraction will do," he said when she told him what she intended doing that day. " Keep your mind on the Hittites. This country has seen a dozen invaders and sooner or later most of them have been absorbed by it. Don't let that happen to you."

" You seem very concerned for my welfare, Nick."

He stood up, looking down at her with the sleepy, mocking gaze that annoyed her so much because she could not fathom it. Even his confession of the other night had only revealed part of him. " It's my nature. I felt the same way about the Indians in Peru."

She watched him amble away, walking with the slow cat-like movement that she found slightly incredible in such a big man. She envied him his impregnability : he had been hurt, but now he had built up a shell that would take him unharmed through any situation. She could only guess at the subsidence within him, the wreckage of his belief and hopes, but he would not let it show on the outside. She would feel safer if her own façade were as strong as his.

Promptly at ten, the arranged hour every morning, Dursun called for her in his car. " I can't get over your punctuality," she said, getting into the car beside him under the appraising stare of Mustafa, the porter, and the fat French priest : she was gathering witnesses to her own destruction, she thought. " People out here are supposed not to care about the exactness of time."

" Depends on the appointment," he said, smiling at her, reaching out to touch her wrist in a gentle gesture of welcome and love.

She was amazed at the evidence of tenderness he had shown towards her over the past few days. " People are watching, Yashar. Do you want them talking about us ? "

He glanced up at the terrace, at the priest in the shadow of an umbrella, the porter in the shadow of the doorway : they watched with the steady unblinking scrutiny of secret police. " They are nobodies. They can't hurt us."

No, she thought, only we can do that. She put her camera and other gear on the back seat of the car with the picnic basket the hotel had packed for her. " We're going out to Kasrik to-day. I'm going to do some work."

" Not Kasrik."

" Yes." He shook his head, his face stiffening ; but she persisted : " Why not ? "

" I do not want to go to Kasrik, that is all."

" Well, listen to you ! What about me ? Look, Yashar, I told you—I'm not one of the local women. I don't do every-thing the master says. Now if you don't want to take me out to Kasrik, I'll go in the Land-Rover——" She reached back for her gear, but abruptly he put his foot down and sent the car shooting out into the street. She sprawled sideways in her seat against the door, but he did not even glance at her to see if she was all right. She composed herself, rubbing her elbow where she had knocked it against the door, swallowing the angry words that frothed in her mouth. They went up through the town at a speed that brought a shout of protest from two men driving their donkeys across the square. Then they were out on the open road that led to the turn-off down into the Kasrik valley. She tried to keep her voice cool and indifferent : " If you want to tear the engine out of this car——"

He took his foot off the accelerator, fumbling to try and find a steadier speed. They drove along the ridge that flanked the valley, the heat coming up at them as it bounced back from the broken cup of the valley. "You are right. I need the car."

"You might treat me a little more gently, too. Or don't you need me?"

He turned his head, suddenly smiling. "You would make a good Kurd. You have such an independent spirit."

She made no reply, but his smile had its effect on her and they drove on in a more genial atmosphere. They went through Kasrik, past the village square where the harvest was now piled in golden hummocks, and on up to where the road ran between the pockmarked rock chimneys. They got out, Virginia setting her straw hat firmly on her head against the onslaught of the sun, and turned up the path that led through the purple cascade of thistles. Dursun carried the resistivity meter and rods for her, but there was no grace in the gesture of help: he obviously considered this a waste of their time together.

Now she was here, exposed to the assault of the heat, Virginia regretted her insistence on coming. But she had to show her independence, she told herself, and she was determined to work for at least an hour or two.

"I wish I had better maps." From her research in the Archæological Museum in Istanbul, she knew what to look for. She had no expectation of a major find, despite her dreams; but even Schliemann had not begun by unearthing Troy. But the maps she had to work from were old and, she had found by experience, inaccurate. A lot of what she had plotted down in Istanbul did not check with the actual region now that she had visually surveyed it. "Some of those new aerial maps would be just the thing."

He hesitated, then he said, "I have one down in the car. You may borrow it."

"Where on earth did you get one? They're top secret or something."

He shrugged. "Nothing is secret if you know the right

people. But you must not mention to anyone that I showed it to you."

" Would it get you into trouble with Ankara ? "

He grinned at some secret joke, and drew his finger across his throat. " I am trusting you with my life."

" Then I don't want to see it."

But he had already turned and was scrambling down the rocky path to the car. He came back with a map case, opened it and handed it to her. " The very latest, taken by the United States Air Force."

" I don't want it, Yashar. I wouldn't want to get you into trouble."

He looked around at the deserted hillside. " Who is going to know out here ? Take it."

" What would happen if Captain Arif found out you had this ? "

" I should probably have to kill him." Then he smiled, but just a little late, she thought. " I am joking. Go on, use it. If anyone should come by, just hide it. I am going for a walk down to the village to see Ahmet." He leaned towards her and kissed her on the cheek. " You are a beautiful flower. You make even these dry hills look like a garden when you are amongst them."

She was not accustomed to such compliments ; but then the poet had never been suspect here in this part of the world as he was in the Western world. Turkish women had compensations for what they were denied in other ways. " You embarrass me, Yashar. I shall have to get used to you."

" Don't you like being called beautiful ? "

" I love it. What woman wouldn't ? But most of the compliments I've had have sounded like telegrams, not poems." Even Tom had been like that : his idea of a fulsome compliment had been : *You look pretty good to-night.*

Dursun squeezed her hand, then went down to the car. He took a black umbrella from the boot, put it up, waved to her, then went off down the road. She smiled after him, thinking how ridiculous he looked, reminded of pictures she had seen of African chiefs walking beneath the modern caricature of a king's canopy. He turned and waved once more, she waved back, then she began to climb farther up the hill.

She could hear the flutter of wings and the soft murmuring of the pigeons, but the birds were too sensible to be aloft in this heat. More sensible than I am, she thought; but she was determined not to retire yet. She reached the top of the path and stood surrounded by thistles that lay among the great profusion of rocks like dark patches of fallen sky.

She looked down towards the village and saw the black mushroom of Dursun's umbrella. He had stopped to speak to a man, someone who stood on the other side of him and was hidden by the umbrella. She wondered if it was Ahmet; then the man moved out from behind the umbrella and looked up towards her. It was one of the strangers, one of the men from the fight in the *lokanta*, the man who had grabbed her in the moment before she had fainted when she had been here in the valley last time.

She was staring down at him, straining her eyes to identify him more closely through the haze, when suddenly the hills around her seemed to come alive. They shuddered, and for a split second she thought it was a trick of the hot bright light, another mirage about to take place in the glassy air. Then the ground beneath her began to tremble; she felt the earth roll like a swelling sea. She heard the thistles pop, exploding with small dull sounds like dud firecrackers; a large stone jumped like a brown frog and went rolling down the path; below her the top broke off one of the rock chimneys and crashed to the ground in a spray of yellow dust. She stood with her feet wide apart, trying to keep her balance. The pigeons had burst from the cliffs as if the earth itself had catapulted them, darkening the sky and adding their terror to her own. The tremor passed beneath her, was succeeded by another; then the earth, with something like a groan, settled back. She saw Dursun drop the umbrella and run up the road towards her, staggering as the tremor passed under him, then regaining his balance and running on. The pigeons swung away, exposing the sky again, and she looked up, somehow expecting a violent storm to break. But she looked straight into the sun and was blinded. She shivered, despite the intense heat, then she heard Dursun clambering up the path.

"Are you all right?" He reached her, took hold of her shoulders and pulled her to him. He said something in Turkish then held her away from him and looked down at her. "I thank God you are safe."

She stood on her toes, forcing herself up within the tight circle of his arms, and kissed him on the mouth. She could feel his lips trembling; indeed, all his body: the movement of the earth still echoed in him. "I'm all right, darling," she said soothingly, surrendering completely at last, becoming at once mother and mistress, the perfect lover for the man. Love was a mutual selfishness, each looking for his own need in the other: she had suddenly seen his need of her and she had found her own need in him: it was the answer to her lone-liness. Love was always a contention, there was always a risk in it; she had learned that from the one and only argu-ment she had ever had with Tom, when for one dreadful hour there had been no love in her at all for him. "Darling," she said again, and the word was a confession of love.

He recognised it; and sank his mouth on hers. Then he lifted his head. "I thought it was going to be worse than just a tremor. An earthquake." He stood with his arms still about her, then unexpectedly said, "Will you come to Brazil with me?"

She laughed, thinking he was joking, that he was trying to calm her with some trivial talk. "To-day?"

"In a day or two."

"I'll go anywhere at all with you. But I'd be quite happy down on the coast at Antalya."

He shook his head, and she realised now that he had not

been joking. " You'd be too close to the past. I don't want it to catch up with us."

Standing here on this rocky hill, shaken by the earth tremor, shocked by his sudden seriousness, she was not prepared to commit the rest of her life. She slid out of his arms. " You mean you're jealous of the Hittites, too ? "

She bent down to pick up the map case she had dropped. And saw the cracked bank of earth between the rocks, and projecting from it the smooth handle of some vessel. With a cry she dropped on her knees, grabbing at her trowel and furiously beginning to scrape away the earth.

By the time she had uncovered the jug she was dirt-streaked and sweating profusely ; but she did not care nor was even aware of how she looked. She had made her first find ! Oh, there had been other finds on other digs, but this was hers and hers alone ! She dragged the jug out of the hole she had dug, handling it carefully as if she were some midwife delivering a fragile infant from the womb of a dead mother. It was almost a foot high, with a delicate long lip to its neck like the beak of a bird. She brushed the dirt from it and saw the faint geometric designs on the body of the jug, black, red and white figures that had faded almost from sight ; it was impossible to distinguish what the designs meant, but now was not the time for close examination. Yet she knew one thing : this jug was pre-Hittite. It could be the first clue to an even greater discovery than she had ever dreamed of.

" Is it interesting ? "

She looked up startled. Then was ashamed, for in her excitement she had forgotten Dursun. He stood above her, arms folded, indifferent : whatever man had made this jug had no message for him. She could have dug up a bone buried by some dog from the village. " I think so. But I can't be sure. It would have to be examined by someone more expert than I am——"

He bent down and took it from her. " It is a nice shape."

He handled it carelessly, as if it were some cheap item he was bargaining for in a bazaar. " It is heavy——"

" Watch it ! " She stood up, sweat streaking the dust on her face, and put out a nervous hand. " Don't go bouncing it up and down like that ! That thing may be priceless."

He raised a quizzical eyebrow. " Really ? How much ? "

" I don't know. Oh, for God's sake, don't be so mercenary ! Here, give it to me."

He handed it back to her. " Would you sell it ? Would it be worth thousands of liras ? "

" I would *not* sell it ! Are you out of your head ? " She was even hotter now with indignation. " Yashar, this is my find ! There may be more——" She gestured around at the wrack of rocks amongst which they stood. " Under all this there may be a village or even a town, a whole way of life buried by time. There could have been an earthquake—something must have happened to throw all these rocks together like this ——"

" Are you going to dig them all out, just to look for a few old houses ? You'll need one of Mr. Meldrum's bulldozers from the dam."

" You don't do archæological digging with a bulldozer ! "

He looked at the jug again, cradled in her arms as if it were a child. " I should sell that if I had found it."

" That's another of the differences between you and me."

" Yes it is. You can afford not to think of its value in liras."

She went to make some angry retort, but bit off the words. Of course he was right. She looked down towards the village, saw the children thin as stick insects in the shimmering glare, remembered Ahmet trapped forever here by poverty. Then remembered something else : " What did the man want who spoke to you ? "

For a moment she thought he was going to deny that there had been a man. " Man ? Oh, *that* one. He was one of the men who tried to stop us on the road the other day. He thought he knew me. But now he knows he mistook me for someone else."

It was a lie, she knew, but he told it so well : relaxed, direct, not a sign of any unease. " Does he live here in Kasrik ? "

He shrugged. " I didn't ask him. I am not interested in him. It's getting much hotter. Are you going to stay up here digging ? "

She looked around her again. Nothing more than the jug had been exposed by the breaking of the earth's crust ; and if she wanted to dig deeper she would need something more than the trowel she carried. She was still excited by her find ; and that, she decided, was enough for one day. The shock of the earth tremor, the excitement of finding the jug, the final surrender to Dursun, had combined with the heat to reduce her to a state of exhaustion. She would come back to-morrow, confident now that she stood on a hill beneath which was buried an ancient settlement. The ghosts of the past would wait for her.

" You won't mention this in Malavan ? This is *my* find. I don't want everyone up here digging away like bandi-coots——"

" Bandicoots ? "

" An Australian animal. Oh, I've got such a lot to teach you ! How to appreciate the past, all about Australia——"

He smiled, then picked up her gear, leaned close to her and brushed his lips across her dirty cheek. " You are like a child sometimes."

" I've thought the same about you."

He chuckled, and they scrambled down the path to the car, she holding the jug to her bosom, as careful of her step as if she were walking on the crumbling edge of a precipice. Dursun retrieved his umbrella, which he had dropped as he had run up the road to her, then he got into the car and headed for Malavan.

2

Dursun drove carefully, while Virginia sat beside him nursing the jug, now and again looking at the design on it like a mother trying to find some recognisable feature in her new baby. Dursun would glance sideways at her and grin indulgently, but said nothing.

" Do you think Ahmet would like to work for me when we start to dig ? "

" The money would be welcome to him," he said, delighted at her suggestion. " It is a very good idea."

" I'm glad you think so," she said, pleased that she had pleased him.

He took his hand off the wheel and pressed her arm, and they rode on through the dazzling day in a mood that made them oblivious of the discomfort of the heat.

They came round a bend below a rock-warted hill to find the road blocked by a tumble of boulders. Dursun stamped on the brakes and the car skidded on the gravel road. Virginia was flung forward, but somehow she managed to hold the precious jug away from the dashboard as she hit it with her shoulder. Dursun brought the car to a halt, switched off the engine and leant towards her.

" All right ? "

" I almost broke the jug."

" Damn the jug ! Are *you* hurt ? "

She sat back, massaging her shoulder. " Just a bruise, I think. No bones broken."

He put a gentle hand on her shoulder. " Nothing must ever happen to you." Then he opened the door and got quickly out of the car. " The earth tremor must have brought those rocks down. I'll move them."

He picked up one or two of the smaller rocks and threw them aside as if they were footballs. She had been aware of the strength in him, had felt it during their love-making, but

113

this was the first time she had seen him display it. He moved to one of the larger boulders, one that to her seemed almost half as big as the Volkswagen in which she sat. He leaned against it and slowly began to rock it on its rough base. She could see the muscles standing out on his arms and neck and could imagine the bulging strength hidden beneath the sweat-darkened shirt. This was not exhibitionism, the male showing off before the female ; this was how he would have moved the boulder even if he had been alone on this road. She could see the strain on his face, the sweat shining on it like oil ; his foot slipped on the gravel, but he dug in his boot and pushed harder. Once more she was aware of the rough peasant in him ; the sensual side of her thrilled to it, but her intellect was chilled once again by a momentary doubt. Then suddenly he gave a tremendous heave and the boulder rolled off the road and went bouncing down into the small ravine at the bottom of the hill.

He turned to give his attention to another of the boulders. Then he stopped and looked up at the hillside above him. She got out of the car, curious as to what had caught his attention. Three men were sliding down the hill and even as she got out of the car they landed with a jump on the roadway. They were three nondescript men, peasants dressed in patched trousers and waistcoats, as much part of the countryside as the goats and sheep Virginia and Dursun had passed coming along the road. They were the sort of men Virginia had seen every day since she had arrived here in Anatolia : silent, anonymous, indifferent. Except that these men were not indifferent : the tallest of them held a gun.

The leader said something to Dursun, who laughed, and the gun was brought up threateningly.

" What do they want, Yashar ? " She was still holding the jug in her arms as she moved up the road to stand beside Dursun.

He was grinning as he looked at her. " They want our money and our watches."

" You mean they're bandits ? Brigands ? " She looked at the three men incredulously ; even the fact of the gun somehow did not make them real.

" Not brigands. These men are amateurs. Look at them, frightened to death by what they are doing." He looked at the three men with amused contempt ; one would have thought he was the one holding the gun. " Poverty has driven them to this. I feel sorry for them."

The three men glowered, doing their best to look threatening. All three were thin, long-nosed and moustached ; their cheeks and jowls were black with a week's growth of beard. The leader had a cast in one eye, but it added no menace to him ; Virginia was not quite sure which eye was looking at her, and found it disconcerting. He raised the gun, an ancient rifle, but Dursun did not even look at it.

Then one of the men, a boy of twenty or so, with broken front teeth and a closely-cropped head, stepped forward and put out his hand, muttering something to Dursun. There was a look of reluctance on his plain dull face ; robbery was a last resort, the end of a road that had been reached too soon. Dursun smiled at the boy for a moment, then he put his hand in his pocket and took out a wad of lira notes and handed it to the boy. He took off his wrist watch and also handed that over, then he said something in Turkish to all three men.

" What did you say to them ? " Virginia was not frightened because she felt that, somehow, Dursun had command of the situation, that he would not allow any harm to come to her or himself. But she felt uneasy and stood a little closer to him.

" I told them to leave you alone, to be satisfied with what I have given them."

The three men were staring at her, as if making up their minds whether to heed Dursun's advice. Then the third man, small and thin, his face covered by a tight veil of pock-marks, a man whose courage was no more than an exhibitionism that he would later regret, suddenly reached out and grabbed at the jug in Virginia's arms. She grasped the handle of it, there was a struggle for a moment, then both she and the man let go of the jug at the same time and it crashed to the ground, splintering into fragments about her feet.

And at that Dursun let out a roar that seemed to bounce back off the hillside. Later she would remember that she had never heard such an eruption of anger : it was animal-like in its terrifying effect. A huge arm shot past in front of her and lifted the small man off his feet. He hung there in front of her startled eyes for a moment, his pock-marked face splitting apart with terror ; then suddenly he was hurled at the leader of the group, hitting him and sending him sprawling. Dursun flung his other arm at the youth, knocking him to the ground, then he went after the other two. Virginia saw him pick up the small man, hold him aloft as if he were a half-filled sack of wheat, then drop him to the roadway. Dursun stamped on him with his boot, stepped over him and picked up the rifle from the nerveless hand of the leader, who was still sprawled on his back. It was brutal, but Virginia had no time to feel shock : it had all happened so quickly.

Then she saw Dursun raise the rifle and aim it at the head of the small man he had dropped to the road. " Yashar, no ! "

Without lowering the rifle Yashar turned his head and looked at her. " Why not ? He deserves to be shot. He touched you after I told him you were not to be touched——"

" He didn't hurt me ! "

He nodded at the fragments of the jug scattered on the roadway. " He broke your jug."

" Please—please don't harm him." For the first time she *was* frightened, afraid of what he might do to the three men. " If you want to punish them, hand them over to Captain Arif."

It was almost as if she had said something remarkably funny. He threw back his head and laughed, at the same time lowering the rifle. The three men still lay or crouched on the ground, staring up at him with a mixture of fear and incredulity ; it was plain that they were now beginning to think they had held up a crazy man who could only be held in check by the blonde foreign woman. Dursun looked down at the men, still laughing; then abruptly he barked something at them in Turkish. The three of them jumped to their feet, even the small man who must have been painfully hurt by Dursun's treatment of him. They stood together like ragged recruits in front of a drill sergeant, terror standing out more clearly on their faces than even their black stubble of beard. Dursun put out a hand and the youth quickly thrust the bundle of liras and the watch into it. Then Dursun barked again, and the men turned and went racing down the road, round a bend out of sight. Dursun laughed once more, then, still chuckling, turned back to Virginia.

" Amateurs are never very good at this sort of work."

" Would you have shot that man ? "

He gazed at her, as if realising for the first time the horror he might have caused her by shooting the man in front of her. He leant the rifle against the car and bent down and picked up the shards of the jug. He gathered every piece, brushing his hand across the gravel to sweep the smaller pieces together. He took a peasant's large red handkerchief from his pocket, carefully put the fragments in it, stood up and handed it to Virginia as if he were presenting her with a bouquet of flowers. He did it without any mock ceremony, almost humbly.

" I am sorry he broke this. It means nothing to me, but I know how much it means to you. That was why I would have killed him."

She took the red cradle of shards of pottery, shaking her head, bewildered by his matter-of-fact approach to retribution, touched by his manner in gathering up the broken jug and presenting it to her. " Don't ever kill anyone for my sake, Yashar. One death is enough to be responsible for."

" Your husband ? " He shook his head. " You did not kill him. It was written by Fate that he should die when he did."

" And that man you were going to shoot ? "

He laughed, picked up the gun and put it in the boot of the car, ushered her into the car and closed the door. " He did not die, did he ? You were his Fate this morning. He will be your slave for life." He started up the car, drove past the boulders that were still scattered about the road, and headed for Malavan. " So shall I, but for a different reason."

She made a moue of her lips, kissing him across the space between them : something she had not done in years, not since she had done the same thing to Tom. She and Tom had reached a stage where they could make love to each other without touching each other : with their eyes, a gesture, a clicking of the teeth that suggested a bite. Already, in a few days, she was beginning to reach that stage with Dursun : the events of the morning had precipitated her feeling for him. She made the full confession to herself : she loved him.

They drove round the shoulder of the hill and down in the field below them, standing there like scarecrows, were the three men. Dursun put an arm out of the car and waved to them, grinning at them, all his anger gone : after a moment the men raised hesitant arms and waved back. Then they turned and went running across the field, skipping shadows that were soon washed out in the bright hot glare.

" Why did you laugh when I suggested handing those men over to Captain Arif ? "

He turned his grin on her. " Captain Arif has enough to worry about without having to gaol some amateur brigands."

" What, for instance ? "

The grin broadened. " Me."

" I know he's worried about you, but—Yashar, please tell me. What have you got to do with Arif ? "

" I cannot tell you now." He was still grinning at some secret joke, but his voice was serious. " Maybe later, some time in the future. A long time." He looked at her again, his face sober again. " But say nothing to anyone about these men. We don't want to get them into trouble."

" You were going to kill one, and now you don't want to get them into trouble ! "

" I am not angry at them any more. Let them go. They are poor men—they probably decided to hold us up on the spur of the moment. They were probably out trying to shoot something for their dinner, a bird or something, saw us there on the road, thought we had money—a man with a car in these hills is a man with money—No, let us forget them. Do not mention them again, I was like them myself once."

She shrugged, appreciative now of the non-commitment that the gesture offered. " If that's what you suggest——"

" What can you do about the broken jug ? "

She looked down at the bundle in her lap and felt a sudden flood of chagrin and disappointment. " I don't know. Try and piece it together—there are experts who can do this. Oh, one thing, though. If I am going to keep quiet about those men, you keep quiet about what I found out at Kasrik. I don't want a horde of villagers up there on that hill digging away for relics to sell to tourists."

" It is their hill, isn't it ? "

" Well, yes. But it may be much more important than the means of their earning a few liras."

" Try and tell that to *them*. In any case, it will not matter, will it ? We shall be gone from here in a few days."

" Yashar, you can be pretty thick in the head sometimes. I'm not leaving here *now*, especially after what I've just found."

" I am leaving." His voice was flat and decisive. " I *have* to. I want you to come with me."

" But I *can't* ! I have commitments to these kids in London. I—well, I have a commitment to myself, if you like. I didn't come all this way to throw it up just when I'm getting somewhere. We can wait a few more months. I'll still be in Turkey. You'll only be down near Antalya."

" No, not there."

" Where then ? "

He suddenly swung the car into the side of the road and

brought it to a halt. A hawk had been tearing at something on the verge of the road, another bird or perhaps a field rat; it took off with an angry flap of wings, circling above the car and waiting for them to move on. Dursun turned to Virginia, his face set hard with the purpose of his thoughts.

"I shall be a long way from here or Antalya. Perhaps out of Turkey altogether."

"Brazil?" She meant it as a joke, but he did not take it that way.

"Perhaps. Or Greece. Somewhere. But at least out of Turkey. And I want you with me, Virginia."

She could hear the hawk screaming as it hovered and swooped. It seemed that the birds and the men in this country did not like being deprived of what they wanted. "Not so fast, Yashar. Can't you see, I just can't drop everything like that and run away with you? You must give me *time*. I'll come with you wherever you want to go—even Brazil. But not now."

"It has to be now. In two or three days, no more."

"What's wrong, Yashar? If you would only tell me, perhaps I'd understand why all the rush. Must you be so damned mysterious? Is that the sort of wife you want me to be, one who never knows the truth about her husband? I can tell you now, Yashar, I'll never be *that* sort. I want to know all about you—oh, not all at once, but in time——"

"You will. In time. But I cannot tell you now."

"Are you in trouble with the government? Is that it? Is that why you laughed when I told you Arif thought you were spying for the government?"

"I am not in trouble with the government. Not yet." The hawk swooped down, brushing its claws along the roof of the car. The drought had made it even fiercer and more daring than usual; it was hungry for its prey. "All I shall say is that I may be. I cannot tell you any more, Virginia. You and I have different ways of looking at things. I must wait till I am sure you will understand——"

" I am not going away with you *now*. That's definite. If you can't trust me, why should I trust you ? "

" You are being very foolish, Virginia. You are destroying our chance of happiness."

" Now watch yourself—don't adopt that high-and-mighty attitude with me." She was perspiring freely, with the heat and her growing anger. The hawk's claws scraped along the roof of the car again, somehow increasing her irritation. " You still think like a Turk——"

" Not a Turk."

" All right then, a *Kurd*. There isn't much difference to a Western woman's eyes. Righto, don't get angry. I'm talking from *my* point of view, not yours. You don't seem to want me to *have* a point of view. You talk about our happiness, but what happiness will there be for me if I'm the one who does all the giving and you're the one who does all the taking ? "

" It will not be like that——"

" It may not be like that all the time. But that's the way you want it to start ! And the way a marriage starts is often the way it finishes. I've seen it happen——"

" You are a very stubborn woman——"

" You just don't know much about women, that's all ! No, I'm not going away with you now, Yashar, and that's final. In two or three months maybe, yes. You go wherever you have to go, Greece, Brazil, wherever it is, and I'll come to you when I'm ready."

" You will never come to me if I don't take you with me now."

She stared at him for a moment. She heard the swish of wings and from the corner of her eye saw the hawk flutter down, careless of them now, and begin to tear once more at its prey. She closed her eyes for a second's relief from the glare of heat and of memory : her lids only turned the day red, the colour of the blood she had seen on the white corpses of the storks as the eagles had torn at them. This land was too cruel for her : particularly its men.

" You may be right at that, Yashar," she said, speaking slowly, opening her eyes but keeping them averted from the feasting hawk. " I love you now, but given time to think I may change my mind. But that's what I want, time to think. Because if I go with you, wherever I go with you, I don't want there to be any mistake. I could not bear a second marriage that ended in unhappiness."

" You will not come with me now ? "

" No."

3

But that night she went looking for him. She had lain all afternoon in her room, oppressed by the heat, depressed by her fight with him. There seemed no escape from the heat now ; it had penetrated every corner of the hotel. The sheets of her bed were as dry and stiff as paper against her naked body ; she sweated only at the roots of her hair. The air was so dry and hot that it made one's nostrils sore ; she kept wetting her lips with her tongue, afraid that they would begin to crack. For a few moments she longed for the grey wetness of London ; then from there went on to remember the tropical downpours that hit Sydney during the summer. Then she stopped thinking along that line : now was not the time to become homesick.

The French pilgrims had gone, as had the German tourists who had come yesterday for a one-night stop-over. The hotel was empty of guests but for herself and Meldrum ; and he had been out at the dam all day. She had heard his jeep pull into the hotel's parking space late in the afternoon, heard him speak to Mustafa, the porter ; but his presence in the hotel offered her no consolation or distraction. She was shackled by such loneliness as she had not felt since the first days after Tom's death ; yet she did not want to break out of it by seeking Meldrum's company. She was conscious of a pain of mind that had never affected her before ; doubt was a migraine that would keep her awake all through the night. She lay on her bed and through the glass door to the balcony of her room watched dusk creep like a brigand band up out of the gullies and ravines, capturing the hills, softening their harsh outlines for a moment before they disappeared in the soft darkness of the Turkish night. A donkey brayed down by the river, a hoarse sound reminiscent of grief, as if the animal had said farewell to its last sunset.

She found it difficult to be objective about her feelings towards Dursun. For the past twelve months, since the affair with Faber, there had been no predisposition in her mind to fall in love ; she had travelled in lonely places, through the mountains of Greece and Crete, where, had the right man appeared, she could have been deluded into thinking she *needed* love. There had been no aversion to such a possibility, only a natural caution brought on by the treachery of Faber. Love, she had come to learn, was not all bliss. She had read somewhere that it was death's brother; and she knew that in sadness it often reached its highest peak. But the tragedy of the loss of Tom, though it had sent her running to the ends of the earth to get away from the memory of it, had not killed her essential optimism. She still hoped for another love that would last.

But would love with Dursun last ? She was not young nor foolish enough to place her faith in sexual love ; bodies could be united by pleasure, but she knew that the heart needed more than that. Sex could be no more than a few minutes of love : one did not have to think of the future if one took the necessary precautions. But what precautions could she take for the sort of love she sought ? What future had Dursun ever mentioned to her ? A dream of Brazil, that was all : it meant no more than the poet who offered his mistress the moon.

She sat up in the darkness of the room, her flesh brushing like dry silk against the stiff cotton of the sheets She got up, showered and dressed, shutting her mind against thought, wanting to do what she was about to do before she could change her mind. If Dursun could give her some promise of the future, some explanation of the mystery surrounding him, she might, just *might*, go away with him.

She went down the stairs and out past the entrance to the dining room. Meldrum sat in there alone, surrounded by a sea of white-clothed tables, like a man drifting in a sea of parachutes ; he sat hunched over his table, his arms spread out, a man trying to stop himself from falling to his death. Two bottles stood on the table in front of him, and she caught a glimpse of the waiter hovering uncertainly in the background. She hurried on out of the hotel, hearing Meldrum call to her as she crossed the terrace, but she did not turn back. She did not want to talk to Meldrum to-night, especially if he was on a bender. *In vino veritas* ; but did she want the truth ?

The last thing she wanted to-night was advice ; it might only confirm her own suppressed fears at her lack of caution. But whatever answers Dursun gave to her questions, she knew she would not be able to sleep to-night till she had seen him. She did not want *all* the answers to him ; she knew the value of some uncertainty in love, the hidden spark that passion always needed ; but she was not prepared to commit her whole future to a mystery. Love needed some sort of landmark.

She had never been to Dursun's hotel. It was not really a hotel, but a *lokanta* with four or five rooms for overnight travellers. She had once asked him why he stayed there, but he had evaded the question ; as, she was beginning to realise, he had evaded so many of her questions. She went up the main street, its street lamps burning with a strange brilliance in the hot still night ; crossed the square, where the surrounding *lokantas* were unusually quiet to-night, as if everyone had been struck dumb by the heat ; and turned up a side street that led up beneath the towering hill that dominated the town. Above her Kemal Ataturk, still without a nose, glimmered in the dark sky like a local constellation. A dog barked at her, then slunk away, too exhausted and listless to want to attack her.

She felt exhausted herself by the time she reached Dursun's

hotel. It was a small two-storied building built into the lap of the hill; from the terrace of the *lokanta* on the street level one could look out across the town and the valley beyond. She turned for a moment and looked back; even in the starlit darkness she could recognise parts of the town: her own hotel, the barracks, the bank. And it was quieter here than down in the centre of town. For one thing, this was a *lokanta* where the men came to drink and talk and play backgammon, not listen to the squawking radio.

She walked across the terrace and into the *lokanta*. At once the murmur of talk stopped, and the men there turned in their chairs to look at this intruder, a woman at that. She felt a flush of embarrassment, and wondered for the first time if Dursun would be angry at her coming here. Thoughtlessly, because of the heat, she had donned a sleeveless, low-cut dress; she was suddenly aware of her arms and the hollow between her breasts, as if she had been stripped naked. She knew that the Anatolian women, and certainly at least some of the men, considered bare arms immoral. The men stared at her, then almost as one turned their backs on her and went back to their conversations and their games. She could only guess at their thoughts, and she raged at herself for her thoughtlessness in wearing the revealing dress. Like a trollop she had exposed these men to thoughts of adultery with her, a sin almost as great as the fact in Moslem eyes.

She had half-turned to retreat from the *lokanta*, when the proprietor, a lean bald-headed man in a collarless shirt and a dirty apron, came towards her. He had the look of a man who would stand no mischief from others, but would not be beyond it himself. He would throw a pickpocket out of his *lokanta* at the same time as he relieved the man of his wallet. Virginia edged out of the doorway and stood in the shadows, and he followed her.

" I am looking for Mr. Dursun," she said, then struggled to find the Turkish words for her question.

The proprietor shook his head, cold-faced, his agate eyes

unblinking, telling her without saying a word that she was not wanted here. But she was pleased to find he had some skimpy English, something left behind by some traveller: "Dursun gone."

"Where?"

The proprietor shrugged: the comings and goings of his customers meant nothing to him, all he wanted was payment for what he supplied them with.

"When?"

If he had shrugged again, she felt sure she would have hit him. But he held up two fingers. "Two hour. In car. With bag. Pay me. Good-bye."

"Is he coming back?"

He shrugged again, but it did not matter now: she already knew the answer. She thanked him, crossed the terrace and began to walk slowly down the narrow street, past the crumbling houses that were part of the hill. And Captain Arif fell into step beside her.

She was not surprised to see him. She was in a suspension of belief, when nothing could surprise her: whatever happened now would be part of a pattern she expected. She had been like this once before, in the week after the initial numbing shock of Tom's death had worn off; it was a pessimistic resignation, in which the effect of the worst that might happen had been dulled before it *could* happen. She turned to Arif, almost welcoming him, as if he were some proof of what she felt.

"You were looking for Mr. Dursun?" He saluted her, meticulous in his manners even in the darkness. His white gloves, belt and gaiters glowed in the faint reflection of the lighted profile of Kemal Ataturk high above them: it was like walking with a soldier's ghost distinguished only by his military accoutrements. She could not think of Arif as a man out of his uniform: he had been born a soldier. "I, too. But he has gone, they say. I am very pleased."

A dog growled at them, a grumbling shadow. "Were you

afraid of him, Captain ? " She was depressed enough not to be afraid to ask the question.

His boots scraped on the cobblestones : he had missed his step. " Of course not ! But I must watch everyone who comes to this town. It is my task."

" Have you been watching me, Captain ? "

Again the scrape of his boots : she was throwing him out of his stride. " Of course not, Mrs. Halstead. I do not watch tourists or foreign visitors. You are welcome."

" How do you know Mr. Dursun was not a tourist ? "

He laughed, a flat coughing sound that was echoed by another dog in the shadows. " Turks are not tourists, Mrs. Halstead. Not in Turkey. Oh, people visit Istanbul or Adana or Ankara. But nobody from those places comes *here*."

" Mr. Dursun did."

" And I wonder why." He walked a few yards in silence. A woman looked at them from an open window with listless curiosity ; behind her in the darkened room a child cried irritably with the heat. " But we do not have to worry about him now, yes ? "

" No," she said, and was unable to say whether what she felt was relief or regret.

Arif escorted her to the entrance of the hotel, saluted her and went across the street to the barracks, walking so jauntily she almost expected him to break into a whistle. His life as a soldier was so simple : all he had to concentrate on was the enemy : love was a complication that never entered into the rules. She wondered if Arif had ever been in love, then dismissed the thought. He was too well protected by ambition to be open to such an ambush.

She was crossing the small foyer when Mustafa, the porter, came towards her from the dining room. " Madame, Mr. Meldrum, he ask for you."

She followed Mustafa into the dining room and found Meldrum sprawled across a table. An empty wine bottle and an almost empty bottle of colourless liquor stood on the table in front of him. She picked up the liquor bottle and sniffed it.

" Raki," said Mustafa, and shook his head.

" Wine and raki. He's really been mixing it to-night."

" Madame ? "

" Nothing, Mustafa. When did Mr. Meldrum ask for me ? "

" A little time ago. Just before——" He rolled his eyes and dropped his head.

" Righto, Mustafa. Will you help me take him upstairs ? "

But then the waiter, who had been staring at them through the kitchen doorway, came through into the dining room. He and Mustafa, both small men, were dwarfed by Meldrum ; but they were strong and between them they carried him upstairs to his room. They laid him on his bed and looked at Virginia for further instructions.

She hesitated, considerate of their moral outlook ; then decided her duty lay towards Meldrum, not Islam. " Leave him, Mustafa. I'll look after him."

They went out of the room without a backward glance, closing the door quickly behind them, as if anxious to protect her reputation should anyone else be passing along the corridor.

She pulled off Meldrum's shoes, wondered if she should undress him, decided against it, and went into the bathroom to get a wet cloth to sponge down his face. When she came back he was blinking owlishly up at the light. He tried to sit up when he saw her, but the effort was too much. His head flopped back on the pillow.

" Drunk or dead, mah prayers have been answered." His speech was slurred, but she noticed that his Southern accent had thickened. She had noticed before how frequently the tongue reverted to type in drink. Faber, who had affected the light English public school accent, had got drunk one night and she had been surprised, then amused at the vowel-distorting London accent that had emerged, the accent that Faber himself had declared was one of the least attractive of all English accents. She liked the American Southern accent, although it was not always easy to understand, especially if the speaker was from the Deep South. And was drunk. " Honey, yo' mah answer."

" I'm flattered, Nick." She wiped his face with the cloth, then bent over him to arrange the pillow under his head. He raised his face against her breasts, and she straightened up quickly. " Don't do that, Nick ! "

" Ah was on'y listenin'."

" Listening ? "

" When did yo' last have someone listen at the keyhole of yo' heart ? "

" Why, Nick, you're poetic ! " She stood up, busied herself about the room, not wanting to walk out on him abruptly but not wanting to be faced with his being maudlin. The room was neater than she had expected a man's room to be ; but then he did not have much with which to make the room untidy. It struck her all at once that a room like this, or even a tent, was probably the only home he had known for several years. Two suitcases, some technical books, half a dozen paperbacks, a transistor radio : a good many of the peasants he was here to help owned more.

He watched from the bed, still too drunk to sit up. But part of his mind was free of the fog of drink : " Ah'm fulla hidden talents, Virginia. Tha's a fine ol' state, Virginia. Carry me back to Ol' Virginny. Ah sing, too. Hidden talents. Poet, musician—Ah also play the jew's harp. Musically, Ah'm pro-Sem—Semitic. Not anti. No prej'ice. No, Ah'm a liar. Ah'm prej—why do Ah bother with that word ? Virginia, Ah don't like friend Dursun, tha's what Ah mean. Watch that man, Virginia, watch him."

She turned out the light and opened the door. " I don't have to watch him, Nick. Not any more. Good night."

Chapter Five

That day Ahmet had accidentally dropped and broken the bottle of medicine that had been left for his mother by Dr. Altinbash. Behije, his mother, had shrugged and told him not to worry; the medicine had been helping her to sleep, but the pain in her belly was no worse than the pain of seeing Ahmet's bitter vexation at what he had done. He was a good son, the best son in the village of Kasrik, and sometimes she longed for death so that he could be released from his self-imposed bondage to her. Then she would look at Mediha, her daughter, and wonder what would happen to her; then she would pray to God to let her stay alive till Mediha was old enough to have attracted a husband who would look after her. It was wrong that Ahmet should have his whole life spoiled by having to look after his mother and sister. God must have been looking the other way the night he was born.

Ahmet had worried about the broken bottle of medicine all day. When he had gone to bed that night he had been unable to sleep, knowing that his mother was also awake in her bed. Before she had got the medicine she had lain awake in her bed almost every night moaning softly to herself; to-night she was quiet, but he knew she must be swallowing the moans so that he would not feel bad about what he had done. Finally he could stand it no longer. At midnight he had got up, telling his mother he could not sleep because of the heat, and had gone out of their house and down to the cave where they kept their two donkeys.

As soon as he had stepped out of the house he had been aware of the disturbed atmosphere of the night. No lights were lit in any of the houses and all the villagers were in bed; but he could hear several dogs howling softly and as he got closer to the caves where the villagers kept their donkeys he could hear the restless stamping of hoofs and almost a chorus of braying. Then he heard another sound, the brushing of thousands of wings against the still night air, and he looked up and saw the black cloud of pigeons pass across the orange moon. He shivered, despite the heat, and remembered the omens of his childhood: shadows across the moon meant a black day to come.

He went into the cave, talking soothingly to the donkeys, smelling the sweat of fear on them. He paused for a moment, wondering if he should go and wake the *Muhtar* and ask the old man's advice about the premonition he felt; then decided against it: the old man had never made him welcome, considering him a rebel against the authority of his elders, a young radical who wanted to change the age-old way of life here in Kasrik. He put a bridle on the stronger of their two donkeys, feeling it trembling as he slid the rope over its head, then he led it out of the cave, mounted it and headed for Malavan.

An hour out along the road, riding with his head lolling on his chest as he dozed, he was passed by a car. He heard it coming up behind him, driving very fast. It flashed by him, its lights blinding him as he turned to look at it; a storm of dust enveloped him, but not before he had recognised the small car that belonged to Yashar Dursun. He wondered what Yashar was doing here on the Kasrik road, then shrugged and rode on out of the settling dust, staring after the disappearing car as its yellow lights lanced the black folds of the moonlit hills. Then the car was gone from sight and once more he went back to dozing as the donkey plodded towards Malavan.

Some hours later he was riding along the ridge that led down into Malavan. Several times he had dozed off and had fallen off the donkey, and now he had a gash on his knee that he would have to ask the doctor to look at. He had passed two or three farms and there he had noticed that the animals were as restless as those back in Kasrik ; dogs had been howling, their cries echoing a misery of some long-dead soul, and donkeys had been braying with a fear that had now communicated itself to Ahmet. The air had seemed alive with birds, wheeling and screaming across the grinning skull of the moon ; and once he had come upon a camel, standing in the middle of the road with its great ugly head flung back as if listening to the warning cries of the birds above it. Ahmet for a moment thought of turning back to Kasrik, to be with his mother and sister if disaster should strike, but hé was now so close to Malavan he decided to finish his errand. The sound of his mother's moaning haunted his ears as much as the cries of the birds and the howling of the dogs.

He looked up as the sun came up behind him, throwing the shadow of himself and the donkey ahead of them along the road. The hills and the road glowed as if they were red-hot, as if the earth were on fire just beneath its crust ; he was riding through a crimson world in which his moving shadow looked like a smudge of ashes. He raised his head still farther, wondering at this bright reflection from the sky, and felt a surge of excitement that flushed him wide awake. There were clouds in the sky, red blankets that seemed to be thickening even as he stared up at them, the first clouds he had seen for months. The drought was going to break at last ! This was what had disturbed the animals and birds. Oh, stupid creatures, if they only knew how much the humans longed for, and not feared, such a thing !

Then the donkey suddenly stopped dead. It opened its legs wide, as if trying to prevent itself from collapsing, raised its head and brayed with terror. Ahmet felt the animal shiver beneath him, and all at once he, too, was shivering, the animal's terror suddenly part of himself. Far up at the end of the valley, beyond Malavan, he saw the hills ripple. He had never seen the sea, but once a travelling cinema show had come to Kasrik and one of the films had been about a storm at sea. Now he was reminded of what he had seen in that film. The hills shook like giant red-brown waves, seeming to rise up against the sky, and he would not have been surprised if they had all at once rolled forward and down into the valley. From a long way away, up near the hills, a noise came to him, carried easily on the still breathless air.

It began as a low thin thrumming, almost a singing sound that was badly off-key. Then it changed to what seemed like the hollow echo of thunder. The donkey brayed again, its terror sawing against the ear; above him Ahmet heard the birds scream and suddenly shoot up into the sky as high as they could climb. Then ahead of him he saw the road beginning to roll like a carpet being shaken; dust puffed up to hang like a red ground mist above the trembling earth. Ahmet jumped off the donkey just as the ground rose up to meet him. He staggered, trying to keep his feet on an earth that all at once seemed to be turning to a thick liquid; he shouted with fear, but didn't hear his own cry in the braying of the donkey, the high faraway screaming of the birds and the crashing grinding sound, as of the rocks of Anatolia being pulverised, beneath his terror-numbed feet. The Devil was about to take over the world.

All round him he could see the countryside, in the red glare of dawn, jumping like a vast sea about to be wracked by a storm. There was no wind, only a stillness in the air such as he had never felt before; it was as if every living creature in the world had suddenly sucked in its breath, taking the life out of the air. He saw the jagged hill above Malavan shake violently, then part of it broke off and crashed down, trailing dust like spray. Just above the rim of the ridge that still hid the town from view he could see the tall minaret of the mosque glimmering like a pink candle; then suddenly it seemed to melt and fold and in a moment it was gone. Again he saw the road rolling towards him, heard the roaring sound beneath him once more, then his legs crumbled as if his bones had dissolved, the donkey fell against him, and he tumbled forward, striking his head against a rock. The earth heaved under him, coating him with dust, then the shuddering passed on and he was left unconscious by the roadside, the donkey braying with terror beside him.

The earthquake had hit Malavan at 5.28 a.m. The only public clock in the town, that on the barracks tower, stopped at that minute, the two black hands hanging together at the bottom of the yellow clock face as a reminder during the following days of the moment of disaster. The main barracks buildings were demolished by the second shock of the earthquake, but miraculously the tower survived the initial shock, the one twenty seconds later and those that followed over the next five hours. But the clock stopped, as did time itself for many on that terrible morning.

The shocks were recorded by seismograph needles in observatories throughout the world. The magnitude of the earthquake was estimated on the Richter scale at 8.2, and geophysicists in those observatories knew at once that, if a town or a city were at the epicentre of the disturbance, then a major disaster had just taken place. They plotted on their charts the probable location of the earthquake, then waited anxiously for word from Turkey as to whether their worst fears were to be confirmed. They were like doctors waiting for a dreaded diagnosis to be verified ; the injury had been done, but would it kill ? They were men of imagination who could turn figures on a scale into a nightmare in their own minds.

At the moment of the first shock most of the townspeople were still asleep, or at least in their beds. On the neighbouring farms in the surrounding valley and hills most of the peasants were awake and up, preparing for a day that held no more promise for them than yesterday or the day before or the months before : another day of heat that would take the strength from them and the life from the land. Many of them had begun to wonder what they had been doing on the day during Ramadan when the course of their life for the year had been decided by destiny. Had they been drunk, thinking like an infidel, looking at a woman with covetous eyes ? They were being punished for *something*, and what God willed, they accepted.

One or two of the older people, those who had known an earthquake in other parts of the country, had had a feeling of foreboding and had spent the night fingering the charms they had bought from the *hojas*. But they had said nothing. The year had been bad enough as it was without their donning the mask of a death's head. The despair of the people had reached a depth where no one wanted to hear of how worse things had been or could be. They were at the nadir of feeling when relativity no longer has any meaning, when the pessimists and optimists alike are told to hold their tongues. So the older people held their tongues during this night, got up early in the morning and went outside into the hot still dawn to pray, and so saved their lives. Their children, those who would not listen to experience, died in the wreckage of their houses. It was the will of God, the older people told themselves, but knew in their hearts that somehow they hád failed their children. Forebodings were warnings sent by God and they had not done enough to broadcast His message. For the next month their weeping would be as much cries of guilt as wails of grief.

In Malavan itself no houses or buildings collapsed with the first shock. The whole town shuddered, and cracks appeared like flung streaks of dark paint in the walls of some of the larger buildings, but nothing fell down. People tumbled out of their beds, screaming at each other to hurry; mothers grabbed for their children in the dark, instinct guiding their hands as if they were seeing them in broad daylight. Then the second shock struck. Some made the doorways before the houses crumbled inwards; only to run out into the narrow alleys and have the houses opposite collapse on them. A mother ran to the first-floor window of her house, screamed to her husband in the alley below and dropped their baby into his arms; then, stricken dumb, stood and watched as the front wall of the house fell away from her and buried her husband

and child. A donkey went galloping by down the alley, jumping the rubble like a steeplechaser, a small boy clinging to its back; it ran straight into a falling wall, disappearing as if under a grey waterfall, and miraculously emerged on the other side; but the small boy was now gone from its back. The *lokanta* and houses built into the lap of the hill above the town cracked open like so many brittle pea pods; but no one had time to observe their secrets and no householder escaped to tell his own. The side of the hill slid down like a giant apron, and the houses and the people in them were buried for ever, the only dead in Malavan for whom no grave had to be dug. The rumbling thunder of the earthquake passed, and a frightening moment of silence followed, as if the whole countryside were catching its breath again. Then there was a welter of sound : that of falling bricks, splitting timber, the crackle of broken power lines, the gush of water, the screams and moans of people, the strangled braying of donkeys, the yelping of dogs and, somewhere under the wreckage of a house, the hoarse mechanical keening of a stuck motor horn : an aberration of sound that the fear-deafened survivors would only hear much later as an echo in their minds.

Pali, the dwarf lottery seller, had been sleeping in a small mud hut right by the wine factory. The hut fell down around him before he could grab his skates and scuttle to safety; it buried him to his neck as he stood up on his tiny legs. Had he been a man of average height he would have been able to wriggle himself out of the mound of debris that held him down; now his great head sat on top of a body of rubble and screamed for help. The factory next door fell inwards, splitting open the wine vats and casks; the wine cascaded out of the factory and down the slight rise past the trapped Pali. It poured over him in a dark red stream, almost drowning him; when it had gone, the mound was saturated with it and the dwarf's hair and face dripped red. He opened his eyes, feeling them smarting as the wine ran into them, and saw the first of the terror-stricken townspeople rushing by towards the open countryside. He shouted, feeling the pressure of the rubble on his chest as he expanded his lungs, but he might as well have saved himself the effort and the pain. The townspeople, blinded by the selfishness brought on by the urge for survival, that most callous yet most understandable selfishness, raced by him, splashing through the wine as it flooded down the street. They had bought lottery tickets from him in the past, hoping for fortune, but to-day the only fortune they wanted was to stay alive.

The dwarf shouted and cursed, his chest bursting with every cry, then his shouting dribbled away to a whimper of self-pity. God had made him a mockery of a man; and now God was still mocking him. He prayed for the Devil to help him; but did the Devil have an ear for prayer? His prayer-beads were in the pocket of his shirt and he could feel them pressing like pebbles against his ribs; it was as if they were a reminder, and after a while he went back to praying to God. He licked his lips, tasting the wine, washing some of the dust from his mouth. He turned his head in the direction of Mecca, and for the first time looked across the devastated town. And gasped at what he saw, the ruin of a town that he had always thought was ageless and would last for ever. He said an involuntary prayer of thanks to God, knowing, even from this distance, that he had been more fortunate than perhaps half the townspeople.

He looked up at the sky, at the red clouds billowing across the heavens like smoke from the burst and burning earth. Birds were still wheeling and screaming like black furies; and trapped as he was here, he wondered how long it would be before the crows came to pick his eyes out. He was alive, but now the deadening thought came to him that it did not matter. The end of the world had come, and by the end of this day everyone would be dead. He began to pray again, that in Heaven he would not be reborn as a dwarf.

2

Virginia had slept only fitfully during the night. She had never known such heat as this, not even in Sydney at the height of the worst summers; there was no humidity, but the air itself was so hot that it almost stifled one to breathe it. Just as stifling was the thought of Dursun's desertion of her; it burned her brain as she twisted restlessly on the bed trying to escape the heat. She was not a romantic, but she believed in a woman's need of romance; after the initial emptiness of despair at Tom's death had worn off, she had come to realise that she would need love again some time in her life. At first she had been suspicious of Dursun, then cautious of him; but last night when she had gone seeking him at his hotel she had been fully committed to him. She had turned her back on logic, which had been her final protection against Faber. It had been Faber who had told her that a good archæologist needed an equal mixture of romance and logic: one to lead him or her to seek the lost and forgotten, the other to chart the route and evaluate the clues that were found. So, her mind giving itself over to her heart, she had gone to find Dursun and tell him she would go with him wherever and whenever he wanted her to go. And had been met with the cold logic of his own decision, to leave without saying good-bye, making the break as clean as that of a swift sword-stroke.

By dawn, through periods of fitful sleeping and waking, she had arrived at an acceptance of the situation. There was still a feeling of loss, that he had come to mean something to her that would be difficult to replace; the loss was more than a physical or sexual one, and she knew that a seed of love for him had been planted in her that might alternately wither and sprout for years to come. It was as if some meaning had been given to her life, a meaning she still had to unravel; despite the happiness, despair and loneliness she had known in her life, the labyrinth of her own heart was still an unmapped voyage that had to be completed. Love was a mystery as much as an awakening, a paradox she was coming more and more to appreciate, if not to understand.

After the long hours of tortured thought there was also a feeling of relief; like someone searching among the ruins of his house, she had salvaged a few treasured possessions. She still had her pride, the treasure so often stolen from the losing lover: Dursun would never know that she had gone looking for him. And she had some certainty of the future, without which even the deepest love can have no guarantee of survival: she would go back to digging for the past, the past that had its mysteries but no threats or risks. But not here in Turkey. No, to-morrow she would cable the students in London that her plans had been changed. She felt a sense of treachery, but there was nothing else to do; she would try and give them a chance to dig with her somewhere else, there was still time. She would go down into Syria, following the old trade route to Carchemish. The past was buried all over the world, there were still plenty of places to escape to.

She turned over once more, hoping for another hour's sleep before the day became even hotter than the night had been.

Then she heard the rumbling with an ear that was only half-awake. She opened her eyes, lost in that waking moment when even the most familiar seems strange; saw the room shivering like a film that had jumped out of frame, and wondered if she were having some sort of brainstorm. She rolled on her back and saw her naked body bouncing up and down on the shuddering bed in an attack of ague which she did not feel. The bed had jumped away from the wall and skittered to the centre of the room; it came up against the heavy lounge chair which had advanced from the opposite wall. Almost as if in a dream, as if she were playing some role in a ballet she did not understand, she reached out and took her dressing gown from the chair. The bed and the chair kissed again in the centre of the room, then each slid back to its wall. The dressing table against a third wall was jumping up and down, its mirror catching the dawn light outside and slashing the room with red lightning flashes. All Virginia's toilet articles on the dressing-table were suddenly swept to the floor as by an invisible hand; with them went the jug fragments in Dursun's handkerchief. The standard lamp in one corner leapt like a one-legged dancer, then fell over with a splintering of its glass shade. All the time Virginia could hear the groaning thunder of the earth, the crashing of houses and the screams of animals, human and four-legged. She was to remember later that none of the screams had sounded as if it had come from a human throat, although she knew that some of them must have. But at the moment of disaster many of the people in Malavan were reduced to the same primitive level of terror as their livestock.

Virginia rolled off the bed and tried to stand up on the shaking floor. She was trying to get her arms into the sleeves of the dressing gown, her legs splayed wide to give her some balance, when the whole opposite wall of the room fell away from her. She stopped, too amazed to be horrified, one arm in the gown, her nakedness forgotten. The wall fell away and with it almost the whole of the hotel : only one end of the building, the width of one room and the stairwell, was left standing. She stood for a moment exposed to the red glare of the dawn, only the bright angry boil of the sun visible to her through the storm of rising dust. It was as if she stood on the precipice of the world and hell was about to burst into view below her.

The floor had stopped shaking, but now it was tilted. She heard the bed begin to slide behind her, and she jumped aside just in time. It went past her and over the edge of the wide-open room, its mattress parting from the iron bedstead like white flesh from a black skeleton. Other things were sliding out of the room : the small table, her suitcase, her type-writer. The dressing-table slid past her : for a split-second she saw herself in its mirror : naked, wild-eyed, a madwoman in a world that had itself gone mad. Then she felt her feet slipping on the dusty wooden floor. She grabbed at the door that had burst open, swung herself out into what remained of the corridor, and crashed to her knees on the steeply inclined floor. She slid backwards, desperately clutching at the wall; she felt her feet slide out into nothingness, felt the jagged edge of the broken floor scrape against her hip and belly. Then her fingers caught a projecting edge of the wall; she clutched at it with hands and hung on. She could feel her arms being torn from her shoulders; dust rose up to choke her as she gasped for breath. Then slowly, painfully, her naked belly and legs scraping against the edge of the floor, she pulled herself up. She lay for a moment, getting her breath, gathering her strength, then she crawled up the incline of the corridor on to the still-level landing in the stairwell.

She stood up, wanting to be sick but too full of dust to be able to get anything into her mouth. She looked down : from her waist down she was one large red rash, and blood ran from a gash over the front of her right hip. She pulled on her dressing gown, shut her mouth and nose against the choking dust that now obscured everything like a thick yellow fog, and groped her way down to the ground floor.

She came to what she knew must be the foyer of the hotel. She gasped with fright when thin dead fingers brushed against her face, then she recognised it as one of the palms that stood in pots just by the front door. Her eyes were sore and half-blinded from the fog of dust and grit, and when she had gasped she had sucked in enough grit almost to choke her. She stumbled across the foyer, her bare feet kicking against fallen bricks, and out across the terrace and down the front steps. She fell down the last of the steps, tripping on the trailing edge of her gown, but she picked herself up at once and ran towards the Land-Rover parked in the area in front of the hotel. She had dragged open the door of the vehicle, was about to drag herself up behind the wheel, before she realised what she was doing. She stopped, shaking her head, then turned round, slamming the door of the Land-Rover behind her, and lurched over to the ornamental pump that stood in the middle of the parking lot.

She had sat on the terrace in the late afternoons and watched the women and girls bring their long slim-necked jugs here to this communal pump. They would stand for a few minutes gossiping, replenishing themselves as much as their jugs; then head for home, the jugs balanced like coronets on their heads, giving them the regal walk which is the only resemblance princesses and peasant women share. But it would be a long time before the women of Malavan filled their jugs and gossiped again at this pump.

The pump and its ornamental base of lions' heads were just a twisted mass of metal and masonry half-buried in a wide crack in the earth. One lion's head, centuries old, lay on its side, its stone eyes staring sightlessly at the ruins of the hotel; beneath it lay the hotel's cat, its back broken, its grey tail caught in the open mouth of the lion. Water was gushing up from the broken pipe, being soaked up at once by the thirsty earth. Virginia dropped on her knees beside the fissure in the ground and scooped some of the water into her face. She succeeded in washing some of the grit from her eyes, although they were still sore; then she dipped her hand in the water and drank from it, careless of any germs that the water might contain. One death was as good as another: she would die from the choking dust in her throat if she did not die from typhoid.

Then she stood up and at last fully collected herself. The town was a mad tuneless opera: people and animals ran aimlessly, screams and shouts mingled with the crashing of buildings, and the whole scene was lit, through the swirling storm of dust, by the blood-red sun. Across the road the barracks were no more than a small hill of bricks and masonry; a dazed and bleeding man crawled out of it like a mole emerging; he looked up at the clock tower, then shook the watch on his wrist and put it to his ear; then he fell down and lay still. Virginia raised her hand and crossed herself, something she had not done since she was a child, not even when she had seen Tom killed ; this was the gesture of someone who still had faith in God, who was thankful for her own survival.

She stood irresolute, wondering where to go, what to do. She had read that sudden unexpected disaster could have this effect on one, especially if one were alone ; all points of reference were suddenly taken away, and it was as if one all at once had to find one's identity again. Then she heard a moan coming from the direction of the hotel, and then she remembered she was not entirely alone. Meldrum was somewhere in the ruins of the hotel, buried God knew where in the wreckage of the fifty rooms that had crashed down. She ran back towards the hotel, kicking her bare feet against the fallen bricks but unaware of any pain.

" Nick ! Nick ! "

She stumbled up on to the terrace, now just a long mound of fallen masonry, steel girders and crushed bricks. One of the striped umbrellas above the terrace tables still stood, a bright flower in the general devastation. The fog of dust had begun to thin and now it was possible to see the full effect of the earthquake on the hotel. The major part of the building was a total wreck ; Virginia turned her mind aside from the thought of what the death roll would have been if the hotel had been full of guests. She scrambled up over what had been the end wall of the dining room and almost stepped on the crushed remains of what had only a few moments ago been the hotel manager. She flung up a hand to her mouth, wanting again to be sick, but again nothing came. She hadn't eaten last night and now she was glad of it. If she were physically sick she felt that the last of her strength would be drained out of her and she would just collapse. And she knew even now, only moments after the disaster, that everyone who had survived in the town was going to be needed.

She turned away from the sight of the manager and put her foot on a sheet of glass from the shattered doors of the dining room. It broke under her with a loud snap, but she lifted her foot just in time to save being cut. She could still hear the moaning, but she could do nothing to help whoever it was till she found something to put on her feet. The rubble was full of broken glass; plates lay everywhere like fallen white petals; knives and forks glinted menacingly among the bricks. She looked wildly about her, then saw one of her suitcases balanced on a pile of masonry. Careful of where she put her feet, she scrambled across to it. She had always been careless of locking her suitcases and now she was glad of it. She opened it and found jeans, a shirt, socks and underwear—but no shoes. She cursed loudly, but wasted no time. She slipped the jeans on under her dressing gown, wincing as she pulled them over the abrasions on her belly and hip; then she discarded the dressing gown and quickly donned a shirt. Any townspeople passing by might have wondered at the foreign woman who stood in the midst of ruins and dressed instead of running for her life; but those people who did pass by were running for their own lives and did not stop to query the behaviour of others. Nothing was strange on the last day of the world.

Virginia finished dressing, then, after a little searching, found her boots and put them on. The whole routine of dressing had taken her less than two minutes, minutes in which the remaining section of the hotel might have fallen on her and killed her, minutes in which the moaning man, whoever he was, might have died. But what she had been doing had not been the eccentric behaviour of a foreign woman, nor of an over-modest woman; her mind was now clear and she was acting in the cool rational way that had deserted her for the past week. She knew that she was not going to be able to help anyone trapped in the ruins if she cut her feet to ribbons trying to get to them. Emotional she might be, but she was also practical.

She grabbed a pair of gloves from the suitcase, gloves she wore when digging; she was aware even then that she was about to dig for something more precious than a Hittite relic, for a man's life. She pulled the gloves on, turned and climbed over the wreckage towards the sound of the moan. Dust still hung in the air, but most of the thick grit had now settled, like grey snow, and it was possible to see clearly for fifty yards or more. The fallen building was still subsiding, and she could hear girders groaning as the weight of bricks pressed down on them. There were other sounds : screams, shouts, the crackling of flames ; but they belonged to the rest of the town, were beyond her immediate concern. She slid down a mound of bricks, ducked under a girder, and then saw Mustafa, the porter. He lay on his back, a heavy beam across his legs, blood pouring from a gash in his head. He was still conscious, but only just, and when she crouched down beside him his dull eyes looked at her without recognition. Then suddenly his eyes closed and his head dropped back. He was dead.

She stood up, feeling a grief for Mustafa out of all proportion to her knowledge of the dead porter ; it was grief built up by an ashamed relief that it was he and not she who had died. She turned, and banged her head against the girder. She staggered, let out a curse at her own carelessness, then heard Meldrum say, " Don't knock yourself out, honey. We may need you."

" Nick ! " She spun round, almost falling over as she did so. Meldrum's face showed through a tiny gap in a pile of masonry and girders, like a man peering out of a fortification. She dropped down beside the hole. " Are you all right ? "

" Don't do any dancing on this heap of stuff that's sitting on me. Believe it or not, I'm under my bed, that's all that saved me." She heard him chuckle. " There are evidently advantages in going to bed drunk. You fall out of bed and roll under it, prepared for earthquakes when they come."

She was surprised at the relief she felt to know that he was alive. " Are you hurt at all ? Anything broken ? "

" I don't think so. I can't move, not even a hand, but I think I'm okay. Unless we get another shock and this stuff falls in on me. Is there anyone around who can give you a hand?"

She shook her head, suddenly becoming frantic: she had not thought of the possibility of another shock. "I'll get someone! Don't go——!"

He burst into laughter, his mirth magnified in the small space in which he was trapped. Half-turned to go, she stopped and also burst out laughing. They were there, she standing as if in mid-stride, he laughing up at her through the tiny hole in his burial mound, mad fools in a graveyard of desolation, when Dursun, face streaked with dust and sweat, his shirt ripped from his back and flapping like an apron over his buttocks, came scrambling over the wreckage and slid down beside Virginia. He grabbed her to him and held her, choking off her laughter and crushing the breath from her with the fierceness of his embrace. He was mumbling in Turkish, emotion robbing him of fluency in any but his native tongue; his hands clawed at her back as in their love-making, as if his fingers did not believe the reality of her. At last she managed to push her face away from his chest, to gasp some air into her lungs.

He stared at her as if he were seeing a ghost, a ghost he welcomed. Then he said in English, "When I came down the street and saw the hotel—oh, Virginia!" His fingers clutched at her shoulders, digging into her; she was being hurt more by his passionate relief than she had been by anything else so far. "I was praying to God——"

"Yashar, you're hurting me." She moved out of his embrace, upset by his sudden appearance, embarrassed by the staring mocking eye of Meldrum right at her feet. She had not expected to see Dursun again, and now for the moment she did not know how to handle him. Within herself she had said good-bye to him, had swept her mind if not her heart clean of him, had prepared to start a new chapter in her life; and now he had come plunging back, tearing up the new pages before they were written, showering her with the disturbing incoherence of the old. A shudder passed through her that had nothing to do with the earth tremors she had survived; she suffered a disturbance at the core of herself. He felt the shiver pass through her and stared at her with even fiercer concern, but she turned away from him.

Then Meldrum, like a disembodied voice piped in from some invisible source, said, " Three's a crowd at a time like this. Would you either move away, or get me out of here so that I can move off and leave you two alone ? "

Up till then Dursun had evidently not seen Meldrum, nor even heard him laughing. He drew in his breath in a hissing gasp, then dropped on his knees beside the hole where Meldrum's face showed. The latter winked at him. " Think you could do something about getting me out of here, Dursun ? "

Dursun, still on his knees, looked up at Virginia. " Get out in the open, Virginia. It isn't safe for you to stay here—that part of the hotel may fall down at any moment." He nodded at what still stood, an exposed cross-section of the hotel. Some of the rooms looked as if they had not been disturbed at all by either of the shocks : the beds were made for guests who would never sleep in them now, curtains still hung on the windows like limp flags, mirrors glinted meaningless heliograph messages at the distant impassive hills. In a bathroom a tap had somehow turned itself on and a basin was now overflowing, the water running across the tiled floor of the bathroom and falling as a long silver ribbon on to a hot stove in the wrecked kitchen in the basement; steam billowed up, somehow making that corner of the devastated building less dead-looking than the rest. But though the standing section of the hotel looked firm enough now, there were huge cracks in the walls and it was plain that another shock, even a minor tremor, would bring the lot crashing down.

Virginia turned and scrambled over the wreckage towards the open parking lot. " I'll be back. I'll get someone to help you——"

But it was not easy to get someone to help. People were

streaming by down the main street, heading out of town, some still in a state of shock, some gibbering with panic. She clutched at a man, but he slammed at her hand and hurried on, bustling his wife and child before him, screaming at them to hurry as if they were impeding his own dash to safety. An old woman went by on a donkey led by her son: all three, the woman, the man and the donkey had the same dull look in their eyes, the mindless animal look that succeeds the shattering impact of terror. Two small girls came running down the street hand in hand, shrieking for their dead parents; they rushed by Virginia like children at play; but their eyes were blind with shock, their minds scarred for ever by horror. Virginia turned to stare after them, torn by the sight of what she had seen on their faces, glad for that moment that she was childless. Then she ran on up the street, the roadway of which was now a humped and cracked mosaic of broken cobbles.

She ran past a woman with a baby tied to her back digging with her bare hands to release two more of her children trapped in the tumbled tomb that had been their home. Past three dogs fighting savagely over a dead cat. Past a donkey being burned alive in the ruins of a house, its screams piercing the eardrums like a saw-edged sword. Past men and women and children still alive under the wreckage of their houses, their shouts and moans and shrieks a babel-call for mercy.

Up here in the centre of town the fog of dust and grit was much thicker, lit by fires and the still-rising sun, turning the whole scene into a nightmare of distortion. Smoke billowed up, turning the air into a smothering veil, making visibility even more difficult; Virginia ran straight into a donkey and spun away just in time to avoid the kick of the terrified beast. Figures loomed up out of the smoke and dust, coming at her as threatening giants against the red glare, going past her as frightened men whose only menace lay in their blind charge to safety. She fell over a man lying in the middle of the road, picked herself up and ran on towards the square, clutching at men as they passed her but unable to get any of them to stop. Then she came out into the square, where the smoke and dust were thinner than down in the streets.

The first man she saw was Ahmet. He stood in the middle of the square, a dark bruise on his forehead, looking around him like a man seeking some direction. He did not look terrified nor as if he were struck dumb by shock; he looked more bemused, a man unable to believe what he saw. He was like a child at a carnival, one who was dimly beginning to see the tragedy behind the Tiniest Man, the Fattest Woman and the Clown whose smile had to be painted on.

Virginia ran across the square to him, grabbed him by the arm. He turned his head, blinked at her, then smiled politely and ducked his head, formal as a butler. " Madame Halstead. You are well ? " Then he ran out of English and said something in Turkish, something that sounded equally formal and ridiculous.

" Mr. Dursun—come quickly ! He needs you ! "

Ahmet shook his head, still smiling; then suddenly he seemed to realise the urgency she felt. " Yashar ? " he said; then he was running after her across the square and down the main street.

When they reached the hotel they found Dursun was already at work trying to clear the debris from above Meldrum. He had found a shovel somewhere and had dug away most of the crushed bricks and mortar immediately above where Meldrum was trapped. But that was only the beginning : there were girders, wooden beams and several bits of heavy masonry still to be moved before they could get a clear view of just how badly Meldrum was caught. It was a job that might take hours.

Dursun looked up with surprise when he saw Ahmet scrambling towards him, then he nodded with approval and gestured for the boy to give him a hand with the girder he was trying to remove. Virginia stood on top of a mound looking down at them as they strained to shift the heavy steel girder. Beneath the men's feet she could see Meldrum's face peering anxiously out of the hole; for the first time she saw the strain in the sleepy-lidded eyes. He was staring up at the straining men above him, his eyes twitching nervously every time a brick slipped and slid down past the tiny aperture. Virginia could still hear sections of the building subsiding: it was as if the hotel were waiting for the earth to make up its mind whether there were going to be any further shocks before it finally settled. She looked along the length of the ruined building, remembering the pictures she had seen of battlefields. War was more terrible than this, because it was Man who caused the destruction; but it was not as terrifying, because Man would never have the force of Nature. She remembered some of the little she had read about earthquakes and eruptions, that no bomb yet exploded had even approached the force unleashed when Krakatoa blew up some time, she could not remember when, late in the last century.

It was lighter now and she turned to look down towards the river, to the jerky procession of fleeing townspeople as it stumbled across the broken bridge and wound its way up the white road between the fields from which the dust rose like a brown ground mist. Then she felt the earth begin to tremble again. The mound on which she stood shuddered like a great heap of blancmange; she sank up to her ankles and only prevented herself from pitching forward by grabbing at a nearby beam. The tremor passed under her, sending up puffs of dust like small land-mines going off; bricks popped out from mounds like corn popping from a hot stove; a girder suddenly rose up and stood on end, then crashed down in a spray of dust. Virginia could feel the mound opening up beneath her, sucking her into it; clinging to the beam, she dragged her feet out of the dry quagmire in which she stood. Then she heard a crack, like a rifle shot, and she looked up. The front half of what remained of the hotel split away and slowly, almost gracefully, collapsed in an explosion of dust, like a woman disappearing in a curtsy into the chiffon folds of some huge grey-yellow ball gown. A bed shot out of one

of the rooms like a bouquet being tossed away, trailing its
sheets like a scarf, a pillow falling from it like the tight bud of
some flower. Virginia stood transfixed, unable to move in
the treacherous trapping blancmange of the mound, waiting
for the rear wall to fall in and bury them all, Meldrum, Dursun,
Ahmet and herself. But, another of the morning's miracles, it
did not fall.

Then she heard all three of the men yelling to her to get out
into the open. She looked down for the corpse of Mustafa,
but there was no sight of it; the porter now was buried under
tons of rubble. That decided her. She was not going to stand
safely out in the open while Dursun and Ahmet risked their
lives to save Meldrum from the same fate as had just overtaken
Mustafa. She let go the beam, jumped to free her feet, then
slid down the mound, snapping at the men as she did so.

" Shut up ! I'm here to help, so don't argue ! " Dursun
went to say something, but she turned on him almost in a
temper. " Shut up, damn you ! Get on with it ! "

Dursun did not argue with her. He bent his legs, pushing
his shoulder against the girder, and strained till it seemed that
every muscle must burst from his body with the effort. Dust
from the tremor still wreathed about him and Ahmet; they
worked in an atmosphere where they could hardly breathe.
Virginia saw the girder beginning to move; swiftly she
shoved a small beam under it to prevent it slipping back.
Bricks were tumbling past her, but she would not feel her
bruises till later. She looked down, and saw with a stab of
panic that Meldrum had disappeared altogether. She dropped
on her knees, clawing furiously at the bricks and rubble that
now covered the only airhole he had. She heaved away the
last of the bricks and saw his yellow dust-masked face staring
out. For a moment she thought he was dead. Then one grit-
lashed eye winked at her.

" Still here." He blew dust away from his lips. She reached
in through the tiny hole and with her fingers wiped the grit
away from his mouth. She felt his lips kiss her fingers, then

as she withdrew her hand he said, " Now get the hell out of here before you get hurt."

She smiled, feeling the dust crack on her own face. " There's time, Nick."

She had no doubt that they would get him out alive ; then she stood up and saw the large crack appearing in the still-standing wall. It crawled up the grey-painted wall of a bed-room like a long snake painting its track behind it. It dis-appeared into the ceiling, then she saw it appear in the room above, still climbing. She screamed a warning.

Dursun looked up, then swung his head to follow her point-ing hand. Then he came lurching up out of the hole he had dug, swept her off her feet, and plunged across the rubble with her to the edge of the terrace. He set her down, glaring at her with a mixture of anger and love. " Stay here ! You can't help back there. Stay here—please ! "

She did not protest. She had the sense to know at once that he would waste time arguing with her, that he was more con-cerned for her than for Meldrum. But he would go back for Meldrum if she would listen to him. " I'll stay, Yashar. But please be careful—and hurry ! "

He pressed her arm, bruising her again, then ran, slipping and sliding, like a man trying to run through snow-drifts, back over the rubble. He slid down into the narrow trench he had dug beneath the girder. He said something in Turkish to Ahmet, but the boy just looked up at the cracked wall, shook his head and went back to helping move the girder.

Beneath the wreckage and rubble Meldrum could feel himself getting weaker now. He was finding it an effort to breathe, and his arms and legs were beginning to go numb from not being able to move them. His head was aching from the effects of last night's drinking, and there was a sour taste of sickness in his mouth. When Virginia had found him he had only just regained consciousness ; there had been no time to despair about his plight. With the arrival of Dursun he had been certain that he would at least be rescued alive ; but then with the tremor of a few moments ago his optimism had suddenly been crushed. He could not see what Virginia had pointed at, but he had seen the fear on her face and now he himself feared the worst. Something was going to happen in the next few moments that would kill him, Dursun and the young Turk.

" Dursun, get out ! Leave me and get out ! " He swallowed grit as he shouted, felt his ribs being crushed as his lungs expanded.

"Shut up ! " Dursun snarled, and his boot stamped down past the airhole as he tried to get more leverage. Meldrum could hea   and Ahmet grunting, could hear the trickle of rubble as it fell away from the slowly moving girder ; then Dursun suddenly fell across the airhole, there was a rattle of bricks and Meldrum felt as if the whole of the wrecked hotel had shifted to press in on him.

He gasped for breath, but Dursun still lay across the airhole. The wire mattress of the bed was pressed hard against his face, cutting into his cheek and ear ; dust and grit had filtered through the wire and he knew it would be only minutes before he was smothered. He tried to move a hand, even a finger, but could not ; and a cry of frustration burst from him, taking the last of the air from his lungs. He had thought of death, been close to it several times, and he had never thought he would be afraid of it when its victory over him would be inevitable. But he had never thought of dying like *this*, of being buried alive, and now cold black terror took hold of him. Sweat broke from him, turning the dust on him to mud ; grit forced its way into his mouth, harsh against his teeth and gums ; his brain began to mist as the oxygen in his blood thinned out. He made one last desperate effort, straining his muscles, seeming even to try and move his very bones ; but the world pressed him down, all but his mind was dead, and that, too, was ready to surrender. He relaxed, and with the last glint of comprehension in a darkening mind said a prayer to a God long ignored.

Then he felt something against his face, claws that scratched the skin from him as they tore at the grit and dust that was smothering him. Then a hand slid in under the mattress, lifting it from his head ; he opened his mouth, gulping in dust and air. He could feel someone else working on the mattress down by his feet ; then it, too, was lifted, and all at once he could move. Light flooded back into his brain, and he could see, even though he had not yet opened his eyes : just being alive, being able to think, was being able to see. Hands were pulling at him, dragging him from under the mattress, working with frantic haste as if there were only moments to spare. His upper torso was dragged free, strong arms grasping him under the armpits and pulling him out ; his face bumped against a brick and something cut into his hip, but he bit back the cry of pain ; dimly he realised that Dursun and the young Turk were being rough because they had no time to be otherwise. Then his legs were free, and he was being half-carried, half-dragged, across the mounds of rubble. He opened his eyes, blinking against the grit that matted his lashes, and turned his head in time to see the last remaining section of the hotel fall inwards, folding in in a cascade of bricks, girders, furniture and dust to bury the spot from which he had just been rescued.

3

Latife Altinbash had been called from her bed at the hospital about an hour before dawn by one of the male nurses. One of the peasant women in the maternity ward had gone into labour and the baby looked like being born within the next hour. The mother was a young woman from one of the more backward villages in the hills, and Latife had congratulated herself on having got the girl into hospital. All her menfolk, including her husband, had been against the confinement away from her home ; but there had been unexpected rebellion by the women against the men, led by the girl's mother, who had lost two children at birth. The husband, a sullen young man, had been to the hospital only once since the girl had come in a week ago, and his tortured thoughts had been easy to read on his thin stupid face. He was torn between genuine love for his wife and fierce resentment of the interfering woman doctor; he wanted a son, but at the same time he wanted the doctor to bungle the delivery. It had taken all Latife's control to keep her temper with the dull-witted young man.

She expected no complications from the birth, but she was determined to make it as easy as possible for the young mother. She had delivered other babies in her time here at the hospital, but never had she had the opposition she had experienced in this case. This was a test, an opportunity to prove to the obstinate hostile men that she, a doctor, was here to help them in their struggle for existence. They had to be made to realise that Turkey, their country, was part of the modern world, that they had a duty to themselves and to Turkey to take advantage of all the modern world had to offer them. Latife had never been a flag-waver, but she had the bést sort of national pride, the sort that came out in her work.

The baby was born at 5.25, without blemish to himself or complication for his mother. He squawled when slapped, then almost instantly fell asleep, careless in his innocence of the world into which he had been born. His mother settled back in the bed, exhausted but happy, smiling wearily but thankfully at the sweat-soaked, blood-stained doctor.

" A fine healthy boy," Latife said. "Your husband will be pleased."

" God is good to me," said the young mother, knowing that a boy would be much more acceptable to her husband than a girl, that perhaps now he might forgive her for having come to the hospital.

Then the first shock of the earthquake struck. The young nurse clutched the still-unwashed baby to her and looked dumbly at Latife, as if expecting the doctor to tell her what to do. The mother struggled to free her ankles from the stirrups that had held her legs apart during the delivery, screaming louder now than at any other time during her labour. Then the second shock struck. Latife had just stepped out of the labour room into the corridor when she felt the floor heaving beneath her feet again. Acting purely on instinct, too exhausted to think of anyone but herself at that moment, she stepped into an open doorway opposite her and stood beneath the lintel; bricks and plaster crashed past her and through the plunging torrent of wreckage she saw the rooms on the other side of the corridor crumble like cardboard, then fall away. She watched it all without horror, almost coldly. It was a nightmare that she *knew* was not real.

Five minutes later she knew it had been a nightmare, but that it *had* been real. The baby and its mother, two nurses and a dozen patients were killed when the entire eastern side of the hospital was demolished. The male doctor, asleep in his small house at the end of the hospital garden, was also killed; one of the male nurses and six patients were seriously injured. The operating room was buried beneath the collapsed section of the hospital, and so was the dispensary. The entire medical service of Malavan, at a time when it needed such service more than at any time in its long history, consisted of one woman doctor, two male nurses, and a small store of medical supplies that would be used within the next hour.

Latife, she never knew how, had found her way down from the first floor of the hospital and out into the garden. She was standing there, feeling the first effects of shock beginning to shiver in her, wondering where to start first, when Captain Arif came running up the path to her.

He snapped questions at her, got the bad news of just what little service she could offer, then turned and ran off down the path. He was back in twenty minutes, panting a little, all his peacock's dignity forgotten. " All the telephone lines are down. But I have got through by radio to Kayseri. Other towns and villages have been hit by the earthquake—which ones, I don't know. I have a man standing by on the radio. Can you tell me exactly what you will need ? "

" I shall have to make a list." Latife was recovering, glad that Arif had come to her so soon ; she did not like the little man, but now she welcomed his reliance on her. She was discovering that in moments of disaster one sometimes finds that one's strength increases in ratio to the calls upon it; the more she had to do, the less were her morale and nerve likely to collapse. " Give me time, so that it can be a complete one."

" Everything to do with health is in your hands, Doctor. That just doesn't mean the medical side. I have no one else to do it——" He leaned one hand against the walnut tree by which they stood, shrinking to become a tired, dispirited middle-aged man for a moment. " I had sixty men last night. This morning I have five." Latife gasped, and he nodded. " Yes, five. How can I keep order with only five men ? And order will need to be kept——" He stopped for a moment, staring straight ahead of him as if contemplating the disorder that would face him over the next few days. He had asked for reinforcements, but he had no idea when he would get them. Then he shook his head and straightened up. " You and I will have to work together, Doctor——"

Then Latife saw Virginia, Dursun, Meldrum and young Ahmet coming up the path. She brushed past Arif and ran down to Virginia. " Are you all right——? "

Virginia nodded. " We all are. Even Mr. Meldrum——" She was about to explain what had happened to Meldrum, when Arif joined them.

" Mr. Meldrum." Arif's voice was sharp ; he could have been talking to one of his own soldiers. Meldrum, his face streaked where he had tried to wash the grit and dust from it in the water from the smashed pump, looked up ready to snap back at the officious officer. Then he saw that this was a new Arif, one with authority, and he said nothing. " Do you know anything about public health ? Sewers, such things as that ? "

Meldrum nodded. "It used to be part of my job."

Arif looked at Latife. " He is your man. Make up your list with his help." He looked back at the three men. " Nobody leaves Malavan without my permission. I need every man who is still alive and able to work."

"You can't order us around like that," said Dursun, his antagonism for Arif coming out in the rasping snarl of his voice.

Arif's reply had bite, but it was not angry. " I thought you, a government man, would *want* to help."

Dursun suddenly grinned, then laughed aloud, dust blowing from his lips like spittle. " You're right, Arif! A good government man should do what the town commander orders." He bowed, but Arif chose to ignore the mockery in the gesture.

" You will all help Dr. Altinbash here first, then report to me at the barracks." For a moment Arif's eyes clouded : the barracks had been his proudest achievement, the symbol of his command even more than the troops he led. Each time he had walked or driven through the gates it had been like entering the only real home he had ever known, *his* home. " I mean, where the barracks *were*."

He saluted and went hurrying off down the path. Dursun stared after him, no longer laughing, but Virginia put a hand on the big man's arm. " He's in charge, Yashar. *Someone* has to be."

" I swore I'd never take orders from a soldier ! "

" Would you take orders from me, Mr. Dursun ? " Latife asked.

Dursun looked at the doctor, then abruptly smiled again. He made a parody of Arif's salute, winking at Ahmet as he did so. " Any orders you wish, Doctor."

It was now full light, the thickest dust had settled and it was possible to look across the town and see the full extent of the damage. Only one or two houses, in the whole town, still stood ; they seemed to be held up by the piled rubble of their fallen neighbours on either side. A mist of dust still hung above everything, and smoke was wreathing up from several fires. Animals were still bellowing or barking, but there were no more human screams or shouts; shock seemed to be taking over the survivors, and all that could be heard were moans from the still trapped. The hill, more jagged than ever from the slides that had occurred with the first and second shocks, still stood above the town; the small mosque that had stood on its eastern edge had disappeared, but Ataturk's profile still gazed sightlessly across the valley, as if keeping his eyes averted from the destruction immediately below him. The blood redness had gone from the sun, and a golden haze of dust covered the ruins.

For the next two hours the survivors had little time to look at the town as a whole. Meldrum, little the worse now for his experience while trapped, went on a tour of the town to check the water supply and the drains. Dursun and Ahmet, working together like father and son, brought the surviving patients out of the ruins of the hospital and set them up in their beds in the garden; then they gathered what mattresses and blankets they could salvage and laid them out to receive the injured who were already being brought up to the hospital. Virginia, who had once done a first-aid course at school, set to work to help Latife and the surviving nurses.

Meldrum finished his tour of inspection down at the ruins of the barracks. He walked into the big courtyard, under the leaning flagpole from which the Turkish flag hung limply like a red and white wreath, and found that Arif had set up a command post under a gnarled olive tree whose twisted branches seemed a reflection of the human agony that had taken place here this morning. Two of the soldiers who had survived were working to rescue any of their colleagues who might still be alive, but so far they had found none. Sixteen bodies lay in a neat rank at the foot of a mound of rubble, looking almost ready to rise up to attention when the order for inspection was given. One other soldier sat at a table near Arif working a field radio transceiver, his blunt peasant's face twisted in concentration as he read from a list in his hand. Meldrum could only guess that the other two surviving soldiers were somewhere up in the town, sketching a weak gesture of authority among the chaos.

Arif sat at a rickety table. He looked up as Meldrum presented himself, blinking a little as if trying to bring the American into focus. The first signs of weariness were showing in his black sharp eyes. It was not physical weariness he felt, but the beginning of an exhaustion brought on by pity : he had been right round the town himself and the tragedy he had seen had taken its toll of him. " Ah, Mr. Meldrum. Good news or bad news ? "

Meldrum shook his head. " Do you expect any good news this morning ? You had better double that order of DDT I asked for. And we'll need more quicklime. Have you counted the dead yet ? "

" How can I, Mr. Meldrum ? Half the people are still buried under their houses. Who knows who is dead ? " He nodded at the two men working stiffly and silently, like automatons, among the ruins that surrounded them. " I do not even know which of my own men are dead. No, that is not true———" He bit his lip : it was as if he had lost a family. " I *do* know, but I do not wish to admit the truth. They are *all* dead."

Meldrum looked up at the sky through the deformed branches of the olive tree. The clouds that had blanketed the sky at dawn had now gone, like frost melted by the hot sun from a blue windowpane, but leaving no moisture ; the drought and the heat were still there to torture those that had survived the earthquake, to remind them of the other, slower ravages of nature. " Well, we better bury those dead we've found pretty quick. They're going to putrefy in this heat. Putrefy, rot. You know———" He held his nose to answer Arif's questioning look.

" Oh, yes. But that will take time." Arif nodded at the man who sat scribbling on a pad as a static-wrinkled voice came over the radio receiver. " That is Kayseri, relaying messages from Ankara. You do not speak very much Turkish, do you ? It is perhaps as well. All that is very bad news." He listened for a moment. " The roads are blocked through the hills—it may take them two days before they can clear them to bring in trucks. Almost all our vehicles here in the town have been wrecked."

" My jeep and Mrs. Halstead's Land-Rover are still okay."

" We have those and three other vehicles. Not very many, eh ? " With something to occupy him, his vanity had now completely disappeared ; Meldrum began to sympathise with the little man, almost liking him. " I have asked for more troops in case of looting. The gaol fell down, and those prisoners that were not killed or injured have escaped. Including a murderer whom we were to take to Kayseri tomorrow. But perhaps they have escaped to the hills and may not worry us again. It is the others I am worried about, the townspeople. Very soon the shock and fear will wear off and the people will be coming back to see what they can rescue from the ruins. When you are poor and your neighbour is dead, there is the temptation to rescue your own and his belongings also."

Meldrum nodded. He had never experienced real poverty himself, but he had seen the effects of it on others : the Indians of Peru still occasionally peopled his dreams. " How are you going to treat them if you find them looting ? "

" We shall have to kill them," Arif said. " It will give me much pain, but it will be the only way. What would you do ? "

" Don't ask me, Captain. I am just glad it's not my problem." Then he changed the subject : " Have you got through to the dam out at Bebek ? Ask the Germans there to send in what they can. Trucks, bulldozers——" He stopped, looked down through the thin mist of dust to the river, now a yellow muddy stream ; then he looked back at Arif. " I wondered if the dam was okay, but it must be. The river would be in flood if there had been a breach in the dam, and we'd be up to our asses in water. That's all we'd need on top of this——" He gestured at the destruction around them.

Arif smiled, the first genuine and not just polite smile that Meldrum had seen from the man ; but it was wry and had no merriment in it. " Let us pray that a flood does not come. Your ass, Mr. Meldrum, is much higher than mine."

Meldrum suddenly grinned, wondering why a man who could smile at himself like this should have hidden himself behind such a wall of pomposity. But then, he told himself, we all have our defences ; and not everyone chose the right defence. Virginia, for instance, who had chosen the past as her defence and now seemed to have laid herself wide open to the danger of Dursun.

" Well, we better think about burying those dead before the sun gets too hot. If you can get your guy to radio the dam, they have a receiver out there, and get their bulldozers in here as soon as they can, I'll have all the dead we can find carted out somewhere and we'll bury them in one common grave. We can have a 'dozer dig it in twenty minutes."

Arif shook his head. " It will not be as easy as that. We are Moslems, Mr. Meldrum. We do not like all our dead being buried together."

" But this is an emergency——! " Then Meldrum shrugged, not wanting to offend the other man. Religion had never meant much to him, but he realised the need of it for some other people. Cynically, he had long ago told himself that a man who believed in Democracy could not sneer at a man who believed in God. " Okay, I guess you're right. But it's the only way. You better find some way of convincing your-self——"

" Not me, Mr. Meldrum. I am a practical Moslem. But the people here——" He, too, shrugged.

" Okay, you better find some way of convincing them. They won't like me, a foreigner, trying to tell them."

Arif stood up. He had lost his white gloves and his blancoed belt ; his tunic hung on him now like a sack. His white gaiters were the same colour as his uniform ; he was coated from head to foot in grey dust. His uncombed hair hung down over his forehead and beneath the grey dust there was the dark smudge of beard stubble on his face. Yet somehow he now had more an air of authority than yesterday when he had been so spick and span. " I shall persuade them. I am in charge of this town and I am responsible for the welfare of those that have stayed alive. It will not destroy their chances in Heaven if I ask them to bend their religion a little in a case such as this."

Then Meldrum said, "How many guys do you have up in the town ? Two ? Not enough. There are five pumps and wells I want guarded. Nobody should be drinking from the town water supply. You better try and rustle up some other guys you can trust among the townsfolk. I'll get some water carts organised and we'll bring in water from springs outside the town."

Arif swallowed. " Mr. Meldrum, you are a very good man. To help us like this—you are a foreigner, but one would think you were a Turk to-day——"

" There are no foreigners in a disaster like this. We're just human beings together."

Arif hesitated, then nodded. " You are right, but I am still grateful. My only hope is that we shall all act like human beings."

" Oh, we'll do that, all right," said Meldrum, but Arif missed his momentary cynicism.

In the next hour two men were shot dead for looting, one of them the escaped murderer from the gaol. Justice was summary : they were shot dead on the spot, with their loot still clutched in their hands like farewell gifts. Their bodies were dragged out of the ruins of the houses they had been ransacking and laid in the street, a little apart from the other dead waiting to be carted out of town : they were the only ones who would escape the indignity of the common grave. Two more tremors occurred, neither of them serious in itself : none of those still alive and in the open was even slightly injured. But the tremors shifted the rubble, and people still trapped and undiscovered died as the tons of masonry, bricks and dust settled down on them. The sun climbed higher and by mid-morning the heat was as intense as it had been all through the past month. A stench now covered the town, as thick in the nostrils as the now-settled dust had been, and everyone who still remained in the town wore some sort of covering over his face.

Up at the hospital Virginia sank down against the trunk of a tree, taking the antiseptic mask from her face as Dursun came up to her with a tin mug of coffee. The hospital garden looked like a slaughter yard; its flower beds bloomed with blood-bright bodies. Three rescue teams, each with a doctor, had arrived by helicopter an hour before and they were now at work. A canvas awning had been stretched between some trees in one corner of the garden, and there Latife and the other three doctors were amputating crushed limbs and performing remedial surgery in an operating theatre that had the look of some macabre bazaar stall. Injured people were still being brought in, and the ear shuddered under a discordant chorus of pain and misery. Virginia took the coffee, shutting both her eyes and ears against the garden of suffering.

Dursun squatted down beside her. He had found another shirt somewhere, but it, too, was now in tatters; there was a gaping hole in one knee of his trousers, and one of his boots had split. Beneath his torn shirt he was smeared with other people's blood, like some primitive savage. He drank noisily from his mug of coffee, then put a hand on Virginia's knee. She opened her eyes and stared at him above the rim of the tin mug she still held to her mouth. " You haven't spoken to me."

" There hasn't been much time, has there ? "

He looked about the garden, then back at her. " We should have gone away together yesterday. You would have missed all this."

" I shouldn't think much of myself, being thankful that I had escaped other people's misery." He wrinkled his brows while he sorted out her loose syntax; and she went on, a little impatiently, " I mean, *I'm* not hurt. I'm *glad* I'm still here to help."

He wiped a hand across his face, smearing the dust and sweat, so that he looked like a caricature finger-painted by a child. "I am not thinking that I wished *I* had escaped all this. But is it selfish of me to wish that you had not been here to see it ? " He gestured towards the dead and injured lying like a red harvest under the pitiless sun.

" No-o. I'm sorry, Yashar——" She wanted to accuse him of his desertion last night, but to accuse him would be to let him know she had gone looking for him ; and she still treasured her pride, it meant as much to her as the few sorry belongings that some of the injured still clutched to them with their mangled arms. She wanted to ask him where he had gone last night, what had brought him back to the town this morning at dawn, but they were questions she had to swallow. She had made a decision during the night, one that had not come easily, and she was not going to go back on it. She had already begun the cultivation of a new defence, one that would have to suffice her not only till she escaped this destruction that now surrounded her, but till she escaped Turkey itself. The past here, too close to the present, would offer her no distraction nor solace : no dead Hittite would, after all, have any message for her. A weeping woman went by, carrying a dead child in her arms, looking for a doctor to perform a miracle : what defence did she have, Virginia wondered, against the nightmare memories to come ? Her own heart had only been bruised, not sliced open and the core of it removed. This hospital garden was a Gethsemane for many, but not really for her. She handed Dursun the empty mug and stood up. " It's all over, Yashar. You can say the earthquake buried it if you like. Tell yourself anything your pride asks. But it's all over."

He stood up, standing close to her, smelling of sweat and dust and blood, smeared with other people's tragedy. Yet there was a look of tragedy in his own eyes : with a feeling of something like pain, she realised he still loved her. " It is not over for me, Virginia. A man like me does not cut off love like a dead vine."

" Then why did you go last night ? " The question burst from her before she could stop it : the tongue was always the snake in the garden of love. " You left your hotel, left town——"

She had expected him to smile mockingly, to be suddenly superior towards her. Instead, he looked at her almost humbly, as if finding it incredible that she should have gone looking for him. " I *had* to go last night. Not far, but I had to leave Malavan."

" Where ? " She was like a shrewish wife : she wanted to bite her tongue, but she also wanted the answers.

He hesitated. " To—to Kayseri." He put a hand on her arm, gently, as if he were handling one of the injured who lay moaning behind him. " Did you think I would have gone without seeing you again ? I shall only leave when you tell me to go. Is that what you are telling me now—to go ? "

But before she could drag the answer out of herself, Latife came up. " I shouldn't be pleased, but I am." She leaned back exhausted against the tree. The front of her once-white hospital gown was shining with blood. Her small face looked even thinner than usual ; the dark eyes were dull with weariness. She searched in a pocket of her gown, careless of the blood, and brought out a crushed packet of cigarettes. She lit a cigarette with blood-red fingers, then slowly blew out the smoke. " This morning the people here at last accepted me as a doctor."

Virginia and Dursun stood awkwardly, still caught up in the whirling current between them. But Latife was too tired to notice the atmosphere. " Even the men let me treat them. It meant more to me than the day I got my degree." She drew on her cigarette again. " But I wonder how long it will last ? "

And as if to answer her, a young man came staggering up the path. There was no visible sign that he had been injured ;

he walked more like a man in shock. His long narrow head turned from side to side, swung on some pendulum of obsession. Then he saw Latife. He stopped dead, oblivious of everything around him, and stared at her. Latife straightened up, throwing away her cigarette.

" What's the matter, Latife ? " Virginia said.

" It's a young man from one of the villages in the hills. He didn't want his wife brought in here to have her baby."

" Is she all right ? "

" She and the baby were killed."

Suddenly the young man snarled and let out an animal-like cry of rage and grief. He lunged forward, his fists raised, his face dark with murder. But before he could reach Latife, Dursun had stepped in front of him. The young man ran straight into Dursun, not seeing him, his eyes focused only on Latife. Dursun raised both hands, grabbed the young man by the neck and flung him back. Then, as if possessed by some rage of his own, he went after the husband. The latter had fallen on his side and now was struggling to get up ; Dursun was suddenly astride him, chopping down with both hands, terrible in his fury. Virginia was paralysed for a moment by the suddenness of the fight ; then she recognised the demon that had taken hold of Dursun, the one that had caused him almost to kill the man who had held them up out on the road yesterday. She rushed forward, grabbing Dursun's arm and hanging on desperately.

" No, Yashar ! No ! "

He stopped, shaking his head like a man coming awake, then looked down at her. He said nothing, but stooped and lifted the battered and now-frightened young man to his feet. He said something in Turkish, his voice low and fierce, and the young man nodded, broke free of Dursun's grip and turned and ran as fast as he could down the path and out of the garden.

Dursun turned to Latife. " He won't worry you any more, Dr. Altinbash."

" Thank you." Latife had regained some of her composure ; she managed a weak smile. " The way you hit him, I thought I might have to admit him as a patient. He wouldn't have liked that—being treated by me, I mean."

" My temper is a bad one." He glanced sideways at Virginia ; then he suddenly smiled. All his confidence towards her seemed to come back : somehow, without knowing how, she had told him that she did not want him to go. " But Virginia knows how to cool me down."

4

That afternoon, on their way back from digging channels to divert the broken sewage drains that were spilling down into the town, Dursun and Meldrum found Pali, the dwarf. He was stupidly drunk from the fumes of the wine-soaked mound that still buried him up to his neck. They dug him out, laughing as the tiny misshapen man rolled crazily around on his stumpy legs ; not laughing at *him*, but just glad of the opportunity to laugh at *anything*. Now laughter took some of the edge off their weariness, relieved the misery that, as if by osmosis, had begun to permeate each of them.

Dursun picked up the hiccupping bundle under one arm. As he did so, a roll of lottery tickets fell out of the dwarf's shirt pocket. " You think that is an omen ? " Dursun, still chuckling, said to Meldrum. " Should we buy them from him ? "

Meldrum extracted some lira notes from his wallet. " I'm a great man for omens, Dursun. How much can we win ? "

Dursun hoisted the dwarf round on one hip, like a peasant woman holding her baby, while he looked at the tickets. "First prize is a quarter of a million liras. Almost twenty-eight thousand dollars. Ten thousand pounds."

Meldrum grinned in surprise. " That was a quick conversion."

Dursun winked, grinning in reply. The two men had lost

their antagonism for each in the shared effort of the work they had been doing for the past three hours. Dursun's rescue of Meldrum had forged the first bond, and it had been further strengthened throughout the day. " Money is my hobby. In my head I can convert liras into any foreign currency just like that——" He snapped his fingers. " I am a practical mathematician. If I am going to add up figures, let it be money."

" Good for you. The practical man is the one who survives to-day."

They had begun to walk back into the centre of town, the dwarf still held under Dursun's arm like a child. " Unfortunately, I am a dreamer, too. The money I convert is money I have only in my dreams. Have you much money, Nick ? May I call you Nick ? "

" Sure. No, Yashar, I haven't got much money. I've got more than I need right now, but that's only because I spend my time in places where I can't throw it away. But some day the government is going to call me home to Washington or somewhere in the States, and pretty soon then I'll be in hock like every other good American. Money and I don't have mutual adhesive qualities."

Dursun looked puzzled by the last remark, but he did not query it. " Mrs. Halstead has money."

Meldrum hesitated before he said, " That's not what you're after, is it, Yashar ? "

He had been expecting Dursun to drop the dwarf and spin round in a burst of temper at the question. But the Kurd just shook his head half-abstractedly, as if he, too, had been contemplating the same question. " I wish she did not have money, Nick. A rich wife is no bargain."

" An old Turkish proverb ? "

Dursun grinned and shrugged. " Is it not true also in your country ? "

" Maybe. Rich women never paid much attention to me." Libby, his wife, had been rich only in beauty ; he felt an ache now as a memory of her stabbed at him. " Anyhow, Yashar, I don't think Virginia is rich."

" She is to a man like me. It worries me." Then he handed Meldrum the roll of lottery tickets. " But if we win first prize—ah, then it will be different. You look after the tickets, Nick. I am man who is forever losing things."

Meldrum took the tickets and stuffed them in his pocket. " Let's hope you don't lose Virginia."

Dursun stopped short, hitching the dwarf further up on his hip. " You puzzle me, Nick. I thought you did not like me, did not like me being with Virginia. I was jealous of you, you know. And now——" He spread his hand.

" It's Virginia I'm thinking of, Yashar. She needs someone and it looks like it's you. Just be good to her."

The dwarf hiccupped and began to mumble. Dursun cuffed him on the ear, all the time continuing to stare at Meldrum. At last he said, " You love her, too, Nick ? "

Meldrum shook his head. " I'm a very careful guy when it comes to love. Just let's say I don't like to see people hurt."

Dursun nodded. " Neither do I. At least, not some people. Others——" He shrugged again, then looked about him. They were now in the centre of the town. Dead were still being dug out of the ruins and laid in ranks in the middle of the square ; mats and curtains had been dragged out of the fallen houses and thrown over the bodies. The bright mats and curtains lent an incongruously gay note to the scene ; but for the wrecked houses that made a bitter joke of such a thought, this might have been a communal spring cleaning party. Even as Dursun looked about him, another body, that of a tiny child, was brought out, laid down and covered by a mat. Dursun took his prayer beads from his pocket and twisted the yellow beads about his fingers. Then he saw Meldrum looking at him. " I pray for the dead, Nick. But sometimes I wonder if prayer means anything. I mean, *now*. These people were all good Moslems. Five times a day they prayed, and what sort of life did they get for their prayers ? "

The Fall of an Eagle

" Aren't prayers supposed to be asking for a good life in the next world ? "

" Yes. But a little of God's mercy would be welcome *now*." The dwarf belched suddenly, and Dursun looked down at the ugly little bundle under his arm. " This man hasn't known much of God's mercy."

Then a bulldozer rumbled by, its clatter drowning out any reply Meldrum might have had. The German driving it, a muscular young blond with a golden beard, waved to Meldrum and pushed the machine on down to where a group of soldiers waited for it. A detachment of fifty troops had come in from Kayseri and had taken over the rescue work ; trucks and more men, from the American Air Force bases near Ankara, were expected as soon as the road through the mountains had been cleared. Dursun and Meldrum followed the bulldozer down the street. It pulled up and the driver switched off its motor as a sergeant climbed up to speak to him. Captain Arif, wearing his cap now, trying to look a little sprucer now that two other officers were in Malavan, came up and looked curiously at the dwarf under Dursun's arm.

" He is dead ? "

Dursun laughed, held the dwarf up as if he were a baby. " He is the only really happy man in Malavan. Drunk and ignorant." Then he looked at the bulldozer, where the sergeant was pointing out to the driver what had to be cleared. " Someone else is trapped under there ? "

" We do not know," Arif said. " That used to be the bank."

" Who would have been in the bank at five-thirty in the morning ? " Meldrum asked.

" The bank manager. And two of my soldiers. The money to pay the workers at the dam came in last night. Half a million liras."

Dursun whistled, and Meldrum looked at him and grinned. " Convert that, Yashar."

" I have done that, already. Fifty-six thousand dollars. Is that buried under there, too, Captain ? "

" We think so. But we must be careful in using the bull-dozer. It is more important to be certain whether the men are still alive or are dead. The government can always print more notes to replace the money. It cannot replace a man's life."

Dursun walked across and put the dwarf down beneath the shade of a tree that still stood in the garden of a wrecked house. Then he came back. " We shall stay and help."

" There are enough men here." Arif had lost or buried his hostile suspicion of Dursun; he was aware of just how hard the stranger had worked to-day; he might be a spy, but he had worked for the common cause this morning and all through the day so far. There were others, townspeople, who had not done nearly so much. " Perhaps Dr. Altinbash could have some help up at the hospital."

" I shall help here," Dursun said, looking at Meldrum.

The latter looked up at the sky, squinting against the bright sun. His sunglasses had been lost in the wrecked hotel, and his eyes ached from the glare and the dust that had filled them this morning. " I think I'll go up and see if Dr. Altin-bash can give me some drops for my eyes." He stopped, then pointed up at the sky. " Look at those birds. Crows, buz-zards—they know when there's a feast on."

Some of the birds were already fluttering down to scavenge amongst the ruins; they served one horrifyingly useful purpose in that they led the rescuers to more of the buried dead. But their numbers were increasing: Meldrum pointed to the flights coming in from the hills, dark guests hurrying to the banquet of the dead. " The quicklime had better be here by the morning, or we're going to spend all day to-morrow fighting those goddamned birds ! "

" I hope not," Arif said. " No more fights. I am already fighting with people who do not want their dead buried in the one big grave. There are fights a soldier does not like."

Then the bulldozer started up again and began to edge its way carefully into the ruins. Dursun moved after it, joining the soldiers as they followed the wide path being cleared into the huge mound that had been the bank. Meldrum stood and watched for a moment, then he turned and walked up the side street which led to the hospital. Halfway up the street he stopped and looked back. The bulldozer had pulled up, halted by the mass of masonry it had piled up in front of it. The soldiers were grouped about the giant blade of the bulldozer, examining something that it had partially uncovered. It looked like the flattened wreck of a Volkswagen.

5

" Did you go home to Kasrik, Ahmet ? " Virginia asked.

Ahmet, eating the stew the hospital cooks had prepared, the best meal he had had in months, shook his head. " I send message to mother. Okay. Stay here, help."

" Tell me when you want to go home. I'll drive you back."

" You won't, you know," Meldrum said. " They've commandeered your Land-Rover and my jeep, too. Lord knows when we'll get them back."

The three of them were sitting in a corner of the hospital garden eating the first solid meal they had had all day. The sun had gone down and the air had turned cooler, bringing some relief from the exhausting heat that had baked the town. One or two of the injured, lying in the sun while waiting to be operated on, had had sun-stroke, adding to their misery. Virginia had sent Ahmet out to scour the town for something that could be erected as shelters, but he had had no luck : by midday most of the townspeople had returned to their ruined houses and, having lost enough, were understandably reluctant to part with anything further. But now, with the cooler evening, the suffering of some, at least, had been lessened.

Virginia was stiff with weariness. She was filthy, covered with sweat, dust and blood : she could not remember when a bath would have been so welcome. But there would be no baths in Malavan for at least a week : what water was being brought into town, in commandeered carts, was only for drinking and for use by the doctors. If she wanted a bath she would have to go out of town, find a secluded spot somewhere along the river and bathe there. She might do that in the morning. It would be a luxury, but it would refresh her and she would work better because of it. She finished her stew and sat back against the trunk of a tree as Dursun, carrying a plate of stew, came up and joined them.

" Was that your car they dug out of the bank this afternoon ? " Meldrum said.

Dursun had a mouthful of stew. He chewed on it deliberately before he answered, then at last he said, " The bank had fallen on it. Someone had stolen it during the night."

" Stolen it ? " Virginia echoed.

" They must have." Dursun chewed another mouthful of stew. " How else would it have got down there ? "

Ahmet said something in Turkish, and Dursun looked at him almost as if he were annoyed.

" What did you say, Ahmet ? " Virginia said.

The boy looked at Dursun, then at Virginia. " I see Yashar's car last night. It come from Kasrik."

Before Virginia could say anything further, Dursun shrugged and spoke. " I went to Kayseri, came back and left the car up near where I stayed last night, at the *lokanta*. Someone must have wanted to go out to Kasrik, so they took my car, then brought it back and left it near the bank. It does not matter. It would have been smashed just as badly if it had been left up near the *lokanta*. It is insured."

He turned to Meldrum, changing the conversation, but Meldrum had one last question : " Did they find the bank manager or the soldiers ? "

" Not yet," said Dursun, and sounded bored by the subject of what might have happened down at the bank. " If the quicklime comes to-morrow, how are you going to spread it ? "

The two men began to discuss what they would have to do to-morrow. Virginia, worn out, began to scrape away the small stones from the spot where she would sleep to-night. Latife, more exhausted than any of them, came over from the operating theatre and lay down where Virginia had cleared a space for her.

" We have amputated twenty-four limbs to-day." She lay on her back, staring up at the dark sky. She was too tired even to notice that the stars were now hidden by clouds ; all day the focus of her gaze had been only a foot or so in front of her, and her eyes were still glazed by the memory of shattered bodies. " They may rebuild Malavan completely, but we shall always have our reminders with us. People without arms or legs." Then she began to weep.

Virginia put an arm about the thin shoulders. She said nothing, having nothing that the comforting sympathy of her arm could not say, and after a while Latife fell asleep. Then Virginia lay back, and soon she, Meldrum, Dursun and Ahmet were also asleep.

Some of the patients were moaning a little, but the garden now was quiet but for the murmurs of the doctors still at work and the hum of the portable generators that had been brought in from the dam at Bebek. Arc-lights had been set up for the doctors to work under in the makeshift theatre, and operations were still being performed. The town's power supply was still cut off, and up on the hill Ataturk's profile was dark. Captain Arif had worked hard to have the power supply repaired, thinking that to have his hero's lighted profile shining through the night would provide inspiration and comfort for the miserable survivors of the devastated town ; but the German engineers had finally come to tell him that they could do nothing, that for another two days at least the town would have to depend on the portable generators. Arif, a man who believed in inspiration since it had been his own source of strength, had thought of suggesting that one of the generators should be hooked up to the profile of his hero, but in the end he had decided against it and said nothing. During the night looters stole all the globes from the profile of the

Father of their country, but it was days before Arif discovered the theft and by then he had something else on his mind.

Virginia woke as the first rain splashed on her face. She had been at the end of her physical resources when she had fallen asleep ; neither the hardness of the ground, the stench of the town nor the noise of the bulldozers still working down in the ruins had kept her awake. Yet she had not slept well : her mind had spun all night with fragmentary dreams : she was stacked to overflowing with memories of the terrible day she had lived. Bodies kept rising in her dreams, strangers who turned into Tom : she moaned and writhed with a mixture of past and present horror. Blood dripped from somewhere, striking her face. In her sleep she put out a pleading hand to the angry Dursun, wanting to borrow his strength ; then the blood turned into rain, waking her, and she found it was Latife's arm she was clutching. Latife rolled over on her back, muttering something in Turkish. Then she, too, opened her eyes as the rain splashed on her face.

Both women sat up wearily. There was no complaint from either of them : the rain, now settling into a steady drizzle, was only another manifestation of the depression and pessimism they felt. Virginia had learned from experience that despair had its own momentum. She ran her hand through her dusty hair, feeling it turning to a wig of mud, and looked at the still-motionless shapes of the three men, then looked at Latife. The latter smiled, her thin face like a yellowed ivory mask in the reflected light from the arcs over by the operating theatre.

"Leave them be. If the rain does not wake them, why should we ? "

Virginia got up, walked away through the rain and a few moments later came back with two blankets. "They were covering two patients who had died. Do you mind ? " One part of her mind was surprised at her own practical, almost callous, attitude ; but to-day had been an education in the need to separate sentiment from expediency. She had felt no revulsion when she had taken the blankets from the corpses ;

any fastidiousness in her had been wiped out in the first hour of working in the hospital garden this morning. "If we lie together, the outer blanket might keep the other one dry——"

They lay back again, close together like two schoolgirls sharing a dormitory bed, the two blankets covering them. Then Virginia turned her head and looked at the still-sleeping men. "You think I should get something and cover them, too?"

"They are so exhausted, I think we could have another earthquake and they would not wake."

"What if they catch a chill? No, I'm going to find some more blankets." For so long she had had no one but herself to look after. To-day all the mother-spirit in her that had been stunned the day she had lost her baby had come alive again; she had never been lacking in sympathy or pity, but to-day she had shown love for absolute strangers. Their welfare had become an obsession with her; the patients in the hospital garden had got more care and attention from her than from any of the other nurses. She was worried more now about the health and comfort of the three men than she was about her own.

She got up, and it was almost ten minutes before she came back with three blankets. She covered the three men, then crawled back in with Latife. "I had to make sure who was dead and who wasn't. Then one of the doctors stopped me— he didn't recognise me in the dark and thought I was a looter or something. Funny thing, I snarled at the doctor just like a looter would, or the way I *think* a looter would. I *wanted* the blankets, I couldn't see what use they were to the dead——" She lay for a while, her face hidden from the rain by the blankets; they smelled strongly of sweat, dirt and blood, but her nostrils had become deadened. "How long do you think it takes to lose all your decent instincts? I mean, become a plain sensible savage again?"

Latife was already settling down to sleep again: she was due back on duty in another six hours. "I have not given a thought all day to scruples or instincts. I am not going to start now. All I want to do is sleep. That is a very primitive instinct of which I am not in the least ashamed."

Virginia smiled and turned into the back of Latife. Somewhere in the garden a child cried, the sound faint against that of the hissing rain : it was one of the babies from the maternity ward, a tiny cry of promise : a few had not been touched by to-day's horror and despair.

Just before she fell asleep it occurred to her that not once during the long day had she stopped for five minutes to consider her relationship with Dursun. Each encounter with him had been interrupted just as some thought was required of her : decision had been brushed aside by the arrival of someone else. She turned away from Latife, and lay looking across at the sleeping shape of Dursun. Doubts cobwebbed her mind, but when she fell asleep she no longer dreamed of Tom : she walked in the lonely hills of flesh calling for Dursun, but her only answer was the echo of her own pleading voice.

Chapter Six

By morning the rain had gone and only a few clouds remained to make the weather slightly cooler. Ahmet left for home, taking a fresh bottle of medicine with him for his mother. Latife, thin and bedraggled, looking as poverty-stricken as he, gave him the bottle and thanked him for what he had done yesterday. "Go home and comfort your mother, Ahmet," she said in Turkish. "And let us hope the rain has fallen on your field in Kasrik."

"It falls where God wills it," the boy said and Latife kept her face blank, trying to hide the mixture of admiration and exasperation she always felt at the stoicism of these people.

There was very little stoicism among the rescuers, the outsiders to Malavan. The road through the mountains had been cleared and a big contingent of troops and salvage workers had arrived in the early morning. They had faced difficulties at once. What had yesterday been dust and rubble was now thick grey mud, making the task of clearing the debris so much more formidable. Trucks bogged down and even the bulldozers found the going difficult. The broken drains overflowed and the danger of typhoid became even more acute. Rescuers who had worked all day yesterday without complaint now began to be short-tempered; yesterday's moans from the trapped and injured had now been replaced by the curses of the rescuers. The air was a tangle of tongues, most of them abusing the conditions.

Virginia, having some time to herself now with the arrival of Turkish and U.S. Air Force medical orderlies at the hospital, went down to the hotel to search for some of her belongings. All her digging equipment had been taken out of the commandeered Land-Rover and put in one corner of the hospital garden under one of her tarpaulins; but her personal things, the change of clothing and the toilet articles that she needed, were still lost somewhere in the debris of the hotel. She had been searching for about five minutes among the ruins when she heard an American voice go on at some length about the mud. She poked her head up over a mound of masonry. " I admire your vocabulary. Are you college educated ? "

He wore U.S. Air Force working drill, a boy of no more than twenty, crew-cut, bony-faced and still unsophisticated enough to blush. " Ma'am, I'm awful sorry. I had no idea—I'd never swear like that in front of my *own* mother——"

Virginia blinked at him. " You've just insulted me, young man."

" Shall I knock him down for you ? " Meldrum, grinning, had appeared just behind the boy. " But to be honest, you don't look like this year's leading debutante."

The boy was still blushing. " Geez, how big can your mouth get ? I got both feet in it and there's still room for more. What can I say, ma'am—there, I oughtn't even call you ma'am. That sounds old, too, kinda."

Virginia clambered up over the mound and slid down the greasy opposite side, finishing up against Meldrum's supporting arm like a skier coming to the end of a run. But her boots had become caked with mud and when she tried to walk she moved like an elderly matron. She saw a piece of broken mirror in the debris and she hobbled over and picked it up and looked at herself. Her hair resembled the nest of a mud-hen, one not careful about its housekeeping; not a trace of her own blonde hair showed through the dried grey mud that covered her head. Streaks of dirt sketched bags under her eyes; each cheek was shadowed by smudges of dirt. The only colour in her ashen, middle-aged face was the finger-mark of dried blood on her chin. She smiled, and somehow even her teeth did not look to be her own.

She looked at the young American. " I don't blame you. I

do look like someone's mother. I've never boasted of my age before, but actually I'm only twenty-eight. That may be old to you, but to Mr. Meldrum here, I'm still a young chick. Right, Nick ? "

Meldrum grinned at the boy. " I'll bring her back some time when she's had a shampoo and got some make-up on. You'll be surprised."

The boy was not entirely club-tongued. " It'll sure be my pleasure. And I'm sorry for the language, *miss*."

" Thank you," said Virginia, and hoped the mud on her hands hid her wedding ring : she did not want to embarrass the boy further.

" What were you doing in there ? " Meldrum asked.

Virginia held up what she had salvaged, a change of clothing coated with mud. " You know a good laundry ? " They had climbed out of the wreckage into the open parking lot, leaving the boy to go on digging. " This ball of mud in my hand is hand-made underwear, with my initials on it, no less."

" I'm always impressed with underwear with initials on it. It makes seduction a little more personal."

" I always thought seduction was a personal thing anyway. But watch it, Nick. I hadn't meant to lead the conversation in that direction. I was just going to say that, in these circumstances——" She looked about her : in the shell of a house farther down the street a line of ragged washing hung, like a row of shot-spattered pennants "—I feel ashamed of the extravagance of hand-made underwear, with or without initials. Is that being too sensitive about one's good fortune ? "

Meldrum himself had had the same feeling at times in his life, although his extravagances had never run to hand-made shorts or T-shirts. The son of a small-town general merchant, he could remember farmers coming during the Depression to ask his father for credit for groceries ; the Meldrums had always had enough to eat, but every meal, including breakfast, had been prefaced with a heartfelt saying of grace by his father.

The Fall of an Eagle

Jeb Meldrum, a gentle man who believed in white supremacy in his own peculiar way, had often said to his son, " Always be thankful, Nick, for what yo' got. The dirt farmers, they got less. And thank God yo' was not bo'n a Nigra. They got the least of all." Meldrum had left home and gone on to meet the under-privileged who lived outside Georgia : the Nigras, as his father would have called them, of Harlem ; the mountain Indians of Peru ; the peasants of the Mezzogiorno in Italy ; the *real* dirt farmers of western Rajputana in India ; and now these peasants of Anatolia. The biggest burden of the man who worked for the good of others was not the size of the task that faced him, but the size of his own conscience.

" An Italian once came to me and kissed my hand for having brought water to his village. I hadn't the heart to tell him I got nine thousand dollars a year for being such a Good Samaritan. When I got my next pay cheque, somehow it looked like thirty pieces of silver. But what do you do ? Does it help them to bring yourself down to their level of misery ? No, I told myself, maybe not very convincingly, I was working to bring everyone in the world up to a nine thousand dollars a year pay cheque. Now I'll be also working for hand-made, initialled underwear for everyone."

" Thanks, Nick. You've made me feel better——" Then she stopped, staring past him at the ruins of the hotel.

" What's the matter ? " He turned round.

" I think I saw a rat——" She shuddered.

Meldrum let out a curse for which he made no apology. He plunged up over the rubble, slipping and sliding, till he came to the mound at which Virginia had been staring. He snatched up bricks, flinging them in all directions as he searched for the rat ; then suddenly he flung one of the bricks down at something that scurried down the mound. He chased it, picking up more bricks and flinging them, cursing loudly all the time like a man gone berserk. It was as if something in him had burst ; the rat was the enemy he had feared all along. Finally he halted on a mound of rubble at the far end of the ruins, flinging a last brick with savage force at the rat as it ran across the road towards the barracks. He stood there on top of the mound, breathing heavily, a stranger in his fury to Virginia: she had never suspected that he could erupt like this: his anger had resembled the wild storm that was Dursun's.

Then he came scrambling back over the ruins and down to where she still stood in the parking lot. The young Air Force boy still stood in the wreckage of the hotel, not moving, but looking curiously at Meldrum; obviously he did not appreciate the danger of the rat as much as did Meldrum. "There's half a dozen of them in there!" Meldrum's face seethed with his concern; the sleepy-lidded eyes were wide awake with frustrated anger. He banged a fist into the muddy palm of the other hand. "God knows how many more there are around town." He shouted to the boy, who was now coming towards them. "Where have you guys set up your supply dump?"

"Just out beyond the river. Why, what's wrong——?"

But Meldrum turned his back on the boy, looked at Virginia. "Honey, do they need you up at the hospital? Okay, then come with me. After you drop me at the supply dump, take the jeep up to where Arif is burying the dead and tell him I want him at once. *At once*, you hear, or he's likely to have a lot more dead on his hands. Bubonic plague is all we need now."

Virginia threw her muddy clothing into the back of Meldrum's jeep, took the wheel and drove down across the hump-backed, but still standing, bridge and up along the cracked and crumpled road that led out of town. Yellow pools of water glistened by the roadside, and the river under the bridge was now a swift-flowing torrent. She swung the jeep in on to a churned up track that led down between rows of vines that covered this field like ranks of stooping humpbacked women. The track led into an open space where a compound of U.S. Air Force tents had been set up.

Meldrum jumped out. " Pick me up on the way back. And hurry ! "

She turned the jeep round and went back down the track as a helicopter, like some great carrion bird, came whirring in over the poplars that lined the river. It hovered for a moment, the trees bending like cowering dancers beneath its down-draught, then it settled down somewhere behind the supply dump.

Virginia drove up the road, now and again having to slow to a crawl to negotiate the wide cracks in the road, cracks that sometimes extended a hundred yards or more into the fields on either side like streaks of black lightning laid on the earth's face. Tents had been erected in the fields, a temporary Mala-van, but they were all deserted now. Every family in the town had lost someone in the earthquake, and this morning all the survivors were out at the mass burial. Virginia had no trouble finding the place : a black half-circle of people, like a huge wreath, hung on the shoulder of a low hill about a mile out of town. The yellow fields, glittering in places with pools of water, stretched away on either side of the hill ; behind it the cloud-marbled sky, scrubbed of the menace it had held for so many months past, shone like an immense cathedral wall. The murmur of prayers only seemed to increase the feeling of loneliness, to push the horizon out to widen the sense of desolation.

Virginia parked the jeep beside the road, jumped out and ran stumbling through the mud to find Arif. The wailing of the mourners came and went like the soughing of a sad wind, a wintry grief in the warm summer day. They stood on the slope of the hill, sun-blackened faces now ochre-coloured with the pain of loss. A woman knelt in the mud, hitting her head on the ground as if trying to dig a grave for herself with her fore-head ; her husband stood beside her, oblivious of her, locked in the coffin of his own sorrow. Three men leant together with arms linked like children, weeping silently, the mud on their faces turned to clowns' masks by their tears. A woman sat cross-legged, rocking back and forth, her mouth open in a continuous one-note wail ; in her lap a baby laughed and gurgled, its eyes wide open to but untouched by the tragedy around it. And all the time the sound of the mass grief went on : the cry of loss, the ashamed ululation of relief that the mourner had been spared. Virginia stopped for a moment, suddenly feeling she was an intruder : she was aware of several heads turning to look at her, a foreigner and an infidel. But then she reminded herself she was here in their interests, and she went stumbling on through the mud looking for Arif.

She found him at the end of the long open trench. The bodies had been laid in the long grave ; a bulldozer stood at one end like a giant steel altar. Virginia had to pull twice at Arif's sleeve before he turned to her ; he had the same look of locked abstraction as many of the mourners. She spoke quietly to him, telling him that Meldrum wanted him, but he shook his head, nodding at the grave. One did not desert the dead in their last moment of farewell.

Virginia looked down into the grave, at the bundles, wrapped in blankets, curtains, mats, that had once been people; and understood why the Moslems hated the idea of mass burial: human dignity became just a mocking phrase when bodies were heaped together like rotting vegetables. The bulldozer started up its engine, began to move forward, pushing the earth ahead of it ; a woman screamed, and suddenly the crowd of mourners surged forward down the hill like a dark landslide. Arif's face contorted, tears sprang to his eyes, then all at once he half-shouted, half-wailed an order. Four soldiers, standing on the opposite side of the grave from the crowd, brought their rifles up to their shoulders and fired above the heads of the wailing, screaming mourners. The screams cut off as if everyone had been suddenly struck dumb ; the surge forward was abruptly halted. Arif, weeping, pleading, shouted at the crowd : they saw the new Arif, and it was that recognition, more than the soldiers with their rifles, that held them. Dimly they realised that the town commander was on their side, that what he was doing was, somehow or other, for their own good. Slowly, silently, they began to edge back up the hill. The bulldozer had stopped, its German driver looking inquiringly at Arif; he was a young man, but suddenly this scene was familiar to him; he remembered with shame films he had seen of other mass burials, at Dachau and Buchenwald. He wanted to climb down from the bulldozer, go and take his place with the mourners; but he was a German, discipline was inherent in him, and so he looked at the Captain for orders. Arif nodded, and the bulldozer began to move forward again, the earth curling in like a yellow and brown wave over the dead. There was a single moan from a woman somewhere in the crowd, but no other protest.

Virginia tugged again at Arif's sleeve. " We must hurry, Captain Arif! There are rats in the town——"

Arif had been staring up the hill at the crowd, all its grief and pain reflected in his own face; but now he looked sharply at Virginia, his expression a mixture of puzzlement and horror. " Rats ? "

He stood for a moment as if trying to comprehend what Virginia had told him. Then he had barked an order at one of the soldiers and was running after Virginia through the mud down to the jeep. As he got in beside her, Virginia noticed that he had taken a string of prayer beads from his pocket and was twisting them like a tourniquet around his fingers.

When they pulled up in front of the supply dump, Meldrum was waiting for them. He jumped into the back of the jeep and spoke urgently to Arif as Virginia drove them back into town.

" They're giving us two helicopters for spraying——"

Virginia pulled the jeep up in front of the ruins of the barracks. Tents had been erected in what had been the barracks square, and a guard with a rifle now stood at the gate. Two other officers had arrived with the troops from Kayseri, but Arif was the most senior of the three. He now commanded more troops than he ever had in his whole career; even the major in charge of the American troops consulted him as town commander. But the increased authority seemed to mean nothing to him : vanity and ambition had been washed out of him like the whitening from his belt. He got out of the jeep, carelessly returned the guard's salute, and said to Meldrum, " I shall order everyone out of the ruins. Bring in your helicopters when you wish."

" They'll be here as soon as they're loaded up." Arif walked away up towards the command tent, and Meldrum turned to Virginia. He sighed, slumping a little in his seat, and for the first time she noticed the ugly dark swelling over one eye. " You better warn Latife we're going to be spraying——"

" What's the matter with your eye ? "

He put up a tentative finger to the bruise, feeling it gently. " I had an argument this morning with a guy trying to steal this——" He slapped a hand against the outside of the jeep. " This is no picnic, is it, honey ? You feel you want out, to pack up, tell 'em all the hell with 'em and head for home ? You think a nine-thousand-dollar-a-year Good Samaritan is entitled to forget his conscience once in a while and have his moments of doubt ? "

" This man really would have stolen the jeep ? "

" He sure wasn't taking it away to wash it for me."

" You're entitled to your doubts, Nick. But there are bastards everywhere——" She used the Australian noun that described every miscreant from a malingerer to a murderer ; the blunt word came easiest when you were weary. " I felt that way when I was looking for someone yesterday morning to help Yashar dig you out. Nobody cared for anyone but themselves. Then last night up at the hospital I saw a woman breast-feeding an orphan baby, cutting down her own baby's food to give the other kiddy a chance to live. You probably know it as well as I do, with conditions as they have been these past months, the women around here aren't overloaded with milk. But she squeezed out enough to feed some strange baby, one that doesn't have a name, we don't even know who its mother was. To-day there's plenty of tinned milk been brought in, but last night she wasn't to know that." She put her hand on his arm. " I don't really think you want to get to hell out of here, Nick."

He looked at her steadily for a moment, then he nodded. " I guess you're right. But you mind if I say something ? The moment the panic is off here, and it should be in a day or two, *you* get the hell out of it."

" You mean because of Yashar ? I'd already decided that."

" I'm glad to hear it. You told him ? "

" Not yet." She got out of the jeep, took her muddy clothing from the back seat. She ran a hand through the stiff nest of her hair, and flakes of mud fell like scurf on her shoulders. She had a slight headache from lack of sleep, and her belly and hip were hurting from the scraping they had sustained yesterday morning when she had almost slid over the edge of the wrecked hotel floor. Yet she welcomed the work that had kept her occupied all day yesterday, would keep her occupied for the next few days : it was like a moving wall between her and Dursun, one that kept pushing him away every time he tried to establish contact with her.

Meldrum moved over into the driving seat of the jeep. " Take care, honey. And if you're looking for a Good, or maybe Not So Good, Samaritan to give you a lift out of town, call on me."

He let in the gears and went speeding up the street. Virginia watched the jeep disappear round a wrecked building, then she bundled her clothing under her arm and began to walk up the main street. Meldrum's concern for her disturbed her; womanlike, she both welcomed and suspected a man who offered friendship, nothing more. He had said nothing ; but now, secretly ashamed at the conceit, she wondered if Meldrum was in love with her. She remembered the touch of his lips against her fingers yesterday morning when she had been trying to scrape the rubble and dust away from his face as he

lay buried : had it been a kiss of gratitude or of something
more ? The thought made her tremble a little, like an added
measure of fatigue ; she knew she would not be able to cope
with another complication, another required valuation of herself. She knew that only through suffering and doubt could
one come to know oneself ; and she had known enough
suffering to be conscious of her own limitations. She was not
equal to the swamping flood of two men's love, if Meldrum
should be in love with her ; she had not even been equal to
Dursun's love for her. She had had to struggle to retain her
own personality, to keep hold of her independence ; and it had
taken all her strength to do so. She had a feeling of inadequacy;
but to be the target of love was often more demanding than
to be the lover. To go through the same battle with Meldrum
would be too much. She prayed that all Meldrum felt for her
was gratitude—for what, she did not know, but she was glad to
accept any reason. She remembered her own early gratitude to
him for his just being here in Malávan. Perhaps it was no
more than that. Two strangers grateful to each other for their
foreignness in an alien country.

"Virginia ! "

She stopped as Dursun, mud-streaked, ragged-shirted, but as
strong-looking as ever, an indestructible man, hailed her from
in front of the ruins of the bank. He had been talking to the
dwarf lottery seller ; now he patted Pali on the back and the
little man went bumping down the road on his roller skates.
Dursun came across to Virginia, grinning broadly, as if their
relationship were back on the same old level.

"Nick and I bought all the tickets from Pali. He has just
been telling me he sent off the butts to Istanbul this morning.
If we win—ah ! "

But she didn't ask him what he intended doing with the
money if he won it : he might give her an answer she did not
want. She looked past him at the ruins of the bank, where four
soldiers worked among the rubble, digging with picks like
prospectors looking for buried treasure. Dursun's car, a

buckled mass of metal on twisted wheels, had been pushed into a side alley beside the bank; a crow was in its front seat, pecking away the exposed stuffing of the seats. " You'll need to buy a new car."

Dursun looked at the car, picked up a stone and flung it lazily at the crow, which paid no heed but went on tearing at the seats. Dursun shrugged, grinned and turned back to Virginia.

" They haven't found the money yet." He nodded at the bank.

" What money ? "

" Of course. You didn't know." He looked away, and she thought he was not going to say anything more; then he looked back and said, almost stiffly, " There was half a million liras in the bank last night. Twenty thousand pounds in your money."

" And that's all you're interested in—the money ? What about Mr. Yusun—have they found him yet ? "

The grin had set on his face, but it was now a baring of his teeth; not a snarl of anger, but the grimace of a man who had been wounded. " Why do you always attack me, Virginia ? We are looking for Yusun, too, but it is not very likely that he is alive under all that——" He gestured at the ruins : four piles of rubble and masonry, pushed there by a bulldozer, stood at each corner of what had been the bank building, like shattered monuments guarding the corners of some wrecked temple. But a large mound of girders and bricks still remained in the centre of the site, and it was here that the workers were working carefully at their prospecting, searching for cash or corpses. " You are wrong about me, Virginia. I have use for the practical things such as money—you learn that lesson when you have been poor. But I think people are more necessary than money. A man needs another man, or a woman——" he paused for a moment to gaze steadily at her "—to convince himself he's alive."

She knew the truth of that. " I'm sorry, Yashar. I'm tired,

The Fall of an Eagle

I suppose—Perhaps I should have a holiday down at your hotel near Antalya."

She was angry at herself as soon as she heard the words in her own ears : her tongue had made another idle, betraying remark. But Dursun surprised her by shaking his head. " I shall not be going back there. My plans have been changed."

" Do you really have a hotel down there, Yashar ? " Somehow she had never really believed that he had : it had always sounded like another of his dreams, another vision of Brazil.

He shook his head again, smiling wryly to himself, making no apology for the lie he had told her. " I have nothing. I've never owned a roof over my head in all my life—no, I'm wrong. Once, for one day, when I was three years old, I owned my parents' house. I've never thought of that be-fore——"

Across the street behind them a chapel of crows were picking clean a disembowelled house ; they swarmed like black smoke in the shell of the building. Hawks hovered above the ruins, occasionally swooping down to send up an explosion of smaller birds. Two dogs, thin as wire sculptures, nosed tentatively at a donkey still buried beneath a mound of bricks. Only the animals, the birds and the rescue squads held sway in the town ; oh, and the rats, Virginia thought, and shuddered. Death lay like an invisible fog all over the town, thick in the nostrils, a taste on the tongue like that of bitter smoke. But Dursun had tasted and smelt death at a very early age, and that perhaps was why he could appear outwardly unmoved by what surrounded them now.

" What are you going to do then ? " All at once she had a feeling of compassion for him ; and she knew he still had a hold on her : love and compassion were part of each other. Pity could trap as easily as the kiss : she had exposed herself to him again.

He sensed it. His eyes seemed to take on the old light, half-mocking, half-loving her ; he opened his mouth to say something that she knew she would not be able to answer. Then the wall suddenly moved in between them, saving her again : Captain Arif said from behind her, " Mrs. Halstead, I think you should go up to the hospital. They are going to spray the town."

Down at the end of town Virginia saw the two helicopters lifting up above the trees by the river. They hovered for a moment, their blades making a dark whirlpool of the air above them, then they came slowly up towards the town, the spray of DDT whirling behind them like long yellow scarves in the bright sunlight.

Then there was suddenly a shout from the soldiers working in the ruins of the bank. Arif and Dursun turned sharply, leaving Virginia in the middle of the street, and ran across towards the soldiers. Two of them were on their hands and knees among the rubble, struggling to shift a large girder that was caught between two big pieces of masonry. Dursun pushed past the other two soldiers and clambered up over the rubble. Arif halted at the edge of the wreckage and Virginia came up beside him.

" What is it, Captain ? "

" They have found another body."

" Whose ? Mr. Yusun's ? "

Arif shouted something at the soldiers, but it was Dursun who answered him. He turned back to Virginia. " Mr. Dursun says they cannot tell who it is. All they can see is his leg."

The helicopters came whirring up on either side of the main street, their engines drowning out conversation, scaring the birds out of the gutted houses. The spray trailed behind the aircraft, misting down over the ruins, softening the jagged wreckage of the town for a moment into a faded watercolour of some landscape seen through a dusty glass : a harvest scene of piled grain, perhaps even an ancient temple of the dead, it was difficult to give the scene a name. Then the spray settled and the ugly reality took shape again.

Arif ran down towards the helicopters, waving his arms at the pilots. He stopped in the middle of the street and pointed towards the ruins of the bank. The helicopters paused in their flight, then they swung up and away, switched off the spray trailing behind them, passed on, and fifty yards up the street began spraying again. The noise of their engines was the only sound now in the empty town.

Dursun and the four soldiers had collected in a group above the spot where the body, whose ever it was, was trapped. Virginia saw Dursun and the biggest of the soldiers bend down beneath the girder, put their backs to it and begin to heave. They clasped hands as if to support each other; their faces contorted in twin expressions of agonised effort. All at once Virginia was ashamed of her condemnation of Dursun : he had worked as hard as anyone else, was still working, to rescue the living, extricate the dead. Slowly the girder shifted ; two other soldiers pushed against one of the chunks of masonry. Then the piece of masonry fell away, rolling down to land with a splash in a wide pool of water. The girder rose up suddenly, and Dursun and the big soldier fell back, grabbing at each other to prevent themselves following the girder as it rolled down the mound.

Dursun picked up a shovel and, working with a furious sort of urgency, as if to rescue someone who was still alive, scooped away at the mud that still buried the unknown man. Then he was down on his hands and knees in the hole he had dug, obscured from Virginia's view by the soldiers bending over to help him. Then she saw them bringing out the mud-shrouded body, carrying it carefully as if in hope that some life still breathed in it. They brought it down and laid it on the cracked and buckled pavement outside the bank. The whole upper torso and head was caked with grey mud, a mass of clay out of which the man, whoever he was, had to be carved.

Virginia took a silk slip from the bundle under her arm ; her embroidered initials taunted her as she dipped the slip in a nearby pool of water. Then she knelt down beside the body and began to wash away the mud. The six men stood around her, silent and curious, and above them a hawk came back to circle slowly in the air, smelling carrion. Virginia herself could smell the body, but she held down the sickness that rose in her throat.

Slowly the dead man emerged from his mould. She looked up at Dursun, Arif and the soldiers. " It's Mr. Yusun."

She wet the slip again and washed away more of the mud. The thin stone-grey face, toothless now, the sunken mouth turned down in a last grimace of pain, stared up at her. The mass of mud at the back of his head hid the ghastly wound where the bullet had come out : the hole in the wrinkled forehead was no more than a small dark deathmark.

2

There was a whirr of metal, and Pali, the dwarf, skated in to stand crouching by Dursun's legs, like some faithful dog curious as to what its master had found. The big head, the face wrinkled as a dried melon, rolled back and forth on the broad shoulders ; the big loose mouth clucked sympathetically. Then the dwarf looked up at Dursun as if he expected the big man to have the answer to what had happened to Yusun.

Dursun was the first to speak. " Who could have shot him ? One of your soldiers, Captain ? "

Arif looked sideways past his long nose at Dursun ; the nose twitched, but not with nervousness this time. " Do not say such a thing in Turkish, Mr. Dursun. These soldiers might kill you. They were friends of the two soldiers still buried in the bank."

Dursun looked at the four soldiers, none of whom seemed interested in a conversation he did not understand ; they had already turned to go back into the ruins of the bank, bent on finding their dead colleagues. The thought of what the soldiers might do to him if they did understand the conversation did not seem to perturb Dursun. " It was only a suggestion, Captain, not an accusation. Your soldiers would be the men with the guns in the bank."

"That wound was made by a small-calibre bullet, Mr. Dursun, not by a rifle bullet. Do you not know guns very well?"

Dursun did not grin outright, but there was a suggestion of the mocking smile on his face as he shook his head. "I never use a gun, Captain."

Virginia had watched the fencing between the two men with misgivings. They were back to their original attitudes with each other; their antagonism, forgotten in the distraction of working together in the immediate aftermath of the earthquake, had come alive again. But there was a difference now. Dursun had all his old mocking expression, but he did not appear to have the confidence he once had; Arif, the suspicious, frightened one, was now the man whose confidence seemed to be growing quietly every moment. Virginia began to worry for Dursun, aware of the four soldiers who backed Arif.

She looked down at the dead Yusun. She wondered if he had any relatives, or if they had survived the earthquake; but their grief or their death meant nothing to the little man now, he was beyond the net of human complications. For a moment she envied him, surrendering to the death urge that circulates in everyone like a germ in the blood: death was the solution to life. But then she shook the thought away, angry at herself for her cowardice: all her life she had fought against the pessimism that one was born only to die. Life was more than a downhill slide to the grave, even when its problems made one wish for the downhill pace to quicken. She was becoming contaminated by the atmosphere of the town, becoming too ready to accept death.

Dursun put a hand on her arm, as if he had sensed the depression that had taken hold of her. This perception of his came and went like the turning beam of a searchlight. Sometimes he floundered in the dark, being almost brutal towards her in his obtuseness ; then suddenly, as now, he would guess her thoughts almost as if she had spoken them aloud. The pressure of his hand was gentle, comforting ; and she looked at him gratefully. He was the biggest factor in the complications that had induced her pessimism, but his strength and energy, his suggestion of the *force* of living, now communicated itself to her through his touch. The exhaustion of utter resignation lifted from her. She had looked at the heaped bodies in the grave out below the hill and thought how they had made a mockery of human dignity. But there was no dignity in self-pity : degradation went no deeper than that.

" It's too late to take him out and have him buried with all the others, isn't it ? " she asked, and was glad when Arif said the mass burial would now be finished. Yusun, she felt, deserved a grave of his own.

" We shall bury him," said Arif. " Perhaps you would dig his grave, Mr. Dursun ? You are strong with the shovel."

Dursun's hand was still on Virginia's arm, and she felt his fingers tighten till she almost had to cry out. She could feel the anger quivering in him, ready to burst out in a fury, the prospect of which terrified her. He would kill Arif, and the soldiers in turn would kill him ; she suddenly hated Arif for his reckless baiting of Dursun. The tables had been turned, but Arif's new confidence had made him giddy. Then she felt the pressure of Dursun's fingers easing on her arm ; somehow he had kept control of himself. He took his hand from her arm and rested it on the dwarf's head.

" Pali and I will dig the grave for Yusun, Captain. But only because he was my friend, and Pali's. I am not going to become the town's grave-digger, no matter how strong I am with the shovel."

" Friend ? " Arif's new confidence had given him back some of his old pomposity. " You did not know him well."

" I knew him better than you think. I once told Mrs. Halstead, friendship is a swift growing flower in the right soil."

" In the soil of a bank ? A good place for friendship."

Dursun suddenly laughed and looked down at the dwarf. " Hear that, Pali ? The captain has quite a wit. I'd never have suspected it."   The dwarf grinned up uncomprehendingly ; he did not understand English, but he was obviously prepared to accept unquestioningly anything Dursun said to him. He was pathetic in his devotion to Dursun : the big man had made a friend who would follow him anywhere.

Dursun looked back at Arif. His own confidence now seemed to be returning. It was as if he had taken stock of the other's attitude and had decided to face it : he was a man who preferred to fight out in the open. " I shall need something to carry Yusun's body in, a truck or something."

" I can give you only a barrow."

" That will do," said Dursun, the half-smile still on his face. " And perhaps a soldier to wheel it. I have not pushed a barrow in years. I am not going to learn again now."

Virginia then decided to intervene. The two men had begun to enjoy their conflict with each other, and the dead Yusun had been forgotten. " Hadn't we better find Mr. Yusun's family ? "

" He had no family, Mrs. Halstead. Perhaps that was why he made friends so quickly," Arif said with another sly look at Dursun. The latter grinned, but said nothing ; and Arif went on, " We shall bury him up in the town cemetery. You may be lucky, Mr. Dursun. The earthquake may have already opened the ground for you, perhaps you will not have to dig."

Virginia turned away, making no attempt to hide her disgust. " I am going up to the hospital."

She had gone a few yards when Dursun came after her. " What is the matter, Virginia ? " His eyes were dark with concern. " You are annoyed."

" Why shouldn't I be ? " She looked back at Arif, who had gone across to speak to the soldiers, who had resumed their digging in the ruins. " You two were arguing over poor Mr. Yusun like dogs over a bone."

" I didn't start the argument."

" No, but you didn't let it lie. Oh, Yashar," she said despairingly, " what gets into you ? Can't you see now we'd never have been happy together ? There's a cruelty in you I could never come to understand—maybe cruelty is the wrong word, a *hardness*——"

" There is something else in me, too. Love. But if that were all that was in me, I'd be a soft man. You are not the sort of woman to want a man who is all sweet gentleness. Men who are full of love and nothing else are holy men. And a holy man has never had women fall in love with him. He stops being holy as soon as one does."

" Those two hundred and eighty or whatever it was books gave you quite an education, didn't they ? You have all the answers. All the answers but the ones I want. Go and dig your grave, Yashar." She turned and went on up the street.

" Not *my* grave," she heard him say, still standing where she had left him. " No one will ever make me dig my own grave."

She could feel the tears smarting her eyes, her lips trembling with the torment of feeling that coursed through her : she suddenly saw an image of him dead, lying in the place of Yusun outside the ruins of the bank. She spun round, wanting to cry out to him. But he had turned away, had gone back and now stood above the body of the bank manager. One hand rested on the head of the dwarf, who nestled close to his leg ; his own head was bent like that of a mourner, remote from her and everyone else about him. It seemed to her then that if she did cry out, he would not hear her. She stared at him for a moment, then went on up the street.

The helicopters came round the hill above the town, one from each side of it. She stood in the centre of the street, wrapping the wet and muddy slip about her face and head as the aircraft roared over her, covering her with their spray. Then they had gone on down the street, the spray had settled and she took the slip from her head. She saw a rat come out from the shell of a house and scurry across the road in front of her, but she ignored it, no longer even shuddering at the sight of it. If the spray had not reached it, had not killed the fleas it carried, there was nothing *she* could do about it. She had reached the state of mind that eventually came to all rescuers in any disaster : it was impossible to do everything, and it was better to settle on one job and block off the mind to all outside it. She had settled on the job of helping Latife, and as soon as she was no longer needed for that she would, as Meldrum had advised, pack up and get to hell out of here. No amount of DDT would obliterate the disease that threatened to plague her if she stayed.

When she reached the hospital Latife was just coming out of the large tent that had now been erected as the operating theatre. She pulled off her rubber gloves and slid out of her blood-glistening medical gown. " Another three amputations this morning. If ever tourists start coming back to Malavan, what are we going to do with all the limbless locals ? Tourists don't like to have to give pity when they're on holiday, am I right, Virginia ? A few coins, perhaps, or a packet of cigarettes. But not pity." She lit a cigarette, drew on it, blew out the smoke and smiled. " I'm sorry. I'm sounding just like Mr. Meldrum, all cynical and sour. What I need is a good bath, to wash the mud and blood and sourness out of me."

Virginia abruptly straightened up. " Are you off-duty for an hour or so ? Good. I'm going to get my Land-Rover back, even if I have to shoot someone for it, and you and I are going out somewhere along the river and have a damned good bath. Here, look after this for me." She shoved the bundle of muddy clothing into Latife's arms. " Get some soap and some towels. And see if one of your nurses has something about my size I can wear. I'll be back as soon as I find the Land-Rover."

It took her only five minutes to find it. It was parked in the barracks compound, outside the command tent. The armed guard stopped her at the gate, but she made such a commotion that Captain Arif came out of the tent to see what was going on. She stalked past the guard and up to Arif.

"Captain Arif, I want my Land-Rover. Righto, I know you've commandeered it—" as he went to protest "—but I want it. Just for two hours, maybe a little longer. I'm taking Dr. Altinbash out of town so that she can have a bath and wash all the muck out of her hair. And I'm going to do the same for myself. You're a man, maybe you don't understand, but a woman can work much better and longer if she feels *clean*. And if you want Dr. Altinbash to go on working, you'd better see she has the chance to be clean."

Arif stared at her, aware of the four or five soldiers standing watching him and this aggressive foreign woman. A week ago he would have ordered her out of the barracks; but he no longer felt compelled to make such petty displays of authority. He smiled and inclined his head in a slight bow. "Mrs. Halstead, you are a very strong woman. You have won your argument. I hope Mr. Dursun appreciates you."

"Mr. Dursun?"

"I am sorry. Of course I mean Dr. Altinbash," he said, but there was no mistaking that he meant nothing of the kind. "Enjoy your bath."

She went across, got into the Land-Rover, drove it out past the suspicious guard and up the street. Ahead of her she saw Dursun, a pick and shovel over his shoulder, walking up the street; beside him, on his skates, trundled Pali, being pulled along like a child by the big man. In front of them a soldier pulled a barrow; on it, like a sleeping man, lay the body of Yusun, a small bag of quicklime cradled in one of his arms. Virginia swung up a side street, not wanting to have to face Dursun again for the moment.

She picked up Latife at the hospital and half an hour later they had parked the Land-Rover in a grove of poplars and were bathing naked in the river. Virginia had wondered if some of the traditional Turkish modesty still remained in Latife, but the latter had taken off her clothes without hesitation and plunged into the river. The water was cool but pleasant and much clearer here than down by the town. They washed themselves, their hair and their clothes, and emerged refreshed and feeling they could cope with whatever work lay ahead of them for the next few days. Virginia had always believed in the therapy of a shower or bath, and none had ever revitalised her as much as this dip in the cool sparkling river. Even some of her doubts about her attitude towards Dursun appeared to have been washed out of her. At least she felt she could now face him with much more confidence than an hour ago.

" I got a clean skirt and blouse from one of the nurses," Latife said. " I hope it fits."

The skirt and blouse were a little tight, but anything was a welcome change after the mud- and blood-smeared clothing she had been wearing. " Do I look Turkish ? It's a very fancy outfit."

" It belonged to the nurse's sister. It was her bridal dress."

" Where's the sister ? "

" She was killed in the earthquake, she and her baby. They were in the hospital."

For a moment some of the warmth went out of the hot sun. " Doesn't the nurse mind ? I mean, doesn't she want to keep it as a memory of her sister ? "

" She's practical. She also admires you, Virginia. We all do."

Virginia said nothing. She liked being complimented, but she had never learned how to respond to it without embarrassment. She dried her hair, combed it, and as she did so momentarily wondered if the young American serviceman would still think her old enough to be his mother. She was lit by an unaccustomed spark of vanity : a compliment from a man, preferably a stranger, would be the final refreshment.

" Have you ever thought of marriage, Latife ? "

Latife had sat down on a rock and was smoking a cigarette. Her head was bent so that the sun could get at her still-wet dark curls. Now she looked up at Virginia from under her brows, smiling a little wryly. " I've been asked twice, by two different men."

" What happened ? "

" I said no, both times. They were old style Turks. They were looking for a housekeeper and a bedmate. I don't want to be that sort of wife. I'd like to go on working as a doctor."

" They expect a lot, Turkish men, don't they ? "

Latife smiled again. " You've found that out, too ? And what have you said ? "

Virginia hesitated a moment before answering. " I've said no."

Latife stood up, crushing out her cigarette with her shoe. A slight breeze had sprung up ; the poplars brushed gently across the sky like green brooms. The weather now was perfect : perfect for burying the dead, for lovers to say good-bye. " It was the only sensible thing to do. I've been worried for you, Virginia, but I didn't feel I could say anything to you. I think it must be the same in Australia as it is here, or anywhere in the world, for that matter. No woman likes another woman to advise her about a man. She can't help but feel that there's jealousy or envy somewhere in the other woman."

Virginia had been combing her hair, but now she stopped in surprise. " Were you envious or jealous of me, Latife ? "

" About Mr. Dursun ? " Latife shook her head. " Not about him personally, although he's a very attractive man. But he would be hell to live with. I envied you, but I wasn't jealous."

" Why did you envy me ? " Virginia asked, but she knew the answer before Latife gave it to her.

" You had someone to take your mind off how lonely it can become up here. A woman doctor in a community like this, it is like being a nun in a Christian community. I can't flirt, I can't have an affair, even go out with a man two nights running—once I do that everyone in the town looks upon me as his. And so would he, probably."

" I think that's what's happened with Yashar. He looks upon me as his."

" Are you ? "

" No." The resolution was quite firm : suddenly she made up her mind she would leave to-morrow, drive south to Adana, then across to Carchemish. There was no chance that the students still waiting in London would be allowed to come to Malavan now ; she would not disappoint them, she would cable them to stand by to go to Syria instead. They wouldn't mind the change in plans : Syria or Turkey, anywhere at all would be a change from fossicking in building excavations in London or skin-diving for Roman ships in the Thames. She would follow the Hittite road south : she would not be the first by several thousand years to have used it as an escape route.

" No," she said. " Not any more."

They drove back to Malavan. Some of the townspeople were walking back into the town, coming back to add to their despair by standing and staring at the shells of what had been their homes. Some were heading for the ruined mosque, looking for the *hojas* who had sold them the charms ; they were not looking for revenge, but only to buy more charms. Some of the men were being recruited for salvage work by the soldiers and were responding willingly, glad to get their minds off their misery. Now one's dead had been buried, one should take up the life that had been interrupted. Life in Anatolia has never been easy and these men were conditioned by inheritance to quick recovery from grief and shock. Already some of the farmers were back at work in their fields, harvesting the grain that waited for no one.

As Virginia and Latife drove up the main street they saw a big crowd had gathered round the ruins of the bank. Men stood on the mounds of rubble, and other men, women and children were pressing forward in a curious throng from the street. Meldrum's jeep was parked across the road from the bank, and Virginia pulled the Land-Rover in beside it.

She and Latife jumped out and pushed their way through the crowd. Meldrum, who had been standing with Arif, saw them coming and shouldered his way towards them. " They've found three more bodies. I think you better get out of here. These soldiers are in a pretty nasty mood."

For the first time Virginia noticed that the soldiers were standing slightly apart from the crowd. They were muttering fiercely to each other and throwing angry looks at the towns-people, who looked frightened yet at the same time resentful of the soldiers' attitude towards them.

" What's the matter ? "

" One of the bodies is that guy who was in the fight that night in the *lokanta*—remember there were two strangers there ? The other two bodies are the soldiers who were on guard the night before last. And they've got their hands and feet tied. These other guys think their buddies might have had a chance if it hadn't been for that. You can't run from an earthquake when you're all tied up.' "

Some of the soldiers were now looking at the two women and Meldrum with the same hostility they were showing to-wards the townspeople. That was it, of course : the soldiers had no time for civilians. It had been the same all through the history she had read : an army always had a second enemy, its own civilian population. The Hittites, the Greeks, the Romans, the Seljuks ; why should these soldiers be different, especially when two of their own men had been virtually murdered ? The soldiers had worked gallantly and tirelessly at rescuing the trapped townspeople ; but now suddenly their attitude had changed. Their whole concern for the disaster that had struck Malavan was now focused on the fate of their two colleagues.

" Had the soldiers been shot ? " Virginia asked.

Meldrum shook his head. " They might just as well have been. These guys look on it as murder, anyway."

" How does Captain Arif feel ? " Latife looked across at the captain standing with his back to them, his head bent and his hands clasped behind his back. Somewhere or other he had found another pair of gloves; his hands moved in the small of his back like white doves making love. He lifted his head, stared at the ruins of the bank for a moment as if contemplating what other explosive secrets they held, then he turned and came towards Meldrum and the women.

He didn't see them till he was almost upon them. He pulled up sharply, blinking his eyes as if coming awake. His long nose twitched and he raised a white finger to rub the side of it. "Ah, you have had your swim? You were right, Mrs. Halstead, it does improve you."

It was an ambiguous remark that could or could not have been a compliment, but Virginia didn't query it. It was obvious that Arif had more on his mind than the exchange of flippancies with her. "Is there anyone else still left in the bank, Captain?"

He shrugged. "Who knows? We did not expect to find *him*." He nodded at the dead stranger, carved in grey dried mud, lying like a stone effigy unearthed from the past.

"He had a friend," Meldrum said. "The dead guy, I mean."

"I know, Mr. Meldrum. At least one friend, perhaps more."

Something in Arif's tone made Virginia look up. She had been staring at the dead man as if at the suddenly discovered key to a puzzle that had tormented her for weeks. But now the key tormented her even more than the puzzle had, there was no feeling of relief or triumph. She looked at Arif, then glanced about for Dursun, but there was no sign of him.

"Mr. Dursun——" Arif spoke to her as if reading her mind. "He is up at the hospital. He hurt his arm getting these men out. It was he who discovered the bodies of my men."

"And the stranger, too?"

"And the stranger. Mr. Dursun has worked harder than anyone here in the ruins of the bank. I do not know how we shall repay him."

" What about the money ? " asked Meldrum. " Is it still under all that rubble ? "

" Who knows, Mr. Meldrum ? But I would think so, eh ? " And he looked slyly past his long nose, confident and unlikeable again.

Meldrum looked at Virginia, then back at Arif. " What are you going to do ? "

" Just keep digging. Mrs. Halstead is an archæologist— she knows it is the only way to discover the truth. Dig out the pieces, put them together till they tell you what you want to know. Am I not right, Mrs. Halstead ? One can dig up the present as well as the past, eh ? "

" Good luck, Captain," Virginia said, and turned and pushed her way through the crowd and crossed the road to the Land-Rover. She took her own and Latife's wet clothes from the vehicle, handed the keys to the soldier who had followed her, and got into the jeep with Meldrum and Latife. They drove slowly up the street towards the hospital.

" What are those men doing ? " She nodded at men who were prowling over the ruins and through the shells of houses, small jerry-cans strapped to their backs and spray nozzles in their hands.

" Looking for rats. That's a stronger concentration of DDT than we used from the helicopters." He looked across at the men scrambling like hunchbacks over the rubble, then he looked back at Virginia. " Are you thinking the same as me, honey ? "

" About rats ? "

" No, you got me wrong there. I don't think he's a rat."

" Oh, you mean Yashar ? " She was silent for a moment, then she sighed. " What else is there to think ? "

" I just wonder how much the Turks go for circumstantial evidence."

Virginia looked over her shoulder at Latife. " Are you envious of me now ? "

" No," said Latife, and smiled at Meldrum, who looked at

them both inquiringly. "A woman's secret joke, Mr. Meldrum. We have been talking."

"About Dursun? So was Arif. To me, I mean. He said, ' I wonder if Mr. Dursun is not a government man, after all?' Then he laughed, at himself, I think, and said something else. 'Suspicion is a form of blindness, don't you think, Mr. Meldrum?' I didn't have an answer to that one. I never do to so many of these local sayings. They're too subtle for me. I'm used to the American ones. Never give a sucker an even break. You can fool some of the people some of the time——" He stopped and looked sideways at Virginia. "Am I talking too much?"

She smiled, a little painfully. "It's all right, Nick. But do you think Yashar knows Arif suspects him?"

"I don't think Yashar cares a damn. Arif can't prove anything." He looked at her again. "Neither can we, if it's any consolation to you."

"No. But it's pretty hard to block your mind to circumstantial evidence, isn't it?"

Meldrum trod on the brakes as something came scudding out of an alley and across the road in front of the jeep. He leaned out and shouted abuse at Pali, but the dwarf did not stop, just went on speeding down the street, his skates occasionally striking sparks from the cobbles. Virginia looked back and saw him shoot in like a dog between the legs of the crowd outside the bank. She wondered why he had been in such a hurry, then it suddenly struck her that he had come from the direction of the hospital. Had Dursun sent him down to act as a watchdog? She could imagine the tiny man being almost pathetically eager to help Dursun, no matter what the latter might have done. Would she be so unquestioning with her own loyalty if Dursun asked for it? All at once her departure to-morrow became even more of an urgent necessity.

They pulled into the hospital garden. More tents had been erected and now all the patients were accommodated under canvas. A U.S. Air Force field kitchen had been set up and lunch, a meal richer than any of the patients had ever tasted, was now being served. Dursun came towards them, one arm in a sling, a plate heaped high with food in his hand.

" Long live America ! " He winked at Meldrum. " I am told even the pigs live better than our peasants."

Meldrum kept his temper. " It's not something we boast about. The pigs are just lucky, that's all."

" Such luck to be a pig."

Please shut up, Virginia thought. He might need friends now, yet he was doing his best to antagonise Meldrum. He was as hearty and unconcerned as if he were no more than a rude guest at a Fourth of July picnic. He could have been unaware of the devastation around him, of what had happened down at the bank ; he could have injured his arm in a game of softball or on a diving board. His total lack of concern disconcerted the three who got out of the jeep. They had been adopting their attitudes towards him in advance, and now they were faced with a man who looked as if he would not understand what they were talking about.

Meldrum and Latife walked away to join the meal queue outside the kitchen, leaving Virginia alone with Dursun ; it was as if they had abruptly switched their attitudes and decided that it was her problem and hers alone. She looked resentfully after them, but it was really only Meldrum whom she resented for his desertion. Then Dursun said, " Do you want to eat, Virginia ? I shall get you something——"

She shook her head. She had been hungry coming back from the swim in the river, but now the thought of food sickened her. A bundle of washing under each arm, she walked towards the corner of the garden where she and the others had slept last night, and where her excavation gear was piled beneath its tarpaulin. She found a length of rope and tied it between two trees, and began to hang her washing on it. Dursun sat down with his back against one of the trees and watched her while he ate his meal. The scene was a domestic one. It reminded Virginia of the two types of commercials that seemed to fill British television screens : people were always eating or hanging out their washing. Any moment now Dursun, his mouth full of the gravy that enriched, would ask her why her clothes were not whiter than white.

" Because they're khaki," she said.

" What ? " He looked up, a forkful of food halfway to his mouth.

She had lost herself in her fantasy, trying to escape him. Now she came back to reality, heard a moan of pain from one of the tents, looked down at him and said, " Why did you do it, Yashar ? "

He put the food into his mouth and chewed slowly, her question marked on his face like the clutch of a hand. I've hurt him, she thought ; but she made no apology, she had to be answered. If she left here to-morrow with no answer, the question of him would hang like an albatross round her neck for ever.

" Why did you do it, Yashar ? "

" Would you understand if I told you ? "

" I might. But murder is a pretty hard thing to understand—or forgive." She hung out her slip, the one with which she had washed the mud and blood from Yusun's face. Her initials, ornate as a royal insignia, fluttered in the slight breeze.

" I didn't kill Yusun, if that is what you mean. Nor the soldiers."

" Why did you rob the bank at all ? "

He looked about him, then stood up and moved closer to her, his plate held like a begging bowl in front of him. They were alone in this corner of the garden ; everyone else was concentrating on his eating. The two of them stood among the flapping washing : Tell me, Mrs. Halstead, are you pleased with our product ? " Tell me, Virginia, how do political parties in Australia raise their money ? "

" Not by robbing banks or murdering people."

" I didn't murder anyone ! " He flung away his plate ; food

spattered the trunk of a tree. " I *liked* Yusun, he was my friend. Why would I want to kill him ? It was an accident. Makal had the gun, it went off when the earthquake happened—he lost his balance——"

" Who was Makal ? "

" The man we dug out with the soldiers."

" Where's the other man ? There was another one, wasn't there ? "

He nodded. " Bekir. He's still buried."

" With the money ? " She began to hang out her panties, and regretted it at once : he put up a rough hand and fingered the soft material as if it were her flesh. " You're dirtying them."

He took his hand away. " I'm sorry. Only a few days ago you didn't mind."

" What about the money ? " she said, turning her face away from him as she hung out her shirt.

He was silent for a moment, but she didn't turn to face him. Then he said, " Bekir had it in two suitcases. It was very heavy, all small bills. The workers out at the dam don't like big bills. Neither do we—they are too hard to get rid of." He had simmered down again ; he talked like a mechanic explaining the difficulties of his trade.

" How many banks have you held up ? "

" This was the third." He looked at her as she turned back to him, sudden suspicion sharpening his eyes to slivers of black glass. " Would you betray me to the government, Virginia ? "

Betray : the word had an old-fashioned ring to it. But this was an old-fashioned country, despite Ataturk's efforts to drag it into the present ; revolution was still a fact and a threat, not something from the history books. She came from a country where a minor skirmish, the Eureka Stockade in which no more than forty had died, was an historical event. " I don't want to take sides, Yashar——"

" Not even my side ? " Then he shrugged, resignation

settling on him like dust. " Why should you ? What do politics here mean to you ? "

" Was that why you robbed the bank ? Politics ? "

" You know what Turkey is like now. No really strong party, lots of small parties—now is the time to found a *new* party——"

" You were going to be the new Ataturk ? "

He smiled, not offended by her soft sarcasm. " Not me. We have a leader, but he's still in the east. No, I was the fund raiser."

" By robbing banks ? "

" How else ? " His frankness was almost an innocence ; she felt she wanted to laugh. " The poor here have no money for politics. The rich wouldn't want our sort of party. There was no other way but to rob the banks. We stole only government money."

At that she did laugh. " Is that more honest ? Yashar, I've been brought up to respect the government, whether it's my party or not. Do you really think what you were doing was legitimate ? "

He joined in her laughter then, and they stood there beside the flapping washing, a gay pair enjoying a huge joke, the washing powder man and Mrs. Suburbia. People across the garden turned from their eating to look at them, smiling at the laughing couple ; it was the first time in two days that laughter had been heard in the garden, it was good to see someone breaking out of the fog of misery.

Then Virginia said, " Who would vote for you ? The poor ? Are you a Communist, Yashar ? "

" You don't know much about the poor, do you ? " he said, and she didn't deny it. " They don't only vote for the Communists, Virginia. Many poor, especially the farmers, are more conservative than the rich. No, I'm not a Communist. You could call us Socialists, I suppose."

" A Socialist who dreamed of being the Sultan of Brazil ? " Her sarcasm was no longer soft ; she cut at him as with a sword. He had betrayed *her*, filled in his time with her while waiting for the money to arrive at the bank : her underwear blew into her face as if to taunt her with how stupid she had been. She wanted to weep, to scream her fury at him ; but across the garden the others were still smiling at them. She looked for Latife and Meldrum, two she knew would not be smiling, but she could not see them. " I wish the bank had fallen on *you*, Yashar——"

" It did," he said quietly. " But I managed to get out. Then I came straight down to the.hotel to find you——"

That was true : he had been at the hotel within five minutes of the first shocks of the earthquake. " To take me to Brazil ? "

She was still slashing at him ; he flinched under each cut. "Virginia, I've hardly slept each night since that first day out in the cave. All my life I've avoided falling in love—oh, I've known women, but never loved them. For ten years politics has been my life, I wanted no one to complicate it. I did dream of Brazil, yes, but we all have those sort of dreams. Even Stalin must have dreamed of something better than the Kremlin."

" If you have been in politics, how could Captain Arif mistake you for a government man ? Couldn't he have checked on your name ? "

" I have a dozen names, Virginia—I've almost forgotten my original name. You need them when you have to work as I have had. I was never in open politics—our party has never yet run a candidate. Next year was to be our year, when we had enough money to start us off. I moved from place to place—Erivan, Trebizond, Ankara, Istanbul, Izmir, Adana—building a political party is like making a necklace, you pick up a bead here, a bead there. Then one day you hang it round the neck of your country."

" To choke it ? "

The unexpected smile broke on his face again. " You're not a Socialist, are you, Virginia ? No, with your money you couldn't be."

" My money ? " She had never thought of her own wealth, modest as it was, in relation to him ; somehow she had never thought of him as poor, he had always had the suggestion of an income somewhere behind him. " Why didn't you rob me of that for your party ? "

" Haven't I robbed you of enough ? " he said, the smile gone, his voice suddenly hoarse with despair. " Why do you think I couldn't sleep ? I loved you, Virginia—I still do—but I was committed to my friends. Every time I met them, they were out at Kasrik, they cursed me for being with you. And I had no excuse other than that I loved you. But that was no argument with them—political fanatics give up love, some of them are as celibate as monks——"

" No one could say that about you." Now she was slashing at herself as much as at him : she wallowed in self-pity, trying to degrade herself as much as he had done.

" Don't, Virginia. Please." Then abruptly his face hardened and his body stiffened ; she had reduced him to abject pleading and that was too much. It was as if he had heard his own voice, that of a beggar, with the ears of a stranger ; something like disgust with himself showed in his eyes. " I was wrong to make love to you when I wasn't free to offer you any more than just that——"

" You're sounding pompous now. Just like Captain Arif."

" That is not the insult you intended. I'm beginning to admire Arif. At least he is more dedicated to his task than I have been over the past few weeks."

" Are you blaming me for that—that you lost your dedication ? " It was a lovers' quarrel, one that went round and round : chance phrases were flung freehand, never fired from the bow of logic. One part of her mind realised the futility of the argument ; but she wanted some compensation for what he had done to her.

" No, Virginia." He was calm now, had the dignity that she had sacrificed with her involuntary urge to prolong the argument. " I don't think anyone is to blame when love happens. I can't blame you for being beautiful, for being all the things I fell in love with: Am still in love with. You Western people don't believe much in Fate. It embarrasses you to talk of it, I think. But we Moslems accept it, it is what governs our lives. Fate brought us together. I wish I knew what it has planned for us from now on."

" Nothing," she said, no longer bitter-sounding, trying to match his dignity with some of her own. " I'm deciding that, not Fate. There's no future for us——"

" Because of what you've learned about me ? "

She hesitated. " Partly, I suppose. But I had made up my mind this morning that I was going to leave here to-morrow—and I still am."

" Where will you go ? "

She hesitated again, wondering how much to tell him. But he wouldn't follow her, she was sure of that : that would be too much like begging. " Down to Syria."

" You wouldn't be safe there. The Syrians are always having revolutions. Go somewhere else, Virginia."

" Brazil ? "

" Somewhere where I'll know you'll be safe."

" How will you know ? I shan't be writing you."

" No, I suppose not." His eyes were suddenly bleak. " Is it really to be good-bye then ? "

" Yes, Yashar." Then she softened a little : " Where will you go ? After here, I mean."

He shrugged. " Back home, maybe. I've been promising myself for years to go back there—maybe now is the time." Then he saw Pali come into the garden. The dwarf looked around, then came skating towards them, his brown gullied face cracking with excitement. Dursun put a hand on Virginia's arm : the strength of his grip made it an order, not a plea : " You won't tell anyone what I've told you about the bank ! "

" Betray you, you mean ? You're like all the men in this

country, Yashar. You don't appreciate your women enough."

He looked at her at that, but she had turned away and was walking across the garden towards Meldrum and Latife, whom she had now spotted sitting against a wall beyond the operating tent. Halfway across the garden she looked back. Dursun, hand in hand with the dwarf, was hurrying out of the hospital gate.

3

By the end of that afternoon the salvage and rescue work in the town had been disciplined into some sort of system. The townspeople were accustomed to military law, and it needed no readjustment to authority to be told by the soldiers what they could and could not do. Street by street they were being brought back in groups to salvage what they could from their wrecked houses; the soldiers stood and watched them like bailiffs, now and again moving to help an old woman trying to retrieve a chair or bed, something in which she had rocked a dead son or had slept in with a dead husband. Several houses, in which dead were known to be still buried, were covered with a snow of quicklime; and the soldiers sometimes had forcibly to prevent people from rushing into the ruins. Other houses had been so saturated with DDT that they, too, were marked out of bounds : their owners stood sullenly by, watching their more fortunate neighbours who moved freely through the wreckage of the houses that were rat-free.

There was now a steady arrival of trucks over the mountain road, bringing more equipment than it seemed one town could find use for. The rest of the world had responded to the government's appeal for help, and the government looked like being embarrassed by the response. Truckloads of blankets poured in; the townspeople of Malavan would never be so warm again as they were in their destitution. Engineers arrived to repair the power supply, bringing with them a year's supply of electric globes; that night the town was to blaze with carnival brightness, Ataturk was to gleam like a jewelled portrait. Out in the fields every family had its own tent, every meal was a banquet from the American field kitchens. Only the occasional truck, heading out of town with another recently discovered corpse, was the *memento mori* at the feast.

Late in the afternoon Virginia and Latife had just been photographed by several newsmen when Meldrum drove into the hospital garden in his jeep. "You on duty, Latife? You better come down to the bank. They've found that other guy, the one who held up the bank. He's still alive, but he's in a pretty bad way."

"Have they got him out?"

"No, that's it. You may have to amputate his leg."

Latife went away to get a nurse and what equipment she would need; and Virginia looked at Meldrum. "Is Yashar down there?"

"With only one arm, but working like a guy with four. I'll say this for him, he doesn't scare easy. But what's he hanging around for? To find out what happened to this second guy, or is he still hoping to grab the money somehow?"

"I don't think it's the money, Nick. He's not just an ordinary bank robber."

"I can see that, honey, even though I haven't had much acquaintance with bank robbers."

"Don't joke, Nick. Can I trust you?"

"You haven't up till now," he said with mild reproach. "Why don't you try me?"

She looked across at the newsmen standing in a group, gazing around like looters, each looking for a story different from that of his colleagues: Dursun's story would be just the one they would all be delighted to have. She dropped her voice and told Meldrum all about Dursun. "It doesn't excuse his holding up the bank, but somehow I'm glad to know he's not just an ordinary bank robber." Then she added ruefully: "Something must be happening to me. I never thought I'd find some sort of respectability in a political outlaw."

" It's just relativity. I'm told that in gaols the man who's killed his mother is considered more respectable than the guy who's raped a little girl." He pushed his bush hat back on his head. He had lost the faded puggaree from it, and one side of the brim looked as if rats might have been at it ; it contrasted oddly with the brand-new khaki shirt and trousers he had managed to scrounge from the U.S. Air Force stores. He stood looking at her for a moment, then he slowly slid the hat forward again. " Do you believe his story about the shooting of Yusun being accidental ? "

" Yes," she said without hesitation. " Don't you ? "

One hand was at the back of his neck, the fingers idly flipping at the brim of the hat. ".Yes, I think I would," he said after a pause. " He rubs me the wrong way sometimes, but I don't think he's a killer. Not a vicious one, anyway, not someone who'd murder a defenceless old guy like Yusun. What are you going to do ? "

" I don't know." She spread her hands in a helpless gesture. " If I don't tell Arif what I know, does that make me a what do they call it ? An accessory after the fact ? Tom, my husband, used to talk about such people. I never thought I'd be one."

" I'm no expert on Turkish law. But maybe Arif won't ask you any questions. Maybe he won't have to."

" What do you mean ? "

" This guy they're trying to dig out, he's still unconscious. But if he wakes up and talks——"

After a long pause she said, " If the man, Bekir is his name, is likely to talk, why is Yashar working so hard to dig him out ? Why doesn't he just disappear ? "

Meldrum himself didn't hurry with his answer, as if he was reluctant to put thoughts into her head that might pain her. " Maybe he's afraid Bekir will talk too much. If they're mixed up in politics——"

" You mean Yashar might try to kill him before he can talk ? Oh, no ! No, not in cold blood——" Across the garden the newsmen broke into laughter : someone had just made a joke.

" Political killing is nearly always cold-blooded. It has to be. I've seen it before. They weigh the cause against one guy's life, and the poor guy always loses out. This feller Bekir is half-dead anyway—we're not even sure we can get him out alive. He's trapped just like I was, only worse. Wait till you see where he is—it would take only the slip of a shovel to bury him properly——"

Then Latife and Ismet Javid, the male nurse, came hurrying across the garden. A moment later the four of them were speeding in the jeep down towards the bank, Meldrum driving all the way with his hand on the horn. The newsmen, sensing a story, came after them in the two large cars in which they had come down from Ankara. When the three vehicles pulled up on the edge of the crowd congregated outside the bank, the newsmen jumped out and pushed through the throng ahead of Meldrum and the others. Their cameras slung round their necks were like badges of rank : the crowd opened up without a murmur.

" Freedom of the Press," Meldrum said with a touch of sourness. " We must never let it die."

" I hope they're not too free with their cameras. They could be more lethal to Yashar than a gun."

" You mean pictures of the heroic rescuer ? I hadn't thought of that. I wonder if he has ? "

" This way, Doctor." An English correspondent held back the crowd with all the authority of a London policeman. " Right through here. Stand back and let the doctor through!"

Meldrum and the others had now come to the front of the crowd, to the circle of soldiers who were keeping a cleared space in the ruins of the bank itself. Here the newsmen had met their first opposition : Arif, his back to them, was shaking his head to all their entreaties to be able to come closer.

" Excuse us," said Meldrum to an American correspondent, and stood back to let the two women and Ismet Javid through.

" Who are you, mac ? " said the newsman.

" William Randolph Hearst," said Meldrum, and followed Virginia through to stand close to Arif. " How's it going, Captain ? "

" Not too well, Mr. Meldrum." Arif nodded towards the big mound of rubble and girders up which Latife and Ismet were clambering. Half a dozen soldiers stood at the top of the mound looking down at someone working below them. " Mr. Dursun and one of my men are down in the hole they have dug there, but they are having no success. The man, whoever he is, is trapped under the steel door of the bank vault and they cannot move it. If they do move it, the whole of the wreckage will fall in on them. Very dangerous." His nose twitched.

" Should Dr. Altinbash be going down there then ? " Virginia said. Latife and the nurse were already sliding down out of sight. " Why not let me go back and get one of the men doctors from the hospital ? "

" Stay out of it," Meldrum said quietly. " If Latife hadn't wanted to go in there, she wouldn't have. She wants to prove she can do a man's work."

" It's a dangerous way of proving it." Virginia looked anxiously towards the mound. Then suddenly she left Meldrum and Arif and clambered up the huge pile of rubble. One of the soldiers turned round as she scrambled up behind him and put out a hand to stop her. But she ducked under his arm and crouched down on the edge of the narrow deep crater at the bottom of which Dursun, a corporal, Latife and Ismet were huddled about a half-buried figure.

" Latife ! " Latife looked up over her shoulder. " Let me go back and get one of the other doctors. It's too dangerous for you——"

" There isn't time." Latife was already at work, fitting a mask over the face of the trapped man.

Dursun, grey with dust, looking like a substantial ghost, looked up at Virginia. He was seated with his knees drawn up in front of him, his feet propped against one side of the crater; he looked as if he were taking a rest, till Virginia noticed that his back was holding up a big steel door that formed one wall at the bottom of the crater. Sweat was running down his face in rivulets, streaking the dust; the arm in the sling was cradled across his chest, but the hand of the other arm was clutching at his knee in spasms of agonised effort. The corporal, a thickset man with a hammer-head nose and a thick black moustache that curled up like horns, was desperately trying to work a prop of timber into position against the steel door, but it kept slipping in the loosely packed rubble that was the opposite wall. At any moment the whole mound might subside, filling the crater and burying all five people at the bottom of it. There was no time to go back for another doctor.

The soldier who stood over Virginia bent down and touched her shoulder. He spoke to her in Turkish, nodding back down the mound. She stood up, understanding that he meant she was only contributing to the danger by remaining here, and went back down to rejoin Meldrum and Arif. The latter looked at her reproachfully, and she said, " I'm sorry, Captain. I just didn't want Dr. Altinbash hurt."

" Only Dr. Altinbash ? "

" I don't want anyone hurt," she said, refusing to be drawn into mentioning Dursun.

" Neither do I, Mrs. Halstead. But I should like to give the trapped man a chance to live. Do you not think he deserves that? "

She made no answer, and behind her the American correspondent said, " Hey, Captain, let's take some pictures, eh ? We won't get in the way——"

But Arif, without turning round, still shook his head. He looked at Virginia and said, " Perhaps the trapped man would not like his picture to be taken. What do you think, Mrs. Halstead ? Or some of the others down there. Mr. Dursun, perhaps ? Do you think he is a man who likes publicity ? "

" Do we have to have small talk, Captain ? " said Meldrum, with a quick look at Virginia's strained face. " Mrs. Halstead is worried about her friends, can't you see that ? "

" I am sorry." Arif made a small bow with his head. " I am always trying to practise my English—it has got better since you and Mrs. Halstead have come to Malavan. But there are times when it is better to be—what is the word?—fluent in silence, yes ? "

Down in the crater Latife now had the trapped man ready for the amputation of his right leg. Beside her Dursun could feel his strength slowly ebbing out of him ; he wondered if he would have the endurance to hold out till the doctor had completed her operation. Occasional spasms of cramp bit into his thighs and he was continually massaging them with his free hand. The steel door against his back seemed to be getting heavier every second ; it was as if the mound of rubble was on a slope and was slowly moving down against the door. The crater had been small enough˙when only himself, the corporal and Bekir were down here ; with the arrival of the doctor and the nurse, it seemed that there was almost no room to move a hand, let alone perform an amputation. Yet Latife, on her knees, bent over beneath the corporal as he struggled to hold the timber prop in place above her, was already at work.

She had never performed an amputation till yesterday ; now she had the experience of a couple of dozen behind her. She could not work swiftly because there was so little room in which to wield her scalpel and the small saw needed to cut through the thighbone. She could stitch no sutures down here once she had done the operation ; she would have to plug the stump as best she could and rush the man at once up to the hospital. Even as she worked she gave the trapped man little chance of living, but she had always had the right attitude for a good doctor : never surrender the patient's life till he is dead.

It was stifling hot down here. Sweat dripped like water

from the four people; several times Latife had to stop and wipe her eyes so that she could see. Beside her Ismet was working without a word; but occasionally, out of the corner of her eye, she saw the shiver in his hand as he gave her what she called for. She did not blame him for his fear; it took an effort of will on her own part to shut out the thought of what might happen if the walls of the crater collapsed. Above her she could hear the corporal grunting, could feel his sweat dripping on her, as he kept lending his weight to the shifting prop of timber. On the other side of her Dursun sat in silence, but once she turned her head and caught a glimpse of the strain that threatened to tear apart the mask of sweat and dust that hid his face.

"I shan't be long," she muttered in Turkish.

Dursun nodded, then winced as the door slipped an inch, forced down by shifting rubble behind it. He tried to shut his ears against the two sounds that abraded them, the slow taunting trickle of rubble and the cold scrape of the saw through bone. He was sitting in a pool of Bekir's blood; his mind went back almost forty years to another day when he had sat in someone else's blood. A mood of fatalism all at once swept over him: perhaps his life was to end as it had virtually begun. For a moment he relaxed, his back bending under the weight of his depression: the weight of his whole life pressed down on him, bending him as the steel door had not been able to.

"Look out!" The corporal desperately thrust at the timber prop as the door leaned in. Dursun snapped back out of the past. He shoved out his legs and pushed backwards, grunting with the effort. His boots slipped in the soft rubble and for a second he lost all leverage; he felt the door give way against his back and he ducked his head, waiting for the wall of the crater to come plunging in on them. Then his boots struck against something buried in the rubble, a beam, a girder, something solid and heavy, and he had leverage. He pushed back, using more strength than he had ever had to call on in all his life before. His eyes were shut against the mud of sweat and dust that now caked his face; his breath tore its way out of his aching chest. He could hear rubble sliding somewhere behind him; then there was a sharp crack, as if a piece of timber had snapped. Almost on top of him, the corporal, grunting and whimpering with a mixture of effort and fear, was frantically working to anchor the prop. Ismet had jumped to his feet and was lending his shoulder to push back the steel door : a small man whose urge for survival, whose fear of being buried alive, had doubled his strength. The combined efforts of the three men could not shift the door back; but they held it. And Latife had now severed the crushed leg and was ready to bring out the trapped man.

She plugged the stump as best she could, then hastily wriggled out from beneath the corporal and Ismet. She stood up, reached up a hand and one of the soldiers up above jerked her up out of the crater. As she climbed out, Meldrum, who had come up to stand beside the soldiers, dropped down into the hole. He reached under the corporal and Ismet, grabbed the unconscious Bekir under the armpits and dragged him out. Swiftly, careless of what he might do to the injured man's stump, thinking now of the other three men whose lives were endangered, he swung Bekir up to the waiting hands of the soldiers on top of the mound. Relieved of the injured man, he turned back to help the others.

" Get out, Ismet ! " He leaned over the little nurse, pressing with outstretched arms against the door; he, Ismet and the corporal were bunched together like three men about to perform some spectacular balancing act as they leaned against the door. Ismet hesitated, then with a quick grateful look at Meldrum he slid out, reached up and was jerked out by the men above.

" You next, Corporal ! " The corporal, the horns of his moustache now down-turned with sweat, giving him a look of utter mournfulness, also hesitated, as if he doubted that Meldrum and Dursun could support the door on their own.

Then abruptly he backed away, threw up both hands above his head and was snatched up as if he were no more than a small boy.

Meldrum and Dursun were now bent almost double beneath the tilting door. Dursun, taking his injured arm from its sling, had got to his feet, but the weight of the door bent him like a cripple : he looked like a huge dwarf, a monster brother of Pali, the lottery seller. Rubble, like a thick grey fluid, was sliding in around the edges of the door, covering their boots, making it more difficult for them to keep their feet. Dursun was ready to collapse ; only his fierce urge to live kept his legs from buckling under him. Meldrum, sweat dripping like a wet veil down his face, grit between the door and his back biting into him like savage ants, the muscles of his thighs burning their way out of his flesh like hot spears, suddenly knew that he and Dursun were doomed. They could not move without the crater falling in on them : by holding up the steel door they were only putting off the moment of death. He let out a gasp, a cursing of himself and of Dursun : what the hell was he doing down here ? Then he knew : he was here because he owed his own life to Dursun.

But now they were both going to die, the account was going to be closed. He was about to give up, to buckle his knees and let himself collapse beneath the weight of the door hoping he would die instantly, when he saw the dark pendulum swinging across the level of his down-turned eyes. At first he thought it was a trick of vision brought on by the sweat and dust that blinded him ; then he saw Dursun's hand shoot out and grab whatever it was. He shook his head, flicking the sweat from his eyes, and saw Dursun swing the short length of timber in under the tilting door. Another prop was swung down ; this time Meldrum grabbed it and shoved it in beside him. A third prop came down, and this, too, was clutched at and jammed in against the door. Four props now held up the door, but none of them looked safe ; at any moment any one or all of them might slip in the loose rubble that now filled the bottom of the crater. But right now they were holding : Meldrum cautiously bent a little farther and felt his back come away from the door. He straightened again, leaning back against the cold steel.

With the props as they were, Dursun would have to go first. He looked at Meldrum. " Has to be me, Nick ! "

" I'm not arguing. Get going ! " He put out a hand and gave Dursun a gentle shove. The latter hesitated, reached down and squeezed Meldrum's hand, then slowly, like a burglar retreating from a silent threatening house, lowered his back from the steel door and crept out. He straightened up, raising his arms, and next moment Meldrum saw him disappear upwards out of sight.

Now it was his own turn. He could hear the rubble trickling into the crater, a soft hissing sound, a hollow gurgle ; now and again there would be a rattle as larger pebbles slipped and fell. Somewhere behind the door there was the creak and groan of timber ; and a blood-chilling sound as metal would suddenly, and for just a split second, scrape against metal. Beyond the crater he could hear nothing : it was as if the whole town were holding its breath waiting for him either to escape or die.

He put out cautious hands and tested the props. They seemed firm enough, but his own strength was still helping them ; as soon as he took his back away, the weight of the door and the rubble behind it might prove too much for the props and they would just collapse like match-sticks. He raised a hand and wiped the sweat from his eyes ; once he decided to move, he wanted to be able to see exactly where he was going ; there would not be an inch to spare for an error of judgment. He breathed in, tensed himself for death or rescue, then slowly, so cautiously that every muscle ached, like a crippled man trying out a body that had been paralysed for years, he bent away from the weight of the door. Every muscle in his back was drawn tight ; as his back came away from the door, it seemed that cold air rushed in to chill him. He turned his head, his eyes strained to the corners, watching the door

H

as if it were a beast about to leap on him. Inches from his face he saw the trade mark in raised letters on the steel surface : *Always Safe*. He tried to grin, but his face was paralysed.

He looked down again. Still bent beneath the door, feeling its weight still on him even though he was no longer in contact with it, he raised a foot from the loose treacherous rubble. He stood there, crouched over, on one foot, and watched the rubble slide like grey quicksand into the hole left by his foot. Six inches from it the rubble slipped away from the foot of one of the props, and he waited, his back tensed to take the weight of the door as it would come crashing down on him. The grey tide went down : something dark was exposed, a stain that he suddenly knew was the blood from Bekir's severed leg. Then he saw the end of the leg itself, and he retched ; not at the ugliness of it, but at the reminder of how he himself would look if the door crashed down.

But the prop held, and he let out a soft hiss of relief. He lowered his foot, stretching out till, when he stood up on it, he would be out from beneath the tilting door. Then, just as cautiously, his muscles burning in his legs, he lifted the other foot, drawing it out of the rubble as he might have drawn the fuse from a bomb. Again he saw the loose dirt and pebbles trickle into the foothole ; again he saw it slipping away from the foot of one of the props. Then he saw the prop itself begin to slide.

He flung himself out from beneath the door at the opposite wall of the crater. He reached up blindly, felt the hands grab at his, then he was jerked up as the door fell, hitting his swinging boot, and the whole side of the crater, a mass of rubble, bricks, masonry and metal, fell in in an enveloping explosion of grey dust.

4

Dursun, sitting with Ahmet on the footboard of one of the trucks parked in the hospital garden, stood up as Virginia came towards them. "Ahmet has come back to help," he said, and the boy smiled shyly at Virginia.

Help whom? Virginia wondered; but did not voice the question. "Your friend is still unconscious."

"Have you told Arif he is my friend?"

"No. But Arif is with him, has been ever since we brought him back up here. If he regains consciousness, Arif will be the first man to speak to him. He is waiting to ask questions. I've never seen a man so patient. He's been sitting there five hours now——"

In the light from the globes slung between the trees, as for a garden party or a ball, Dursun's face was that of a man ready to admit defeat. The death of Makal and now the possible death of Bekir had scarred him grievously. He had worked for two years with these men, and though they had often argued, especially over the past few weeks, he had come to look on them as brothers. He raised a hand and wiped it down the thick black stubble of beard that covered his cheeks and jaw. His arm was back in a clean sling, but he still wore the torn and dirty clothes he had been wearing for the past two days. One of his boots had burst its stitching, and a thick straggle of sock stuck out like a gangrenous toe. If he had any strength of spirit left, it was not evident.

"Does Dr. Altinbash think Bekir will live?"

Virginia shook her head. "He may not even last the night."

Dursun slapped a hand against his hip and half-turned away. "Bekir was always a religious man—he was always talking of God being on our side. And now look at what God has done for him!"

"He wasn't the only religious man around here," Virginia said quietly. "Nor the only one hurt."

Dursun looked as if he were about to make an angry reply. Then Ahmet put a sympathetic hand on his arm, and he turned and looked at the boy. He stared for a moment, as if looking at Ahmet for the first, or perhaps even the last time; then he nodded, raised his hand and grasped the boy's shoulder.

" We were doing it for you, Ahmet. For people like you. Mrs. Halstead doesn't understand, but you do, don't you ? "

Ahmet had had difficulty in following all the English words, but he caught the gist of their meaning. " I understand, Yashar."

" I didn't say I didn't understand," Virginia said. " I don't agree with what you did, but that may be because I come from another way of life, one very different from this. You can understand something and still not agree with the reasons for it."

Then across the garden, beyond the twisted shapes of the walnut and olive trees, she saw Arif come out of the tent where he had been keeping his vigil with Bekir. He looked about him, then strode, almost ran, down to the two soldiers who lounged on duty at the hospital gate.

" Yashar, I think you'd better go !" Down at the gate Arif had turned back to face the garden ; his gesticulating white-gloved hand flashed like a knife in the air. " Bekir must have recovered consciousness ! "

The truck hid them from Arif's view. Dursun glanced down towards the gate, then bit his lip. For the first time he appeared disturbed by what Arif might do ; the little captain had suddenly become a threat. He looked back at Ahmet and said something in Turkish. The boy hesitated, then he spun round and was gone quickly over the low wall behind them and into the darkness of the olive grove beside the hospital. Dursun turned back to Virginia.

" This is not the way I should have chosen to say good-bye, but I have no choice."

" How will you get away ? Have you any money ? " But then she remembered she could offer him none at all. All she had were travellers' cheques, and there was no bank to cash them : she was as poor as he.

He grinned. " I'll be all right. I've been without money before—I've learned how to get along without it when I have to."

The Fall of an Eagle

She put out a hand and he took it. She could feel the callouses and cuts in his palm, rough as sandpaper against her fingers ; it was difficult to believe that this same hand could have been so tender in their love-making. A flood of physical memories came back, and she trembled under their onslaught ; but he mistook it for emotion, and just pressed her hand as he might that of a child who was about to weep at their farewell. Then he raised her hand to his lips, kissing her palm, and she said, " Don't, Yashar. Please go before it's too late ! "

Too late for her to turn back, she meant, before she left everything behind her and vanished with him into the darkness of the olive grove and the future that lay beyond it. But he had turned and looked down towards the gate. " Arif doesn't know I'm here. But you are right, I must go. Good-bye, Virginia. I love you."

He leant forward and she felt the rasp of his beard on her cheek as his mouth felt for hers. She pressed against him, returning his kiss, using his mouth to gag the words that threatened to burst out of her. Then he had broken away from her, and was gone over the wall and into the darkness, merging with the trees, merging with the countryside. She leaned back against the truck, drained-of strength and feeling. She had said good-bye, fighting against the wild temptation to go with him, and that last kiss had taken more from her than all the kisses of passion with which he had bruised her over the past weeks.

" You are ill, Mrs. Halstead ? " Arif, with the two soldiers behind him, stood by the corner of the truck, silhouetted against the string of lights behind him.

She straightened up, rubbing the back of her hand against her mouth. She was wearing no lipstick, so there would be no smeared evidence of Dursun's kiss. " Not ill, Captain. Just worn out." She was surprised at the calmness of her voice. " Did you want me ? "

" No." Arif looked about him, then snapped something in

Turkish at the soldiers. They vaulted the wall and went running off into the olive grove, their rifles held at the ready in front of them. Arif looked sideways at Virginia, as if waiting on some reaction from her, but she kept control of herself. Arif sighed, took off his cap and sat down on the footboard of the truck. " No, I am looking for Dursun, Mrs. Halstead. Do you know where he is ? "

" Why should I, Captain ? "

" He was here in the garden half an hour ago. One of my men saw him."

" I don't know where he is, Captain." That was the truth : so long as she could stick to the truth, no matter how tenuously, she felt she could face Arif.

" I, too, am worn out. Why is it always so difficult for the man who represents the government ? Is it like this in your country, Mrs. Halstead ? I do not enjoy having to administer military law in a town. I doubt very much if the government enjoys ordering it. But it is necessary in our country now— no, not just because of the earthquake. Because we are a country and a people caught at a border." He looked up. " Do I bore you ? "

" No," said Virginia, one ear cocked for a rifle shot. " What border ? "

" The border between yesterday and to-day, between East and West." He tilted his head and looked up at the hill above the town. Ataturk blazed there, a constellation in the Turkish zodiac : but not everyone could read the sign. Perhaps, she thought, that was why the late dictator had always looked an unhappy man in his photographs. " Kemal Ataturk was a great man. I would lay down my life even for just the memory of him. But he was too impatient. He tried to change Turkey too quickly, in his own lifetime. One does not advance a man a hundred years just by ordering him not to wear the fez. One needs more than a lifetime, perhaps two or three. That is one of the reasons why I am worn out, Mrs. Halstead. Or perhaps unhappy is the better word. Unhappy because even by the time I am ready to die, Turkey will still not be across the border."

"What has all this to do with Mr. Dursun?" She could hear the soldiers coming back through the olive groves: Dursun had got away. She resisted the temptation to lean against the truck, even though she was weak with relief.

"Very little, I suppose." He stood up, smoothed back his hair with a gloved hand and put on his cap. "He is just part of the problem. A bank robber belongs to both sides of the border, to-day and yesterday, in the West as well as the East. I read of the mail train robbery in England. Two and a half million pounds, over six hundred million liras! How envious Mr. Dursun and brigands like him must have been."

"How do you know Mr. Dursun was a brigand, that he tried to rob the bank?"

"His friend has just died, Mrs. Halstead. But before he did he said just one word. *Dursun.* I need no more proof than that." The soldiers came back over the wall, shaking their heads in reply to Arif's questions. He snapped an order at them, they saluted and went off down to their post at the gate. Arif shrugged and looked back at Virginia. "Do not get involved, Mrs. Halstead. Leave him to me. I shall catch him sooner or later. And even if I do not catch him, someone else will. No brigand ever dies in his bed. It is a point of honour with them. Good night, and sleep well. You do look worn out."

He saluted and went off across the garden. He walked with no spring in his step and the old pomposity had slipped off him again, like a cloak that no longer fitted; but there was no mistaking the new confidence that had taken its place, the air of authority that now depended more on the man himself and less on his rank. Virginia watched him go, suddenly unable to hate him even though he had promised death for Dursun. Arif, too, was caught at the border: he had to administer modern law with old-fashioned methods. Justice still wore a peasant's garb.

Chapter Seven

" You're not going, Virginia ? "

" I can't, Latife. Not till I know something definite—I mean whether he got away or not."

" How will you know ? "

" I'll know, all right, if they catch him. Captain Arif will make sure of that. If they haven't caught him by the end of the week—well, then I think I'll leave."

" You would do better to go now."

" No advice, Latife, please. Remember what you said, that a woman should never advise another woman about a man ? I just have to *know*, that's all there is to it."

Latife had taken down some of the washing that Virginia had hung out yesterday and was folding it. " Do you really love him so much ? "

Virginia sat on a large stone with her back against a tree. She was abstracted, lost in a vortex of her own questions. An olive dropped from the tree, landing in her lap, but she seemed unaware of it. At last, as if surprised by her own questions, she said, " I don't know. I don't really know." She looked up, a frown creasing her brows. " Does that make me sound shallow, Latife ? As if I was having no more than an affair with him ? " Then, as if having voiced the question she knew the answer, she said with some emphasis : " I wasn't ! "

Latife carefully folded Virginia's slip and laid it on top of the other washing, the initials turned upwards. " No, if it were just an affair, you would not be feeling like this."

" No, I suppose not." She sat back, took the olive from her lap and began to roll it round in her fingers. " But what makes me angry with myself, even a little disgusted—now I come to think of it, I never really thought about how it would all end. I was like a young girl in her first love affair. To-morrow couldn't come quickly enough, but there was never any day after to-morrow. Oh, we talked about Brazil——"

" Brazil ? "

She smiled, tossing the olive in her hand. " Sounds silly, doesn't it ? But that was his dream, not mine. I don't think I once mentioned where we would go, where we'd live. I talked about Australia once, but nothing definite, just idle chatter——" The idle talk of lovers after the spent passion : she remembered the poplars standing still as green columns against the sky, heard the scream of the fighting eagles and storks. She knew now that she did not have to fear pregnancy : no tree would be planted for Dursun's child. Suddenly she had a moment of regret : a child would have been something saved from the shattered romance. She was like one of the wrecked houses of the town, a shell from which the life had been taken. She said listlessly, " I think I must have known all along that it was going to end right here in Malavan." Then she angrily threw away the olive. " But not this way ! Not like this ! "

Latife folded the last of the washing. " I really think you should leave here, Virginia. What if they do catch him ? Will you feel better to know they have shot or hung him ? "

" Don't, Latife ! " She stood up, scraping her back against the tree but not feeling it. But even as she protested she knew that Latife was only trying to help, performing another amputation, trying to cut off further suffering.

" I am sorry, but that is what they will do to him. You can't shut your eyes against it. They found the money this morning, did you know ? Buried under the bank, in his suit-cases, with his name on them. The law in Turkey is harsh, it has to be. We can't afford the luxury just yet of trying to rehabilitate our criminals."

" He's not a criminal ! "

Latife's voice was gentle. " I know he's not, Virginia. But

Arif thinks he is. He did try to rob the bank. And poor old Mr. Yusun was shot. Even in your country I think they would call that a criminal act." She put a hand on Virginia's arm. " I am just being realistic, trying to make you be that way. I haven't known you long, but I have always thought you were practical and realistic. But now——"

Virginia nodded slowly. " You're right, Latife. It just isn't easy, that's all."

" Then will you go away ? Now ? "

" No. But don't be angry or disappointed with me. Just be thankful it hasn't happened to you."

" Thankful ? " Latife's voice suddenly cooled, not at Virginia's remark but at the prospect of her own life. " You think loneliness is better ? "

The days passed, and Virginia began to experience a recurrence of her own loneliness. After Latife's remark, though she knew it had not been intended as acrimonious and against herself, she felt she could no longer confide in the doctor. She knew Latife would still continue to give her sympathy, but now she felt she could not repay Latife by exposing the latter's own bleak future here in Malavan. Some of the men hurt in the earthquake had grudgingly recognised the woman doctor, but not all of them. And there were no men here who would offer her the sort of marriage she wanted.

Meldrum was on hand to comfort Virginia, but now with the town trying to get back to some sort of normal routine he was working from early morning till late at night supervising the repairing of the town's water supply and its drains. The rats had been driven from the ruins and the danger of disease was now rapidly fading. Birds during the day and jackals at night were still picking the ruins clean, but gradually the townspeople were coming back to claim their own.

Virginia continued to work at the hospital, but she went about her tasks mechanically, only using them to fill in the time till she heard something definite on Dursun. How she expected to hear, she did not clearly know : like the aborigines back home in Australia, she waited for some word on the wind.

Arif came to see her several times. " You have not heard from Dursun, Mrs. Halstead ? But perhaps I should not ask. I do not enjoy putting you in the position of having to lie to me."

" I haven't heard from him, Captain. I don't have to lie."

Arif was now once more the spick-and-span dandy who had commanded the town before the earthquake ; he gleamed with whiteness at his extremities and round his middle. He bent down to adjust a spotless gaiter with a spotless glove, then straightened up and thrust both thumbs into his belt : he bloomed confidence, a man with a spotless reputation. " I shall get him, Mrs. Halstead. But I think it would be best for you if you left Malavan. It will not be pleasant for you when he is caught."

Everyone wanted her to leave : it was as if there were a conspiracy to protect her. " I should like to know what happens to him, Captain."

He took his thumbs out of his belt and folded one hand into the other. " Mrs. Halstead, I should not like you to be in- volved in Dursun's trial when we catch him. But if you stay, I shall have to call you as a witness. You could be kept here in Turkey for many months. Do you not see ? " He spread his hands.

" I see, Captain," she said after a moment, grateful for but embarrassed by his concern for her. " And thank you. I shall leave at the end of the week."

" Good. It will be best for you." He saluted, but before he turned to go he stepped out of uniform for a moment, forgot he was military commander of the town and became a man. " I do not like to see women suffer."

The rest of the week passed without incident and without news of Dursun. Help was still continuing to arrive for the stricken town ; the fields across the river had now become huge storage dumps. Some rebuilding had already begun ;

it was good therapy to have the townspeople doing something constructive. The shock of the disaster had now worn off; the people shrugged and came back to rebuild the town; history had left them a heritage of misfortune, it was part of the climate. Bulldozers were clearing sites for new houses, and the air quivered with the crack of blasting as explosives were used to loosen some of the wreckage. The clock in the barracks tower had been repaired and the hands once more traced the hours; the moment of disaster was no longer marked for all to see and the people soon forgot the grim reminder that had haunted them. Rain fell again during one night and the farmers began to believe that the worst of the year was over. Next year might be the same or even worse, but that would be the will of God and a man could do nothing by anticipating it.

On the Sunday morning, Meldrum came up to the hospital in the jeep. He had been sleeping out with the U.S. Air Force officers at their headquarters on the other side of the river, and Virginia had not seen him for two days. "I'm taking the day off, I figure I need it. You want to get out of town for a while?"

"Where shall we go?"

"I was thinking of going out to Kasrik." He fumbled in the pocket of his shirt and pulled out a piece of paper. "A lottery ticket. Yashar and I bought a bundle of them off Pali, the dwarf, the day of the earthquake. The little guy came to me this morning and told me one of them had won a prize. Fifty thousand liras, almost six thousand bucks."

She put a hand up to her forehead, feeling a little dizzy. "Half of it is Yashar's, you mean? Oh, isn't it cruel! To win it now——"

"He wanted more than this. This wouldn't have gone far, not for his purposes."

"No, I suppose not," she admitted after a moment. "But it's a bitter sort of joke, isn't it?"

"I think he might have enjoyed it."

She nodded, remembering Dursun's capacity for laughter. Then she said, " Why are you going out to Kasrik ? "

" What would you suggest I do with the money ? Half of it is his, I can't keep it. We're not going to see him again——" He stopped and looked at her, his eyes blank behind the Air Force dark glasses he wore. " You know that, don't you ? "

She nodded slowly. " I suppose so, Nick."

" You're making a mistake hanging around here. I told you to get the hell out of here."

" That's what everyone is telling me." She smiled wryly. " I'm beginning to think I'm not wanted."

" That's not true, honey. Not as far as I'm concerned." Then, as if he felt he had said something he should not have, he pushed his hat forward, half-hiding his face, almost a bashful gesture. " About this ticket. What do I do with Dursun's half ? I asked myself. Then I remembered Ahmet. Dursun told me about the kid, how he wanted to go somewhere to learn teaching. Well, maybe I'm doing the wrong thing, but I can't think of anything better. I'm going to give Dursun's twenty-five thousand liras to Ahmet. Not this morning, I haven't got the cash yet, but I thought I'd drive out there and let him know. A kid living his kind of life, good fortune can never come too soon. You want to come with me ? I thought you might like to, sort of represent Yashar."

" I'd love to, Nick. I think it's a wonderful idea. I'm sure Yashar would agree with what you're doing."

" Well, we'll never know whether he agrees with it or not. But I'm not going to lose any sleep over it," he said a little brutally. He took off his glasses and squinted at her almost angrily. " And I think you've lost enough sleep, too."

She stared back at him, calm and composed. " Do you want me to go out with you, Nick ? "

" Yes, goddamn it," he said, and walked round and got into the driving seat of the jeep. " Get in."

" An old Southern gentleman," she said, and got into the jeep beside him.

" You'd have made my old grandpappy spit." He put on his glasses again, and pushed his hat back on his head. " Okay, I apologise. I don't know what gives me the right to bawl you out."

She knew that he did know, or anyway felt, what gave him the right; but she said nothing, wanting no more involvement than already had her bound and helpless. If Meldrum was in love with her, she did not want to hear him confess it. Love, even unreturned love, could make too many demands. It was an octopus whose tentacles never stopped growing, never let one go.

They drove out of town, up round the crumbled hill and out along the road that led to Kasrik. Once up on the ridge, with the town lost to view behind them, the countryside looked just as it had looked for the past month, possibly for the past ten centuries. Only an occasional wave in the road or a fissure in the yellow-brown earth of the fields showed as evidence of the earthquake. They passed a hedge of thistles running across a field like a blue stream; one could imagine that from time immemorial these same thistles had appeared to brighten the dun-coloured fields with their colour. The heat had increased again and a haze shimmered on the far side of the valley; the hills quivered like naked dancers about to rise against the vast empty background of the sky. A man followed a donkey across a field, walking a track that his grandfather and *his* grandfather before him had trod; in the wide bright glare he and the donkey looked as if at any moment they might be smudged out of existence. A hawk hung in the blue, fixed as a dark star. Far beyond it, so high that only their vapour trails showed as chalk scribbles, two planes headed north, removed in time as well as space from this ancient landscape.

" Do you think it will ever change ? " Virginia said, shutting her eyes against the dust that blew into the jeep as a truck passed them on the road. " The country, I mean."

" I hope so. Otherwise I've wasted my time coming here. It's got to change, it can't avoid progress."

Back down the road the truck had come to a halt and its driver was turning it round. But neither Virginia nor Meldrum noticed it.

" Do you think that's a good thing, that it has to change ? "

" Wouldn't you want them to live better ? "

" Of course. I don't mean *that*. But to live better, do you have to change your way of life, your way of thinking ? "

" I don't know that you *have to*. But you usually do. Improve a man's condition and, God knows why, he has to pay in some way. Usually by sacrificing the ethics he once lived by. I've seen it happen in other places and I'm sure it'll happen here. But I'm a type of fundamentalist. I've learned I've got to be one. I can't see a man's diseased morals or the ulcers on his mind, everything that seems to happen to him when he opens the door and lets progress in. But I *can* see a kid blind with glaucoma, or a baby crippled by rickets, or a woman starving herself to death to keep her family alive. That's the way I make myself look at a country. *You* see some drawings on a cave wall, the remains of an old fort, maybe some pieces of pottery, and you grieve—well, maybe that's the wrong word—you *regret* the ruins of some old civilisation. You dig up the skeleton of some Hittite or Roman or Seljuk, and you like to think you're digging up some part of yourself that died before you were born. That's not for me. I look around me and I see the *living* ruins of humanity, and *they* are the ones who are part of me. Anything I can do to change all this—" He waved a hand at the dead countryside that stretched away on either side of them, an endless brown winding-sheet "—I'll do without any regrets at all. All of us need something to keep us going. That's the carrot that dangles in front of my nose. Progress. Not two cars for every family, central heating, all that. Just the guarantee that a man can *live*, not just exist. That's my idea of progress."

" You sound just like Yashar."

" Could be. I guess we're not so unalike, at that."

" I still think there are lessons for us in the past."

" I'm not denying that. But I haven't got time to learn them. You learn them, honey, and some day maybe you can teach me."

" You never will have time, will you, Nick ? You'll never really go home, will you ? "

He drove in silence for almost a quarter of a mile, then he shook his head. " I guess not. I've been bitten by the bug of conscience. I couldn't sit at a desk again in Washington."

" Not conscience, Nick. I think it's the bug of charity that's bitten you."

" One is only another name for the other."

" That's the cynic showing off. And I don't believe you're really a cynic. It's just a convenient disguise."

" What's yours going to be ? "

But she did not answer him, took her eyes away from him as they went slowly down the steep winding road past the caves where she had first met Dursun. When he heard the jeep the one-eyed boy who had served Dursun and her with their first drink together came out from beneath the faded awning above the roadside café. He looked up the road expectantly, but they went by him without stopping; he stared resentfully after them, then went back into the dark cave of shadow behind him. All visitors had been stopped from the district since the earthquake, and the parking level opposite the café was empty. The caves had once more been returned to their ghosts.

Now they could see the rock chimneys of Kasrik, white as bone, lifeless as gravestones, rising from the floor of the valley. Beyond the naked hills, that once again brought the image of a profusion of flesh to Virginia's mind, the snow-bleeding peak of Erjiyes Dagh rose like a mocking landfall, a horizon that would never be reached no matter how long one travelled. It had glimmered through the haze of just such a day as this when the first Hittites had come down through this valley. All at once, even more than the caves they had passed, the buried settlements she had hoped to unearth, it became for her a symbol of the past. A mountain of silence that would never speak to`her, that past that was never fully attainable, that would forever hold secrets locked in the dead brains of the men who had died with it. She knew then, though she would not confess it to Meldrum, that she had lost, had possibly never possessed, the faith that kept a true archæologist forever searching. It had been only a disguise.

When they drove up the main street of Kasrik, Meldrum looked in his driving mirror. " There's been a truck following us. Must be one of the village trucks."

She looked back, just in time to see the tail of the truck disappearing as it turned up a side alley. " Who would be following us ? "

" I thought it might have been Yashar."

Her heart leapt, then she shook her head. " If it was Yashar, he'd have come after us. Anyhow, he's miles from here by now."

" Are you happy or sad about that ? "

" Both," she said, and was glad he did not ask her to weigh one feeling against the other.

Ahmet was just coming out of the small mosque that stood at one end of the village square. He hesitated when he saw them and looked as if he was about to turn and run ; then slowly, reluctantly, he came across towards them as Meldrum parked the jeep beneath the shade of the big walnut tree. The old men, squatted about the base of the tree like ancient frogs, raised incurious eyes, then went back to the muttering that passed for conversation among them.

Ahmet greeted Virginia and Meldrum politely, but he looked both surprised and uneasy to see them. He glanced back towards the mosque ; Virginia saw the white-bearded figure of the old *Muhtar* standing in the doorway of the mosque. Had the *Muhtar* seen her and Meldrum coming up the street and told Ahmet that he was not to speak to the foreigners ? Even at a distance and though he stood in shadow, the old man's antagonism was plainly evident in his fixed stance and the unwavering stare with which he looked at them. She knew then that the old man would never have agreed to her digging on the outskirts of the village, would have put every obstacle he could think of in her way. He was a man with his face set both ways against change, against the lessons of the past and the promises of the future.

" I say prayers," Ahmet said, but it sounded more like an excuse than a statement : once again he glanced uneasily at the watching figure in the mosque doorway.

" For yourself, Ahmet ? " Virginia said.

He hesitated. " For Yashar."

" Do you know where he is ? "

The boy shook his head, his thin face blank. " Yashar is not here. You come to wrong place to find him."

" We didn't come to find him," said Meldrum. " We came to find you, Ahmet."

Something like fear flashed in the boy's eyes. " Me ? Why, Mr. Meldrum ? I do no wrong——"

Meldrum smiled and put out a gentle hand to the boy's arm: it was a gesture Virginia had seen Dursun make several times. " Relax, Ahmet. We have brought you good news, not bad——" And he went on to tell the boy of the money won with the lottery ticket and what he intended should be done with Dursun's half of the prize. " You and your mother and sister can go to Ankara or Adana, wherever you like——"

Ahmet's face threatened to crumble like a thin shard of pottery. He raised a hand to his mouth, and Virginia would not have been surprised if his trembling lips had come away in his fingers. He seemed to be having difficulty in seeing : his eyes blinked with tears that were still hidden behind the lids. He reached for Meldrum's hand with both of his, and a mumble of Turkish broke from the quivering mouth. From the corner of her eye Virginia saw the *Muhtar* come out into the small forecourt of the mosque, but Ahmet suddenly seemed to have forgotten the forbidding old man.

" My mother——" In his emotion Ahmet had forgotten almost all the little English he knew. He grabbed Meldrum's arm and began to pull him across the square and up towards the alley that led to his home.

Meldrum hung back, looking at Virginia. " Come along——"

" No, he wants to thank *you*, Nick. And so will his mother. I'll wait here."

Meldrum paused, then nodded. " I won't be long." He grinned at Ahmet and the latter's excitement, then he looked back at Virginia. " I wish Dursun could see this. I think I've done the right thing, eh ? "

" Just the right thing," said Virginia, and watched with mixed feelings as Ahmet, still clutching Meldrum's arm, pulled the big American after him across the square and up round the corner of the alley. Then she once more felt the old *Muhtar* staring at her with silent hostility ; and now she was aware of the antagonism of the old men squatted round the tree. She looked down at the men, and they turned their heads away from her ; but she had no feeling that she had out-stared them, they had just dismissed her as a woman, someone of no account. Across the square the *Muhtar* was still looking at her, his head back and his white beard thrust forward like a broad dagger raised for the kill. Then slowly, with a dignity that she had to admire even while she disliked him, the old man began to move towards her.

She snatched her peasant's bag from the front seat of the jeep and walked swiftly out of the shade of the walnut tree and up the street. Four women on donkeys came in a file out of a side alley ; she crossed quickly in front of them as if rushing through a closing gate. When the women had passed and she looked back, she saw that the *Muhtar* had stopped beneath the walnut tree. He stood, still staring after her, and the old men had risen to stand in a group around him ; their hostility came up the hot bright glare of the street like flung spears. She turned and walked on, trembling a little with anger and frustration, not wanting to be an enemy of these old men but knowing that, no matter how long she might stay here, they would never accept her as a friend. She was a woman and an infidel, a combination they could never approve.

She had reached the end of the village before she was aware of how far and how fast she had walked in her effort to get away from the old men. She was sweating with both the heat and the emotion that had gripped her, and she could feel the sun beating down on her bare head with an intensity that burned the roots of her hair. Her dark glasses were coated with dust, and when she took them off to clean them the glare punched at her eyes like a huge white fist. She put the glasses back on, turned to retrace her steps, intending to follow Meldrum to Ahmet's house, and saw that she was opposite the twisted narrow path that led up to the hill on which she had found the ancient jug. The jug itself was now buried somewhere in the rubble of the wrecked hotel, lost for ever: she did not have even that as a souvenir of her stay here.

Suddenly she forgot the heat and the old men, and she stepped off the road and began to scramble up the path. By the time she reached the top of the hill she could hardly see for the sweat that poured down her face. Her throat was parched, and one palm itched savagely from the bite of a thistle when, halfway up the path, she had put out a hand to stop herself from falling. She took off her steamed-up glasses, squinting against the glare, and stood, her legs quivering, her breath coming in deep gasps, and looked about her, wondering now why she had come up here at all and at such a pace. The top of the hill was bare but for the rocks and thistles that lay on it as they had for centuries. The earthquake had moved some of the rocks and had swallowed some patches of thistles, but it had exposed nothing. The past was still buried deep in the bosom of the hill.

She heard the scrape of a boot on the path behind her. She

spun round, blinded for a moment as sweat stung her eyes. She blinked, dabbing at her eyes with her hand; when she took it away, Dursun was standing right in front of her. He looked like a dying man who, in a desert, had just seen the promise of water.

" Oh, Yashar ! "

His arms closed about her with a hunger that threatened to crush the breath from her. She could smell the sweat and dirt of him, feel the heat of him; his thick beard scraped against her chin, his fingers clawed at her back. She struggled in his arms, but she might just as well have tried to fight off a dozen men. Then, all her meagre strength gone, she went limp; and that won the battle for her. He let her go and stood back, beaten by her lack of response.

" Virginia——" He was a huge scarecrow : the one or two birds fluttering listlessly in the hot sky would not alight on the hill while he stood here. His face was half-hidden by his black beard, and he looked as if he had not washed for a week. His long hair was matted with dust and sweat, and his shirt and trousers were ragged. His injured arm, no longer in a sling, was marked by a long blood-encrusted wound, and through the rents in his tattered shirt she could see another dried cut and several dark bruises. He had lost weight, and his eyes had the dull glaze of a man who had not had a good night's sleep for over a week.

" I thought you had gone——! Yashar, why have you stayed around here ? Why didn't you go back home as you said ? "

" It wasn't as easy as I thought. It's a long way and I would need to have stuck to the roads, got a lift from some truck or car. But they have patrols holding up all the traffic——" He smiled, gullying the dirt on his face. " I underestimated Arif. He's a good soldier."

" I didn't see any soldiers on the way down here."

" They are around somewhere. Ahmet has seen them——" He smiled again at her look of surprise. He seemed to have lost all his old mocking confidence, but his air of resignation, if that was what it was, was not a melancholy one : he had not lost the capacity to be amused. " How do you think I have managed to stay alive out here? By stealing from those people down in the village? "

" Have you been here all the time? "

" For the first two nights I stayed in the caves, in the church where we first met. Remember? The skeleton kept me company—sometimes I imagined I could hear him laughing at me. I kept hoping you might come back there."

" It never occurred to me," she said, regretting her lack of sentiment.

He smiled as if he had read her thoughts. " We're a sentimental people, we Kurds. Aren't Australians? "

She turned the question aside. " Does anyone else down in Kasrik know you are here? "

" No, just Ahmet. He has fed me. Not much, they don't have much, but enough to keep me alive." He glanced up at the few pigeons as they fluttered down to their nests in the pockmarked cliffs across the narrow gorge. " Once or twice I've been tempted to wring the necks of a couple of birds. But I never did steal from the poor. It's too late to start now."

" They wouldn't have missed one or two birds out of all these thousands."

" I feared I might go down in Ahmet's favour." He sat down on a rock, stiffly and wearily, like a man suffering from arthritis. He grinned up at her, and it came to her that all that still looked strong in what she had once thought of as a rock-like face were his big white teeth : the cheeks had become lined and even the bones beneath the almost blackened skin seemed to have lost their hardness. But the grin was the old grin, although it was now self-mocking and another sign of the weakness that was eroding him. " One voter. That's all I gained here in this district. It won't win an election, will it ? He has shared his food with me, risked his life for me, and what can I offer him ? A cause that never even got started."

" You *can* offer him something," she said, and told him of Meldrum and the lottery prize. " Or do you want the money for yourself ? You could use it to get away from here— Ahmet wouldn't mind, he hasn't really got it yet——"

" Twenty-five thousand liras." He had put his hand in his pocket and absently taken out the yellow prayer beads. He ran them through his fingers as if counting the beads of an abacus. " I have never had that much money. A small fortune."

" Not that, Yashar. It won't go too far, not even here."

" Far enough to take us to Brazil ? " He looked up at her, and shook his head in answer to his own question. " We were never really meant to go there, were we ? "

Reluctant to hurt him, but unable not to tell the truth, she, too, shook her head. " I don't think we were meant to go anywhere, Yashar. Perhaps we should never have met."

" No, I'm glad we did that. No matter how it has ended, I'm glad we met." He looked at her for a moment, then he dropped his head and stared down at his cracked boots from which his toes peeped like crabs from their shells. " I shan't take the money. Let Ahmet have it. He needs it more than I do. Just ask Nick to give a little of it to Pali too. I forgot him. He was also a voter."

" Is that how you think of them, as voters ? Not as friends?"

He stood up, rising with the weary resignation of a man who knew that the longest part of his journey still lay ahead of him. " Of course they are friends. A voter is only your friend on polling day. Ahmet and Pali, I hope, will be my friends for ever. The pity of it is that after I leave here, I shall never see them again."

" You are still going home ? "

" There's nowhere else to go. Perhaps it is where I have been heading all along." He looked up, then nodded at a speck in the sky, crawling slowly eastwards. " There's one of our friends, an eagle."

" Not mine."

He grinned. " No, you were on the side of the storks. But

this is a country for eagles—perhaps the storks should not come this way." She said nothing, and he looked back at the vanishing speck in the sky. " He's heading for Erjiyes Dagh. There's a legend here in Anatolia that no matter how long a drought may last, the eagles will never die. They fly to the top of Erjiyes Dagh and there they will always find snow, enough to drink and keep them alive. It is the same back home in the mountains where I come from. Where the eagles drink is where the brigands always survive. Perhaps I'll become a brigand again, steal sheep and take them across the border into Iran, just as I did long ago——"

" Will you be safe there ? "

" Till Judgment Day. Then——" He shrugged, the old gesture that was a philosophy. " Who knows what then ? "

Then down on the road they heard Meldrum shout. " Yashar ! Arif is down in the village ! "

Dursun straightened up, throwing off his weariness as if it had been a disguise. He turned his head towards the village and saw the half a dozen soldiers, led by Arif, coming at a run up the road. He looked down at Meldrum, now scrambling up the path ; then he looked back finally at Virginia, and saw the tears in her eyes. " What's the matter ? "

" I led them to you ! They must have been in the truck that followed us here——" It was just as it had been with Tom : her kiss was a kiss of death.

He put out a hand as big and rough as a rock, and gently stroked her cheek. " Don't blame yourself for anything. Whatever happens, it was written for me long before we ever met. You Christians still don't really trust your God, do you ? Good-bye, Virginia. Remember me."

Then he was gone, stumbling across the rocks, as Meldrum came panting up the path. Virginia stared after Dursun till he had dropped down out of sight below the curve of the hill, then she looked at Meldrum. " Thanks for warning him, Nick."

The Fall of an Eagle

" I shouldn't have. I'm not here to take sides against the government. It just slipped out. I came up here looking for you. Are you all right ? "

" For the present——" She looked back in the direction in which Dursun had disappeared.

" He'll get away," said Meldrum.

Down the road the soldiers had turned up a side track that led up round the shoulder of the hill. Arif was leading them, scrambling up the track, his white gloves flashing like heliographs in the sunlight. Suddenly he stopped and pointed. One of the soldiers dropped to one knee, raised his rifle and a shot rang out. A hundred yards away on a hill round and white as a skull, a puff of dust flew up behind Dursun as he came into view.

The soldiers took up the chase again. With the shot the pigeons had burst from the cliffs in a tempest of wings. Dark rustling clouds swung and swooped above Virginia and Meldrum as they stood and watched the soldiers closing in on Dursun. Black shadows washed like a dark surf over the hills as Dursun, as if knowing now he had gone the wrong way, twisted and turned looking for a way down from his exposed position. The two watchers on the hill, Meldrum now with his arm about Virginia as if he expected her to collapse, saw him run down one smooth white hill, leap across a narrow gully and begin to climb another equally smooth and treacherous hill. He appeared to slip, but he regained his footing and kept climbing with a desperation that was evident even at this distance. Bullets were now hitting the hill all round him, and above him the storm of birds had turned the sky black. He reached the top of the hill and stood for a moment, looking about him as if not knowing which way to go next. Nothing offered him protection or cover : he was just a dark figure in the white glare as the cloud of birds swung away for a moment, naked among the round naked hills, as exposed as a man nailed against a firing wall. Three shots rang out, and two puffs of dust exploded close to his feet. Then slowly he folded in the middle, his arms wrapped across his chest as if he were embracing the third bullet to himself. His knees buckled and he went down, his head bent to touch the ground in the Moslem attitude of prayer. He remained like that for a moment, facing not Mecca but the east, the direction of home. Then he rolled over and at first slowly, then quickly gathering pace, he slid down the slope of the hill into a dark blue patch of thistles that closed over him like a grave.

The birds came back, bringing their shadow to darken the hill where Virginia and Meldrum stood. She turned and buried her face against Meldrum's chest, glad that she was not alone.

2

Next day Meldrum drove her up to Ankara in the Land-Rover. They stayed there the night and next morning left for Istanbul.

Arif had come up to the hospital in the afternoon of the day Dursun had been killed. He was as immaculate as ever, but he had lost one of his gloves in the chase after Dursun and now the other was tucked in his belt, like a posy worn in a woman's waistband. Meldrum, Virginia and Latife were seated on camp stools drinking coffee when he arrived, and he took a cup of coffee and a fourth stool when Meldrum offered them to him. He sat stiffly, with his knees together and his cap perched on his thighs, and once again Virginia got the impression that he was waiting for a photographer to spring from somewhere. He had acted like this the first night he had come to interview her in the hotel. Except that he was no longer frightened, no spies waited round the corner for him : Ankara would be pleased with him for what he had done this morning.

He sipped his coffee and nodded, as if satisfied that it was not poisoned. Then he looked at the three of them in turn. " You were all friends of Dursun, was it not so ? " Even his English had gone back to its old stiltedness : he had retreated to the other side of yet another border, the soldier who could not trust the civilians.

" That's right," said Meldrum. " But we had nothing to do with his holding up the bank, if that's what you mean."

" No, I do not mean that, Mr. Meldrum."

" What do you mean then, Captain ? " asked Latife.

He took another sip from the coffee, then put the cup down on the small folding table between them. He rubbed a finger along the side of his nose, smoothed down his small moustache; he seemed to be debating whether he should go ahead with his next words. Then abruptly he relaxed, almost as if he had changed identity. He leaned forward, one hand spread on the table like a man offering them something. " Mrs. Halstead, I think you should leave here to-morrow morning. If you are gone from here, I shall not have to call on you as a witness. Dursun is dead, so there is nothing more to be said about him. He was just a bank robber——"

" Yes, that's all he was," said Meldrum, noticing Virginia's silence.

" I do not want you to be involved, Mrs. Halstead. You did not know Dursun was out there at Kasrik, did you ? "

" No." Virginia was still suffering from the shock of what she had witnessed that morning. There had been no tears : numbness of feeling could dry the eyes like a thirst.

Arif nodded as if she had given him the answer he wanted ; then he looked at Meldrum. " Why did you shout a warning to him, Mr. Meldrum ? "

" I'm sorry I did that, Captain. I hadn't gone up there to warn him—I was like Mrs. Halstead, I didn't even know he was around there. It slipped out—maybe because I was a friend, like you say. A friend sometimes forgets what's right and what's wrong. Instinct isn't always law-abiding, Captain."

Again Arif nodded, still the man and not the soldier. " Could you perhaps find some business elsewhere for a few days, Mr. Meldrum ? Till we have buried Dursun and I have sent off my report to Ankara ? You have done excellent work since the earthquake. If anyone should come down from Ankara asking for you, I can say you were worn out, that you had to take a few days' holiday. On Dr. Altinbash's orders, perhaps ? " He looked inquiringly at Latife.

" A good idea," said Latife. " I'm ordering you to be out of Malavan by ten o'clock to-morrow morning. And don't come back till you have put Virginia on a plane to wherever she is going. London ? "

" I don't know," said Virginia. Any place was as good as another : destinations would mean nothing from now on. " I'll think about it to-night."

She did think about it, most of the night, and in the morning she told Meldrum : " I'll go to London first and close up my flat there. And see the kids—I don't know how I'm going to face them, tell them the dig is off, but I'll have to do it somehow. Then I'm going home to Sydney."

" The wisest choice."

He loaded all her gear into the Land-Rover, and then Latife came across to say good-bye. " Good luck, Virginia. And write to me some time. I'll be kept occupied here for quite a while yet——" She looked about the ruined town, at the townspeople pecking like dark birds among the shells and wreckage of their homes, digging for something of the old life on which to build the new. " But in the winter I may need something to take my mind off myself. A letter is often better than a book to read." She smiled. " Another aphorism. Anatolia must be getting into my blood."

Virginia kissed Latife on the cheek, afraid to say something for fear that she would break down in tears. She climbed into the Land-Rover beside Meldrum, smiled with trembling lips, then turned away. They were sisters in the loneliness that faced each of them, but they could not offer comfort to each other.

Meldrum took the Land-Rover down the side street and turned into the main street. As they drove up past the barracks, Arif came to the gate. He saw them and snapped to attention.

His hand, gloveless, flew up to his cap in a salute, and Virginia bowed her head in acknowledgment.

"Somehow I think he got nothing at all out of killing Yashar," said Meldrum. "I think he even regrets a little that they were on opposite sides. Yet I can't imagine Yashar ever being a government man, even if he had lived and his party had some day got into power. He was never meant to be anything else but a rebel." He looked carefully at her, as if pondering whether to put the question. "How do you feel about him now?"

"I'll get over it, Nick."

"Him or his death or both?"

"Both, I hope."

They had begun to climb the winding road round the hill. A squat figure came speeding down the hill and went by them with a screech of skates: Pali the dwarf, a pennant of lottery tickets flying from his mouth, once more selling fortune to the unfortunate.

"He and Ahmet were the only two who really got anything out of this."

"No," she said. "I got something, too."

They went up the hill, past the gaol where the recaptured prisoners lounged like privileged sheikhs in their newly rebuilt stockade, past the mosque with its shattered minaret like a jagged tooth, then Malavan was behind them and they were out on the main road for Ankara. Virginia looked back, but the town was gone from view and all she could see was the far end of the valley and the flesh-coloured hills lying whore-like beneath the rape of the blazing sun. She turned back, wondering how long such images would continue to haunt her.

"I'm glad you're going home," Meldrum said. "Sooner or later, you always have to go back. If only to make sure you did the right thing by leaving it. Some people do, some don't do—the right thing by leaving, I mean. I still have to find out myself."

And then two days later in Istanbul he was putting her on

the BEA plane for London. Yesilkoy airport hummed and crackled with waiting passengers and the announcements of departing and incoming planes. An English family went by loaded down with purchases from the airport shops ; to-night a maiden aunt in Beaconsfield would curl her toes into a pair of harem slippers and dream of what she had missed. Two young American girls, as sure of themselves as a couple of Marines, strode past with two sleek young Turks in tow. An old man and an old woman, peasants dressed in their stiff best, sat hand in hand like a young couple, waiting fearfully for their first flight. A group came through from outside the lounge, a party of Americans on a guided tour, wide-eyed and yet suspicious. One of them, a woman in her forties with gem-encrusted dark glasses, stood and looked about her.

" So this is Turkey," she said, and sighed.

But this isn't Turkey, Virginia thought. Istanbul was Istanbul, Stamboul, Constantinople, call it what you like, a city of romance ; but it wasn't Turkey. Turkey was still a village in the hills and an old *Muhtar* standing in the shade of a mosque ; it was not even Dursun, a brigand who had grown up to believe in progress. The men who had inherited the dream of Ataturk still had a long way to go. Ahmet, packing his bags in Kasrik, was just beginning a journey that was more than just the road to Ankara or Istanbul. Go to the hills, Virginia said silently to the American woman, go to Anatolia to find Turkey. But take care : don't fall in love.

Meldrum picked up Virginia's small bag and followed her down the steps as her flight was called. He went out through the door with her and stood in the bright sun just inside the gate.

" I'll see the Land-Rover is shipped okay."

" Thanks, Nick. You've been too kind as it is."

The sun flashed on his dark glasses, but his eyes were a blank behind them. " I'm due for some leave in three months. I'm thinking of going home. Just to make sure, remember ? I think I'll go the long way, across the Pacific. If I came through Sydney, would you come out to the airport and say hallo ? "

" Please hurry, madame," said the hostess at the gate, an emancipated Turkish girl, one who had never known the prison of the hills.

" I'll come out to the airport, Nick."

He bent and kissed her softly on the cheek. " Take care, honey."

" I'll do that," she said, but wondered how one took care against memories.

Urgup—London
August, 1963-January, 1964